Charlie's Ghost of a Chance

Also by VJ Cooper

Fiction
A Sense of Jane
Scandal at Balfour Hall (sequel to *Charlie's Ghost of a Chance*;
to be published 2025)

Poetry
Life as I Know It: A Wee Book of Poems

Charlie's Ghost of a Chance

by

V J Cooper

First Published in Great Britain in 2024

Published by First Spark Publishing

Copyright © 2024 VJ Cooper

The author has asserted their right under the Copyright, Designs and Patent Act 1988 to be identified as the author of this work. This book is a work of fiction and any resemblance to actual persons living or dead, is purely coincidental.

All rights reserved. No part of this publication may be reproduced or transmitted in any form or by any means, electronic or mechanical, including photocopy, recording, or any information storage and retrieval system, without permission in writing from the publisher.

A CIP catalogue record for this book is available from the British Library

ISBN 978-1-7394501-4-4 (hardback)
ISBN 978-1-7394501-5-1 (paperback)
ISBN 978-1-7394501-6-8 (ebook)

Cover Design by Creative Covers

Typesetting by Book Polishers

For the Cooper Troopers

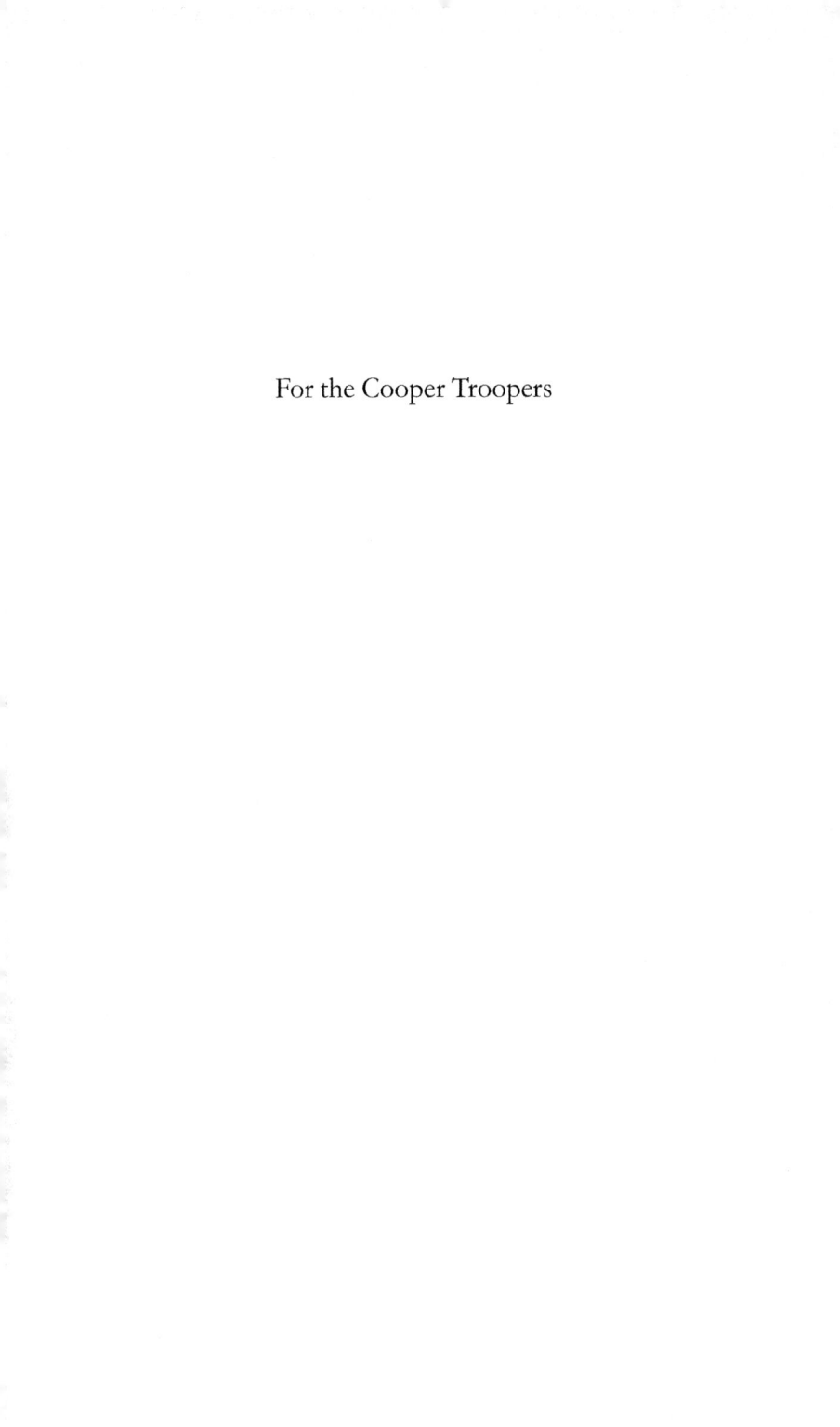

Contents

Character List	9
Charlie	11
Part One: Dufftown 1881	13
Grace	18
Family	22
The Great Divide	30
Black Tendrils	35
The Scattering of Bairns	44
Nae Rabbits	48
When Hope is Lost	52
Willowbank	55
Dinner for Breakfast	65
Pummelling	75
The Auld Fox	78
Cousins at Redwood Manor	84
Alice	95
School	101
The Photograph	108
A Time of Blossom	121
A Birthday	135
Part Two: The March of Time 1899	140
Aspirations	150
Strong Quines	156

Robin Hood	162
Success	168
An Unfortunate Incident	176
Celebration	183
A Beating	186
Enquiries	203
Seabank	209
Answers	213
Cat and Mouse	221
Patriarch	231
Nymphs	236
Games	243
Discovery	253
Threats	263
Consequences	267
Revelations	285
Charlie	290
Epilogue	292
Glossary of Scots Words	293

Character List

Grace and **David Robertson**
Children :
David	died aged 3 months
Hugh	emigrates
George	emigrates
Donald	
Gordon	
Helen	
Grace	
Peter	
Jessie	
Charlie	

Robert and **Ann Ross** - Charlie's grandparents
Children:
Grace (above)
Gordon - wife **Mabel** - Children: Victoria, Ruth, Ann, Agnes, Joseph
James - wife **Edith** - Children: Archie, Ian, Eleanor
Rose - husband **Andrew Milne** (Charlie's new parents)

Dr David Buchan & wife Shona
Children: **Alice** and **Fraser** (twins)

Charlie

My name is Charlie and I am dead.

My life began in 1878 in the rural town of Dufftown, Scotland, at a time when social and industrial advances were being sewn but the plight of the poor was ever prevalent. Alexander Graham Bell had demonstrated his telephone to Queen Victoria, Sophia Jex-Blake had set up practice in Edinburgh as the first female doctor, and a company called Shanks in Barrhead had begun to produce porcelain toilets.

Of course, being a newborn at the time, I had no knowledge of these events and although they may well have been recorded in the local newspaper what good was that type of news to my mama and papa when struggling to feed eight mouths, not including their own, and me now bringing the total number of bairns to nine? It would have been ten had David lived past the age of three months.

Some would say that my early years were tragic: fraught with hunger, cold and loss, but others would say that I was fortunate to have known such riches that I later came to experience and the chance to be highly educated. The chance to be a gentleman.

I remember running in the fields with my siblings and searching for rabbits.

I remember the wonder of school and the bustle of Aberdeen.

I remember Alice.

Part One

Dufftown 1881

Charlie's wee toes were so cold. He stood on the station platform with tears trickling down his cheeks. His brothers assumed the tears were for them, but they belonged to his bare feet. It had been a long, coorse winter and it seemed to have returned, with folk waking up to frost on the ground that June morning. Young grouse had died in their droves, their plumage insufficient for the unexpected cold weather, and farmers were wary, yet again, that it would be another bad year. The previous year had seen crops not harvested until October, much of it still green and completely worthless.

The train waited, hungrily devouring coal, as folk clambered aboard, eager for their journey to begin. Charlie had seen the train many times across the fields and heard its melodic sound but had never before been on the platform and stood so close to it. He was aware of its size dwarfing him and the hissing sound from the boiler unnerved him. Perhaps if he had not been so cold he would have enjoyed the experience and revelled in the wonder of the engine and the coming and going of folk, but as his wee body shivered under his thin coat he felt sorry for himself and fearful of the noises coming from the metal horse.

His lips trembled and his teeth chattered of their own accord but were relieved momentarily, as first Hugh and then George, lifted Charlie and enveloped him in a warm hug. Their voices were gruff with emotion and their beards soft against his skin. He breathed in the earthy scent of tobacco and willed his body to soak in warmth from the coarse jackets.

Not yet four years in age, Charlie had little understanding of the parting or the meaning of never seeing his brothers again.

Words were whispered in his ear but the wind whipped them away before he could decipher them. Their mother was stony faced but hugged her loons tight and each young man took turns to shake their father's hand, with a brief nod of the head, before climbing onto the train, both carrying a cloth bag with a change of clothes which was all they owned. With their tickets, for the ship bound for Canada, safely tucked away in their pockets, the two brothers leaned out of the window as the engine slowly pulled away amidst the clacking of metal, shrill whistles and billowing steam. With a final wave Hugh shouted the words, "We'll make ye proud. We're going tae be rich."

David, with a heavy heart, lifted his wee loon up, popping Charlie's feet into his pockets. "Come on, Charlie. Let's go home." Grace took his arm, her tears coursing, they began the mile's walk from the station back to their cottage on the outskirts of Dufftown.

Charlie burrowed into his papa taking what warmth he could. "Are ye going tae work now, Papa?"

David shook his head. "There was nae work yesterday or today." His words were heavy as David felt the weight of responsibility on his shoulders, Grace having borne ten bairns. Wee David had passed away from whooping cough fifteen years previously and now their two eldest were off to find their fortune in Canada, but there were still seven bairns to feed.

If tenacity was food they would have had full bellies indeed.

Charlie could hear the train but he could no longer see it, hidden by the woodland that bordered the track going north towards Keith. As the path began to ascend more steeply his papa placed Charlie back on the ground and he felt the abrupt coldness seep into his toes and tears threatened to appear once more, but sensing the emotion emanating from his kin he squeezed his eyes tight for a moment and imagined that he was sitting by a roaring fire with a steaming bowl of soup. His belly rumbled but he was unsure if it would be filled as some days his mama just shook her head and turned away with tears in her eyes, muttering, "I'm sorry ma loon."

As their home came into view Charlie ran ahead eager to be inside. The low stone cottage slumped into the ground like an old woman weak on her legs. Its grey stone walls held a dejected air, its sense of pride battered by years of bad weather and neglect. One small window peeked out from the side of the low hung wooden door as if conscious of lacking another eye and the grass roof undulated, emulating the waves of the sea.

David put his arm around Grace's shoulders and the couple followed Charlie up the track that led to their home. "It surely has tae be a better life for our loons than that of paupers living in Scotland."

Grace found her voice. "Aye, but their young minds are full o' a better life, lured wi' the promise o' land and money in their pockets. What if it doesn't turn out that way?"

David had no answer so did not reply and they continued on up the track.

Hillside Cottage was nestled halfway up a hill to the west of the station, on its own, surrounded by a combination of farmland and woodland and cocooned in the glen by the surrounding Conval hills, which themselves were lorded over by the majestic Ben Rinnes on one side and Ben Aigen on the other. The brown hills enveloped Dufftown cradling it in a bosie and quenching its thirst with the soft water of the Fiddoch River and the Dullan water, which converged into the River Spey further north at Craigellachie.

It would have been a lonely house if it were not for the bonny wild flowers that surrounded it and the love within, that radiated more warmth than the low fire, which only smouldered in the hearth. From its only door you could see for miles across fields and woodland with the grand houses of Dufftown spread out below with a square in the middle - a clock tower at its centre. The observer looking to his right would see the long, low buildings that formed the first legal distillery named Mortlach, producing the smooth whisky that to some was golden nectar and to others: poison. The ruin of old Balvenie Castle stood proudly on the other side of Dufftown to the left of Hillside Cottage, which had held the imaginations of bairns for many years as they conjured up games of long ago battles and kings and queens.

It was a fine spot in the summer but too exposed to the cold, westerly winds in the winter. With the weather being as it was all the wild flowers were withering and nature was confused. Charlie had heard folks' angry voices berating the cold and although he did not understand much of what was said he knew that it meant less work for his father and less food to eat. Farmers were struggling from the aftermath of the previous year's disastrous crop and tried to get by, employing less folk and offering lower wages.

The fire was almost out when Charlie burst into the cottage but there was some warmth in the kitchen and the sun was trying its best to peek through the window. He flung himself under the blanket on the box bed where his folks slept, opposite the fire, and cooried down til only the top of his head was visible. His older siblings were either at work or school, a rare event, as often there was no spare peat to take as payment, but today their mama had hurried them out the door following a brief goodbye to Hugh and George as she wanted the day to grieve with less eyes on her.

Grace collapsed onto the kitchen chair and emitted a long, slow moan followed by an awful howling noise that frightened Charlie as he buried his head under the blanket, covering his ears. David too sat and encircled his wife in his arms as they gave into the sadness in their hearts.

It was a type of grief to mourn those who still lived.

Grace

As Grace's tears subsided she rose to begin making some porridge for their dinner. Adding another peat to the fire the warm glow emanated some warmth into the subdued atmosphere and Charlie allowed himself to peek over the top of the blanket and check that the world had righted itself again. His mama beckoned him over and Charlie burrowed into her skirts as she held him with one arm as the other slowly stirred the porridge.

As Grace stood by the hearth, spirtle in hand, her mind wandered back through the years, something that she usually avoided doing, but feeling so bereft she took stock to wonder how it was that her life had turned out as it had.

Her father, Robert Ross, owned the Don Woollen Mill in Aberdeen and had employed her husband, David Robertson, as a carter, transporting the cloth between the factory and both the railway station and the harbour where it continued its journey throughout Britain, and indeed across the world. The mill had a reputation for producing high quality cloth and through hard work and determination Robert Ross had succeeded in building a lucrative and successful business from nothing. He had not come from a wealthy family but tenacity, ruthlessness and greed had driven him forward, and he had done whatever needed to be done to fulfil his ambition to have money and status.

He had married one Ann Ferguson, an amiable creature, several years his junior who had few ideas of her own languishing in her mind but fulfilled the role of an attractive, bidding wife quite satisfactorily. She had proved fertile and a charming hostess and Robert had commended himself on his choice of bride. Ann herself was content with her life, blissfully unaware of the plight of the poor and oblivious to the need for emancipation of women.

Grace's hand stroked Charlie's head as she thought, *I have shown love to my bairns, unlike my own parents. Father was only interested in how we all looked as a family in the eyes of the gentry and Mother had no maternal feelings in her. She focused, like Father, on being seen to do the right thing in society. I was known as the 'sickly child' to friends and acquaintances, though there was nothing wrong with me other than not being able to read and write properly, despite various punishments over the years. I was kept from being seen. An idiot, they called me.*

Perhaps I am, perhaps I'm not.

"Are ye alright, quine? Ye are very quiet," David said.

"Aye. My mind is just thinking back. We may not have much but we love our bairns."

David sighed. "I'm sorry, Grace. I have not been able to provide for ye and our bairns. We are too often hungry these days. If ye had married someone from yer own class and stayed in Aberdeen…"

"Stop, David. I made my choice and I don't regret it. It's not your fault there is little work."

"Perhaps I should have listened to you and written to yer kin asking them for help. My pride wouldn't let me and now we hae so little."

Grace faced her husband. "I was foolish to suggest it. Put it out o' yer mind. We will get by." She turned back to the porridge stirring it as she thought of the letter she had

had the minister write to her mother many months ago and the reply that consisted of a single sentence, '*You have made your bed, so lie in it.*' She had not told David and no point in doing so now. If she had known the address of one of her siblings perhaps the answer would have been different but there had only been one choice of recipient.

Grace wondered what kind of folk her younger siblings had become. Over the years news of her family had come by way of the newspaper, read to her by David. The mill was now run by Gordon, being the eldest son, and his marriage to a Mabel Fraser had been announced. *I hope ye married for love. Ye were a quiet loon, living under Father's shadow with no choice as to yer profession. I always thought ye would have made a good doctor.* Her thoughts turned to James whom she had heard had married an Edith somebody or other. *No doubt a marriage of convenience as ye were cut fae the same cloth as Father.* Rose was the youngest and had only been twelve in years when Grace had last seen her. *You were the daughter Mother always wanted me to be: a bonny, amiable child who spoke only when spoken to and knew how to read poetry and fit into the world of the gentry. Ye married well, I hear, so no doubt ye have bairns o' your own now.*

The spirtle slowed and the porridge began to stick to the bottom of the pan as her thoughts continued to wander down an old road.

I was tolerated, sometimes pitied, by you all. I was a disappointment and told so at every opportunity by Father who blamed Mother for producing an idiot. I lived on the outskirts of the family and left largely to my own devices and the kitchen became my safe place where I was mothered by the cook. She taught me kindness and compassion. But we had one thing in common as siblings: we all feared Father. It was not his hands we feared, but his tongue. I have never regretted running away with David. Becoming Mrs Robertson enabled me to forget that I was ever a Ross.

Grace shook off her memories and thought of her loons

off to find their fortune in the world. Her heart would not recover from not seeing them again but she prayed their lives would be better and not fraught with hunger and lack of money.

Family

Nature continued to be confused. Summer had not yet arrived despite the arrival of August, and crops lay dormant in the cold, wet soil. Flowers too refused to flourish and the countryside was bereft of their colour and scent. With the lack of warmth within cottages chests suffered with bronchitis and both the young and old struggled to keep warm, so when snow appeared on the twelfth of August in that same year, 1881, folk believed that the world had gone mad and mother nature had lost her mind.

The cottage door would normally have been left open over summer, allowing fresh air to circulate and the smoke from the fire used for cooking to dissipate, but with the weather being as it was the door remained steadfastly shut, imprisoning the black smog as it did in the winter months. It filled the lungs of its inhabitants and the wisps strangled from within. Grace developed a slight cough that seemed to linger until such time that no one noticed its constant presence, so used they were to hearing it.

A September Sunday morning dawned bright and clear with few clouds, a welcome relief to the end of what should have been summer. The Robertsons were gathered around the low fire each with a bowl of porridge in his or her hand that was eaten without hurry as Grace allowed no lack of good manners. "Helen, take the bowls and wash them please and Grace help yer wee sister to dress. Then ye can all go out and play."

Peter's eyes lit up. "Are we nae going tae kirk?" His excited tone was shared with his siblings whose lack of flesh on bottoms felt the hardness of the pew as they sat for what felt like half a day listening to the minister.

"Nay today, loon."

"Why not?" asked Gordon.

"God has sent us the sun today so make the most of it. Go on now. You too Donald and Gordon. Ye may well be working now but yer nae too auld for playing with yer family." Donald had been lucky to find himself under the tuition of Mr Thompson, a shoemaker, who, having no sons of his own, had taken him on as an apprentice. Gordon had not fared as well and was employed by a cruel, ruthless farmer to work as a farm labourer.

All seven Robertson bairns scurried outside, four in bare feet, and charged down the track towards the woods. David and Grace stood by their door and watched. "God may well have sent the sun but I'd rather he'd sent some food."

"Aye, quine. My days o' praying are over, the little good it does. Damn the weather, damn the wealthy who do nothing to help those in need and damn the Lord above who lets bairns starve and die o' disease."

"Poor wee Mary, I couldn't bring myself tae tell the bairns their friend died last night. What's to become o' us, David? I fear for us all."

David drew his wife into him. "I don't ken what lies ahead, Grace, but we will face it together just as we've always done."

THE BAIRNS SCURRIED through the woods to their den

which Donald and Gordon had built several years before. It stood between two large oaks and had been built with fallen branches and dead wood honed by a pocket knife and slotted and weaved together like their mother's knitting. The roof was covered with layers of bracken and the inside was draped with old sacking to make a floor.

The den was damp still as summer had refused to appear and the walls needed to be shored up again thanks to the strong winds earlier in the year. Donald, being the eldest, took charge. "Right, we need tae find some dry wood and replace this side o' the den where the rain has gotten in. Me and Gordon will take this side completely down. Charlie, you and Peter drag this sacking from the inside to the dyke by the field so it can dry oot in the sun and Helen you take Grace and Jessie wi' ye tae find some dry branches."

No one grumbled at their orders as all were keen to fix the den. Not only did they want to play but they needed to ensure that it was in good shape for the winter ahead. Unbeknownst to the Robertsons, being a good size, it was occasionally used by the ghillie to shelter from a sudden downpour or a poacher to hide from the ghillie.

The bairns worked well together running to fetch and carry whatever wood and bracken they could find, which was passed to their older brothers, who successfully repaired and replaced branches with the help of an old hand saw that they kept in the den for such purpose. Layers of bracken were interwoven to form another thick layer of roofing - insulating and protecting the space within.

An hour or so later the den was once again strong and the seven bairns huddled together inside excited that it was finished. The old barley sacking was still drying on the dyke, so the floor was still damp but the mood was good till wee Jessie began to complain of a wet bum prompting a change of plan. Gordon poked his head out of the den and looked up at the sky. "How about we skirt the woods and enjoy the sun and see if we can catch a rabbit for dinner? We dinna have a trap but it might be fun."

Charlie's ears pricked at the sound of his favourite animal and he set off at a pace remarkably fast for an underfed three-year-old. The others followed and were soon back in the open countryside where the sun was caressing the earth.

Grace sat on a dry hillock overlooking Dufftown and began to dig in the soil with a small stick. A long, fat worm wriggled upwards and she gently pulled it from the earth and showed it to Peter. "Ooh that's a long one. I'm going to find a bigger one."

Gordon picked up wee Jessie and spun her around in a circle who responded with squeals of delight, her wet clothing forgotten. He had a soft spot for Jessie and happily let her sit on his knee whilst she picked at the wee wild flowers that grew sporadically.

Donald looked at his brother. "I thought we were going to hunt for rabbits."

Jessie snuggled into Gordon as he replied, "You go. I've been working in the fields all week and want tae rest a while." His leg still ached where his master had struck him with his horse whip and crouching to fix the den had not helped. Most farmers were just as sorry for the lack of work on offer as they were for the lack of money and prayed for an upturn in the weather and a return to normality. The close knit community stood together to face poverty but folk such as Gordon's employer had a different outlook and took to blaming employees instead of nature. If David had been aware of his loon's predicament he would have intervened but Gordon, all too aware of the need of a wage, kept quiet and hid his bruises.

"Right ye are. Who's coming wi' me?"

"Me! Me! Me!" shouted Charlie as he again sprinted off towards the path that followed the edge of the woodland.

"I'll come," announced Helen, rising from the hillock

and walking with Donald behind Charlie. Helen was the eldest quine and still in school and would probably enter domestic service or perhaps the Fife's Mills lay in wait for her and her sisters where other dangers lurked, with machinery that grabbed long hair and wee hands as it weaved wool into cloth.

Charlie stopped at the path and put his finger to his lips to hush his brother and sister as they approached and pointed to a burrow just off the path. A wee wooden rabbit that was forever clutched in his hand was slid into his pocket. Now with both hands free he stayed to the left and knelt down. Helen edged along the path and entered the wood behind the burrow whilst Donald lay on his stomach directly above it, hands poised.

The three bairns waited.

A rustle was heard above them as a bird left its tree but no one moved. A vole scampered past Charlie and his eyes followed it for a second before once again glueing themselves to the entrance of the burrow. Eventually Charlie saw a pair of ears twitching - sensing - and gave a tiny nod to his brother. Donald's arms very slowly glided forward, his eyes locked with Charlie's and when Charlie nodded again he lowered his head and thrust his arms downwards onto what he hoped would be a rabbit's body.

Donald felt the softness of rabbit fur as it slipped through his fingers and bolted towards Charlie who dived onto it landing heavily on his stomach as it escaped. The rabbit darted left and circled round to where another burrow entrance lay, marking safety, but Helen was there and having removed her shawl launched herself at the entrance of the burrow just as the rabbit was about to enter, successfully capturing it in her shawl. Holding tight to the wriggling garment until Donald reached her and put the rabbit out of its misery within its woollen prison, Helen triumphantly carried it home by its hind legs.

Quite how she managed to do it would never be answered and it was with considerable disbelief that the bairns returned home with a rabbit for dinner having been caught by a woollen shawl knitted by her mama. Laughter ran out in the cottage that afternoon as bellies were tended and love filled the cracks in the walls.

Charlie rubbed his belly. One rabbit was not nearly enough for nine folk but the tender morsels of meat had sated the yearning within and with a decent dollop of tatties alongside, mixed with a little butter, it had felt like a feast. "When I am growed up I will eat rabbit and pheasant every day. What's the other thing called that we have sometimes, Papa?"

David smiled. "Ye have had pork, Charlie, which comes fae a pig. Beef comes fae a cow but ye have never eaten that."

Grace spoke aloud unthinking. "I used to love beef. Cook made it so lovely and tender and it melted in my mouth."

Eight faces turned and stared. "Cook?" Donald and Helen asked simultaneously.

Grace hesitated and glanced at her husband who nodded. "I have never told ye this, bairns, but my life was quite different when I was wee. I lived in a large house in Aberdeen and my father was a wealthy man and we had servants but it was not a happy home for me and when I met yer papa I left home and never returned."

Gordon sprang up from his chair, sparks of anger embedding themselves into his mother as he spat, "Ye mean we dinna need tae be going hungry and working for cruel folk? Why do ye not feed us if ye hae money?"

Grace flinched as her loon's words stung. "Gordon, there is nae money. I left that old life behind."

"Sit down, Gordon. I will not hae ye speaking tae yer mother in that way. There are things ye dinna understand.

We are sorry that sometimes there is little food but that is down tae me and nae yer mother. It's my responsibility tae provide for ye all."

Gordon glared at his kin and left the cottage as tears threatened to escape. Donald rose and muttered, "I will go after him." His own anger building as he thought of his mother's words.

The air in the cottage hung heavy and thick with words both spoken and unspoken causing the younger bairns to look at one another unsure and confused. Charlie asked his mama, "Can we hae a cook who makes beef?"

Helen intervened before either of her parents could answer. "Come on a'body, let's go oot and play a game o' hide and seek." She grabbed Charlie's hand and shooed everyone out the door.

Grace let her head fall into her hands as David sat staring into the embers of the fire.

It was never mentioned again.

*

THE FAMILY GATHERED round the table as David read the long awaited letter.

Dear Mother and Father,

We hope this letter finds you well. We wanted to let ye know that we have arrived safely on Canada's shore and have been very fortunate to secure both lodgings and employment immediately upon arrival. The journey on the ship was rather unsettling on the stomach, especially for Hugh, but we have both found our land legs again. The first thing to strike us was the heat. Now being August we are in the peak of summer and it will take some getting used to but it is wonderful at the same time to experience such warmth having left Scotland so cold.

We have both been employed by the Canadian Pacific Railway Company and charged with helping to build a railroad from the east of Canada all the way to the west! It is quite a feat and will take several years to complete. At the moment we are both labouring as construction workers, clearing and levelling the land in readiness for track. It is heavy work, especially in the heat, but the construction manager is a quick witted Irishman and there are many folk here from Scotland so there is much camaraderie.

It has only been a week but it feels right to be here. Don't be worrying about us - we have food in our bellies each day and decent lodgings. You can reply to this address. Kiss the wee bairns for us.

We will write again soon with more news. Till then, with fond wishes, your sons,

George and Hugh.

Grace let go of a breath she had been unaware of holding. "It's so good to hear from them and they sound in good spirits."

"Aye, quine, they do. It must be some adventure travelling across the ocean and landing in a foreign land."

"But I do miss them so," Grace said as tears welled in her eyes.

David patted her hand. "Aye, we all do, but they will surely hae a better life and that's we want for our bairns."

Charlie butted in, his brow furrowed. "Did they lose their legs?"

"What?" laughed Donald.

"They said they found their legs so where did they lose them. Do they hae wooden ones like the minister? I saw the minister's one once when his breeks got caught on a nail."

Grace's tears turned to tears of laughter which spread around the table like wildfire and she lifted wee Charlie onto her knee and hugged him tight. Once the laughter had subsided his papa explained to him the concept of sea legs.

The Great Divide

No sooner had the summer, that had not been a summer, filtered away the Robertsons found themselves in the midst of winter. The wind blew them into 1882 much like it had the previous year. The residents of Dufftown fought the elements as best they could, worked when work was available and hunkered down in the evenings sheltering from the bitter cold. Some believed the weather was punishment from God, others believed it to be the work of the fairies. Whatever the cause, folk were fed up of poor harvests, prevalent cold and lack of both money and food.

The great divide between rich and poor caused unrest and the working class movement campaigned and protested for better work and living conditions throughout the land. Politics were changing and the old way of doing things was under threat. A further assassination attempt, the eighth, on Queen Victoria by one Roderick Maclean also spoke to the Government of a country's unrest at the establishment.

As Easter arrived the countryside saw a time of unrest and social protest as landowners denied grazing rights to crofters who decided that enough was enough following the Highland Clearances and years of hardship. This culminated in the Battle of the Braes on Skye bringing support from across Scotland which paved the way for future legislation to protect crofters.

But no amount of protesting could alter the course of the weather. The wind howled, the rain battered crops and bellies remained empty.

Charlie was now four in years but lacked the energy of a young bairn due to sometimes having only two meagre meals a day. Grace took in sewing for the folk of Dufftown earning herself a few pennies here and there. She would walk down into Dufftown to deliver some garments she had sewn and Charlie would accompany her but walking a mile there and back with little food in his belly seemed an awfully long way sometimes, especially as they lived on a hill. On one such day his older sister, Helen, was off school as she had been required to help her mother with the sewing so Charlie was allowed to stay at home whilst their mother walked into town.

Annie Clark, the minister's wife, had employed Grace's services to alter a dress for her. Although quite adept with a needle herself, she liked to offer work where she could to help those in need. Grace, having delivered her package to Mrs Clark, hesitated by the door.

"I was wondering, Mrs Clark, if you would make a point of writing down a message from me in case anything ever happens to myself or my husband."

"Goodness, Mrs Robertson, ye are both young and surely don't have to be thinking of such things."

"It's just that… I have a feeling in my bones… and I would like my bairns to be cared for. If ye would be so kind I would like ye to take note of a name for me. Yer husband has the name and address of my mother but I would not wish her to be informed if anything were to happen to me. I have a sister, Rose. Rose Milne is her married name and I wondered if perhaps ye would contact her on my behalf if the occasion should arise. I do not have an address but it may not be difficult for you or the minister to find it, her being a lady in Aberdeen." Grace's eyes were both serious and sad and Annie felt somewhat moved by her words. She moved to the bureau by the window and removed a piece of paper. She sat down and wrote on the paper.

"There, Mrs Robertson. It is written and I will keep it safe in my bureau."

Grace nodded. "Thank you. It is a weight off my mind. Good afternoon, Mrs Clark."

"Good afternoon."

CHARLIE'S BROTHER, PETER, was three years older than Charlie, with Jessie sandwiched in between. The three bairns were often together whilst their older siblings were employed in chores. The weather followed a pattern of dreichness, month after month, but bairns being bairns, play continued without thought, unlike empty bellies whose loud rumblings complained to the air.

As summer came around, rain prevailed and crops were yet again delayed. Where the time for harvest would have meant work for all - young and old - folk resigned themselves to another poor harvest and lack of money. The younger Robertson bairns were shooed outside unless the weather was too coorse and the fields and woodland that surrounded their cottage held many delights. Peter was a climber of trees and set out each day in pursuit of reaching higher into lofty branches and calling down to Jessie and Charlie when he spotted something of interest. Although he was but seven in years he had soaked in the teachings from his father regarding wildlife. He could name every bird in the sky and took great delight in peeking into a nest whenever the opportunity arose.

Where Peter's eyes were forever upwards, Charlie's were concentrated on the ground. His love of rabbits was so strong that if he had been small enough he would have crawled right inside a burrow and followed the trail of tunnels to see his beloved creatures snuggled warmly in their homes. He had tried once, much to the laughter of his kin and the disappointment to himself.

The three bairns were playing by the burn early one evening when Donald returned from working at the shoemakers carrying a letter in his hand and he beckoned his siblings inside.

"News fae Canada, Mother," Donald announced.

Grace came away from the pot hung low over the fire and sat herself on a stool. "Open it, loon. I can't wait till yer father returns. Read every word now."

Donald tore open the envelope and Grace was disappointed to see just one page had lain within it. It had been many months since they had last heard from Hugh and George. Donald sat by the table and proceeded to read,

Dear Mother and Father,

We hope this letter finds ye all well. We are sorry that we have been unable to write as often as we would have liked. Travelling with the railway company has meant moving frequently as the line extends westwards and the days have been so long and tiring. Both of us have decided to bide here in Winnipeg and have found work as construction labourers. Winnipeg is a rapidly growing town with good prospects, now that the railway line is here, so we are taking our chance to put down some roots. There is a need for many houses here so we should be in work for a long time to come. We will not miss the back breaking work on the line or the poor wages. We hoped for a better life here in Canada and finally we may have it. The work is better and far less dangerous and we are earning a decent wage.

We will write again soon when we are more settled. Love to all,

Hugh and George.

The family looked at their mother for her reaction. Sometimes the letters caused a sigh and a smile and at other times, a steady flow of tears. Grace closed her eyes for a moment bringing to mind her loons faces. "It is good news. They will no longer be living like lost souls with no abode."

The bairns sighed with relief and the soup bubbled in its pot as if dancing to the rhythm of a reel. Charlie had no sense of where Canada was, or indeed how different it was there, but he felt an excitement in his chest to think of his brothers having been on a train and a ship and were now to bide in a place with such a funny name. "Maybe I'll go on a big ship, Mama, and-"

"No! Ye are to stay close, Charlie. Two bairns in Canada and one in his grave is enough for me to bear."

Her look was hard and her words stern which Charlie was not used to. He lowered his head. "Aye, Mama."

Black Tendrils

Folk in the North were beginning to think that the sun would never again bathe the glen in its comforting warmth, so absent had it been throughout three consecutive summers and the persistent cold and rain had blighted crops and robbed men of work and a wage. The dreichness of the grey sky had an effect on folks minds and often tempers flared or tears flowed in exasperation. Human nature being what it is, those with a dour disposition fared better as they lived life in a constant state of negativity anyway but those who erred on the side of positivity struggled to see past the facts in front of them and stared at empty plates disheartened and disillusioned.

The snow buried the land in the north east of Scotland in March 1883. The dwellers of Hillside Cottage fell asleep huddled together for warmth and opened their weary eyes in the morning to a white blanket which smothered their home. The cottage groaned with the weight of snow pinning it down and straining its already buckled knees. The air felt eerie as all sound was muffled and the silence lay heavy and thick as the snow itself.

Grace rose to stoke the fire and set about making a potful of porridge for her family but as was so often the way she was taken over by a bout of coughing so loud and persistent that all six bairns woke and David gently helped his wife into the fireside chair.

"Here, quine, drink a little milk."

"Nae need tae fuss, David, it will pass. It…" She was taken again by an awful wracking cough and Helen, wrapping herself in a shawl, made her way to the hearth and began to stir the porridge for her mother.

"Dinna talk, Grace, just rest a while."

Grace sat back in the chair and allowed her eyes to close. She had been so very tired and could never quite catch her breath. David rubbed the small pane of glass in the kitchen, clearing the thin layer of ice on it to peer out onto the land lit only by a bright moon. "The snow is deep but I will need to make my way to town to see if there is work."

Grace nodded. "Aye."

"There'll be nae school today bairns as I doubt yer wee legs would manage to plough through the snow and anyway we need the peat for the fire. It looks a lot deeper than yesterday so stay indoors and help yer mama wi' chores. Donald ye can walk down wi' me to yer work after we've had our porridge."

"Aye, father. It's just as well Gordon had the mind tae stay at his work last night. Farr's farm is higher up the glen and he would have had an awful job trying to make it there in time."

"He may well be stuck there for a few days by the look o' things."

Charlie cuddled into Jessie and the two stayed under their blanket in the hope that the porridge would come to them where they lay instead of having to go to the table. Mama was a stickler for manners but Mama wasn't well so there was a spark of hope.

Helen set about ladling porridge into bowls and sure enough two bowls were passed to the youngest bairns snuggled in their shared bed. "Dinna spill it." she said, which echoed her mother's tone to perfection. Charlie and Jessie held tight to their bowls and with spoons too big for wee mouths managed to take in every hot, sticky morsel and even surreptitiously licked the bowls clean.

"Grace, you can wash the bowls when a'body's finished and Peter it can be your job today to tend the fire." Two disgruntled faces nodded but no reply was given. Helen glanced towards her mother and noticed her shiver so fetched Donald's blanket from the bed and wrapped it around her shoulders receiving a small smile in return.

Father and son rose from the table, their bellies as sated as they could ever be on a cold morning. "We'll be off now, quine," David said as he kissed the top of Grace's head. The door was opened letting in a rush of icy air and David kicked away the snow that had accumulated up the door and he and Donald stepped out into a day where the sun was yet to rise.

If you had asked Charlie about that day he would have said he remembered a good day where he stayed in bed to keep warm listening to stories told by his older siblings and playing imaginary games. His mama spent the day by the fire as Helen acted like mother, giving out chores and making broth for dinner out of the last of the neeps and carrots that were in the cottage alongside a handful of barley. If Papa was unable to find work that day it would be porridge and bannocks till more food could be purchased.

Grace felt cold and was visibly shivering. Helen was trying to keep her warm by tucking in her shawl and blanket but still her mother shivered. "Will ye eat some soup, Mama? It will warm ye."

Grace turned her face away. "Nae hungry," she muttered as another bout of coughing took her and she clutched at her chest. Her breath came fast and short and Helen bit her bottom lip as she looked upon her mama.

As David and Donald ploughed their way through the snow the folk in Dufftown were clearing a path from their homes to various stores and places of work, each with a shovel in their hands or a large broom. For those living in the grand houses such work was for the servants as the wealthy looked upon the snowy hills from the comfort of their blazing hearths and exclaimed how wonderful and beautiful nature could be. Of course, this fact did not bypass the poor; they were as aware as any of their homeland's beauty but when it endangered lives it was another matter. Roads and rail tracks had to be cleared so food and other essentials could be transported, not to mention folk had to get to their places of work or no money would be earned.

It had been a slow trudge into Dufftown from Hillside Cottage for the Robertsons and what would normally have been a twenty minute walk took more than double that as first they had had to dig themselves out of their own house where the snow had drifted forming a wall five feet high. The gas lamps from the streets below them reflected off the white snow and as they neared the town there were many folk out clearing roads and paths and the air had a buzz of comradeship. Donald left his father and headed towards Mr Thompson's shoemakers workshop and David followed the road into the square where folk in need of work gathered. The three storey clock tower lorded over its surroundings and at its base a group of eight men were being addressed by the station master, Mr Duguid.

"As far as I can ascertain, it is one large tree that is causing the problem and the snow has drifted high up against it. It's nae too far along, just passed Balvenie Castle before the bridge. I have informed Keith station to stop all trains from leaving there till we have managed to clear the line. Unfortunately the laird's lumberjacks are away on some other job so we will hae to do our best. I dinna have experience o' tree felling but how hard can it be. We will have to walk along the line with our equipment and according to the laird he is waiting for some important shipment fae Aberdeen so is willing tae pay each man the handsome wage of two shillings if it is cleared afore noon. He's also lending us his son to help but what help an Edinburgh scholar will be I can't say. He's meeting us at the station."

An agreeable murmur ran through the group and David breathed a sigh of relief that he would earn a good wage that day.

"Right men, follow me and gather what ropes and saws ye have alongside yer shovels." David knew most of the group, a mix of day labourers like himself and railway employees. He fell in line with the men as they made their way back towards the railway station and lowered themselves onto the snowy line alongside the laird's son, Angus McNaughton, dressed in a long, gentleman's, woollen overcoat as if about to take a walk in the park with a young lady. The men doffed their caps but said nothing.

The tree had only partially come down and hung low over the line with snow backed up behind it. One of the men walked round behind the tree.

"If we dig away the snow here at the back we can see how much root is left in the ground. It might be better to cut it away at its roots and let it fall onto the line and then cut it."

A few heads nodded but young Angus interrupted, "When I was younger my father indulged my passion for all things trees and allowed me to spend a summer shadowing the lumberjack on our land. I learned much from him and I even own my own pair of hobnailed boots. I can tell ye that cutting away at the roots is highly dangerous."

Mr Duguid scratched his head. "Time is of the essence so if ye have a plan I will hear it." His tone was curt. He had little idea of felling but he was damn sure that it was more than an upper class scholar.

"There are several cuts we will need to make into the tree in order to control how and where it falls but first let's clear the snow behind and see what we are dealing with."

The men shrugged and began to shovel snow away as Angus had suggested. No one was going to argue with the laird's son but they hoped he knew what he was doing as two shillings was too good a wage to lose.

Once the tree was free from snow the men could see that half the tree roots were still in the ground. Angus surveyed the angle.

"We need to cut a chunk away from the side in which we want the tree to fall which weakens the tree." He pointed to an area about two feet from the base. "Then we need to cut into it from both sides to prevent it splitting and going backwards."

"Surely if we just take a Crosscut saw we can saw it right through in one cut. We dinna have time for several cuts. It's a high tree but not overly thick."

"I can assure ye, Mr Duguid, that if ye do that ye will have at least one death on yer hands. I think my father would like his only son to survive him."

Silence befell the group as Mr Duguid struggled with his temper. He didn't want to hang for letting the Laird's son be killed. "We'll do it your way but you will stand way over there out o' the way. I dinna care if ye own a shop full o' hobnailed boots ye are not going near that tree."

Angus laughed. "Ah but Mr Duguid I own the tree as it's on my family's land."

So a plan was made and work started, directed by Angus. Once the initial cuts had been made he helped the men to cut into the back of the tree in order to encourage it to fall forward. Rope was tied around the girth above the cuts and the men pulled hard, encouraging the tree to turn and fall in the opposite direction. Slowly and steadily the plan worked and the tree fell away from the group, landing safely, adjacent to the track.

A cheer went up as the men realised that they would indeed be paid well as the time was only eleven o'clock. Mr Duguid shook the Laird's son's hand. "Thank you, Mr McNaughton."

"Not a bad result for an Edinburgh scholar," was the answer, to which a sheepish Mr Duguid smiled.

The tree having been cleared, the men made their way back along the track to the station. Mr Duguid sent his telegram to Keith to inform them that the line was now safe and the Laird who had arrived at the station in time to hear the news had brought with him the men's wages, as promised, and a basket of freshly made scones his cook had baked earlier that morning.

David whispered to Mr Duguid, "I wonder what important shipment the Laird is waiting on to afford such generosity."

"Nae idea. I'm just glad that his loon is no longer my concern."

It continued to snow so David found himself clearing roads for the rest of the afternoon. It felt good to earn a good wage for once and although he had berated the weather, today it had resulted in work and money in his pocket. As darkness fell all roads were clear and the snow had finally stopped so David decided to go by the shoemaker's to see if Donald was ready for home. His loon was walking towards him as he turned down the main street so the two trudged once again across the fields to home with money in their pockets and a pheasant slung over David's shoulder that had come a cropper at the side of the road. "Yer mother can cook a feast the morn' if she is feeling better."

As they entered Hillside Cottage bringing in the cold air again the house breathed a sigh of relief as the tense air emanating from Helen evaporated out through the door at the sight of her papa. She ran to her father. "Oh, Papa, Mama is breathing funny and will not eat."

David crossed the floor to where Grace sat, unmoved since the morning, and he felt the clammy, white skin of her cheek and heard the short rasping breaths forcing their way from her chest. Panic flared in him and he turned to Donald. "Run and get the doctor, loon. Tell him yer mother is struggling to breathe. Hurry now."

"Aye, Father. I'll be as quick as I can." He bolted out the door that he had just come through.

David knelt down by his wife. "I will help ye into bed, quine. It will be more comfortable than the chair." Grace did not answer and he gathered her into his arms and placed her on the old thin mattress that lay in the box bed opposite the fire and covered her with a blanket.

In the act of lying down Grace was unable to catch her breath at all and seeing the panic in her eyes David sat her up and held her against his chest as she coughed. A green coloured phlegm trickled down her chin and David shuddered as a memory appeared in his mind.

Sensing that things were not right the bairns huddled together on their shared bed, remaining quiet and unsure. The clock on the shelf ticked. Its constant tick, tick, tick signalling the passage of time that David had no control over. Grace's head lay on his shoulder and he was aware of each short breath that came sporadically, and sometimes not at all, and at such times his heart constricted and time did indeed stop as he willed her to breathe again.

His eyes constantly flickered towards the door, willing it to open and bring the doctor through its splintered frame. An hour passed and still no one came. Darkness had long since descended and all David could do was hold Grace and whisper what he hoped were words of comfort.

Grace's last breath was but the flutter of air that an eyelash creates and David knew without looking upon her that she had gone. He sat completely still, as still as she, and closed his eyes. His arms were unwilling to let go and he took comfort in the warmth that was still present in her.

When Donald returned with the doctor some time later, David was sitting in the same position, holding his beloved Grace.

The Scattering of Bairns

The snow drifts reduced and turned to slush over the following days. Mrs Clark arrived first thing on a cold but bright morning to collect the bairns who were to live in the orphanage. Her husband being the minister, it was her role to work alongside him to help those in need, but this was one task she did not relish. Alongside her stood Mrs Grant, her widowed sister in law who helped with the running of the parish. She looked around the small dwelling with its damp walls and foetid smell and shuddered. It was not right that so many lived as the Robertsons did. The weather had been so cruelly bizarre and with crops destroyed no work was to be had which meant little food for bellies. Some landowners were better than others in providing decent living quarters for workers but others cared only for their profits and did not think of how folk were living.

Wee Peter and Jessie were huddled by the fire playing whilst Helen and Grace, aged ten and nine, were at the table with their father, haunted looks on their faces. It had only been two weeks since Grace had died and grief and confusion was etched onto faces. David did not look at her and Mrs Clark was unsure as to what to say under the circumstances.

Annie Clark had indeed remembered her promise to Grace and had contacted Rose Milne with the sad news of her sister's passing. A letter had come back stating that they would take the youngest child into their care. Annie had passed on the news to David who had merely nodded and arrangements had been made.

The pony and trap waited outside but only the four bairns would be travelling in it as they owned nothing but the tattered ill fitting clothes on their backs and a rag doll or wooden animal toy that fitted in a wee palm.

"Shall I settle the bairns in the buggy, Mr Robertson?"

David closed his eyes and dragged himself from his chair. "Aye, come on bairns it's time ye were off. Tonight ye will hae a hot meal and a warm bed." His words were cajoling but his eyes were dead. Wee Peter and Jessie clambered off the floor oblivious to where they were headed but Helen spoke, "I dinna want to go. I can stay wi' ye Papa. I can cook and help wi' chores."

David's heart constricted with her pleading. Someone had told him what he needed to do, he couldn't remember who, and he had agreed. His bairns needed tending and with little work there was scarcely any food so what choice was there but to have others take care of them. The orphanage in Aberlour had a good name and four of his bairns would be together at least. Donald and Gordon already had employment and could bide at their place of work.

"I ken how able ye are, quine, but that's why ye need to go to the orphanage so ye can look after yer wee sisters and brother there. It will be strange for them and ye can help to reassure them."

Helen's lip trembled and she clung to her wee sister by her side. Mrs Grant placed her arm around Helen's shoulder. "Yer father is right, dear. Come away now and help me get everyone into the buggy."

So one-by-one Helen, Grace, Peter and Jessie, ten, nine, seven and six in years, scrambled up onto the seat followed by Mrs Grant who was to accompany them to Aberlour. David had held each one briefly and Charlie had stood alongside him not understanding why Helen had squeezed him so tight he could not breathe and had burst into tears. The only words to come from their papa were, "I'm sorry."

Mrs Clark had to fight back tears herself at the scene but was conscious of her role and her breaking down would not help the situation.

David turned from the trap not wishing to watch it descend the track and took Charlie back inside with Mrs Clark following behind. "Is there any luggage to travel with us, Mr Robertson?"

"Nay. He has what he stands in."

David stood in the middle of the cottage and cast his eyes around what was his home. With no kin left to bide in it it was no longer a home, just four stone walls, an earth floor and a fire. The love and tenderness that had soaked into the walls over the years and cocooned them now seemed to have soaked so deep that they were no longer tangible. All David now felt was cold, hard stone. A stillness came over him and he turned to Charlie. "Come on, loon, it's time we were off. Ye dinna want tae miss yer train."

Charlie looked up at his father, his eyes wide and unsure. "Are you coming on the train, Papa?"

"I told ye already. Mrs Clark is taking ye."

The day had dawned fair, if still a little cold, and the three of them walked the track that took them into Dufftown and they turned left towards the station. No words were spoken. Mrs Clark opened her mouth to speak but no words would come and she closed it again. It was just before nine o'clock when they got there and several travellers were waiting to embark the next train to Keith. As they heard the engine approach David knelt down in front of his son.

"Your aunt and uncle will look after ye, Charlie, and ye'll go tae school and…" His words became caught in his throat and he swallowed them back. Taking a letter out of his pocket he placed it into Charlie's jacket pocket. "Keep this safe, loon. Promise me now."

"I promise," Charlie whispered and his father pulled him in for a swift embrace before standing and abruptly turning away, walking back the way they had come.

Mrs Clark saw the haunted, defeated look in David's eyes as she took Charlie's hand and led him up the step and into the carriage.

Nae Rabbits

Mrs Clark sighed as she looked upon Charlie's bewildered face but determined that she would make the train journey as enjoyable as possible. She settled Charlie and herself in their compartment on a long single bench seat. Another identical seat lay opposite, which was empty, and a large window allowed the passengers to watch the passing landscape.

"Come, Charlie, sit on my knee so that ye can better see out the window and we will count how many animals we see." Charlie settled himself on Mrs Clark's lap sending up a waft of his unwashed body which caused her to wince and cough. There was only so much that a handkerchief and some spit could do but at least his face would be cleaner on arrival. Annie scolded herself. If only she had thought, she could have picked Charlie up early from his cottage and taken him to her home for a bath first. Goodness knows what his aunt would think. She would also have tried to source some shoes.

A long shrill whistle was blown and the train moved off with a jolt. Charlie's eyes widened and his mouth opened as the engine picked up speed and left his hometown. The melodic sound of the wheels sang to Charlie and his whole body jostled with the rhythm as excitement took over and a love of trains was born.

"Look, Charlie, there are two rabbits running in the field, can ye see them?"

"Aye. Ooh they're fast. I can run fast too. I'm faster than Peter and he's much bigger than me."

Mrs Clark's eyes closed momentarily and her arms squeezed Charlie as the thought ran through her mind that he may never see or run with his brother again, but surely the life that lay ahead of him in Aberdeen would be a better one in so many ways: a full belly each day and regular baths, at the very least. She had heard stories of the unsavoury and spiteful Mr Robert Ross but she hoped with every fibre of her being that his daughter had nothing but kindness in her to bestow on wee Charlie.

Charlie wriggled on Annie's lap. "Are there rabbits in Aberdeen?"

"Not as many, no, Charlie. Aberdeen is a big city wi' lots o' houses and buildings."

His eyebrows knitted together. "Why?"

"Well, rabbits live in the countryside."

"Why?"

Annie frowned. She had forgotten how many 'whys' could emanate from a child. "Aberdeen is like lots of Dufftowns altogether with many buildings and no fields, just gardens."

Charlie's head spun round and his wide eyes locked onto Mrs Clark's. "Nae fields? But where do the coos and sheep live?"

Annie smiled. "Yer new home will be very different, loon. Aberdeen is a busy place wi' lots o' folk and hustle and bustle but I'm sure that biding there wi' yer aunt and uncle will be fun and exciting and maybe sometimes they will take ye oot into the country and ye can see rabbits and cows and sheep."

Charlie's head turned back to face the window still clutching his wee wooden rabbit.

The two alighted in Keith half an hour later to await their connection to Aberdeen. Charlie's expression was no longer baffled at his father's goodbye, his perplexed thoughts having been dispersed by the sights and sounds of his first train journey. He hopped from one foot to the other as he waited, nodding to each fellow traveller and touching his cap as they passed. "Morning," he said to one man. "Fine day," he said to a woman of some means, his infectious smile teasing a small smile in return as his reverent and genuine tone was noted and his good manners belied his look of an urchin. The Robertsons had brought their bairns up well.

"The next train will have more carriages, Charlie, carrying folk all the way from Inverness. We will arrive in Aberdeen just afore dinner time and someone from yer aunt's house will meet us at the station."

"Will there be dinner today?"

Annie's heart constricted. "There will be dinner every day, Charlie, and breakfast and supper too."

The wee loon's face lit up. "No rumbly belly? Ever?"

"No rumbly belly. Yer aunt and uncle hae enough money for food every day."

"Oh. I think my belly will like that, Mrs Clark."

The train came into view, grabbing Charlie's attention and saving Annie from having to speak again which was just as well as a lump had formed in her throat.

Only a handful of folk got off the train and Annie took her charge's hand and they climbed aboard a carriage for the second time that morning finding seats opposite an elderly couple. The air was cool but the sun shone into the carriage and warmed wee toes. Charlie sat with his nose pressed up against the window and as the conductor raised his flag and blew on his whistle his wee face lit up and he waved at the man as the train gathered momentum.

"Well, Charlie, I wonder what things we will see from this train."

A wee tongue blethered as fast as a spark leaping from the fire. "I can see folk waving and they're getting smaller and the horses and traps are along there and… oh the station has gone. The trees are hiding it. Look, Mrs Clark, a farmer is moving the sheep and one is going the wrong way. The dog is getting it back. My papa says sheep are daft and some folk are like sheep."

The old couple laughed. "Aye, lad, yer father is right."

"He said I need to be like a stag and I will do just fine."

That lump returned to Annie's throat. *What is it about this particular bairn that tugs at my heart? I have known many poor folk and witnessed their plight but Charlie's innocence and way of being is different somehow and I dearly hope that the life that lies ahead of him will be a good one.*

The train journeyed on and eventually the repetitive motion and mellifluous sound of the train lulled Charlie to sleep and his head gently nuzzled into Annie's arm.

When Hope is Lost

David turned from his loon, leaving the station before the train had departed and walked towards Lettoch Farm. He felt nothing but a calmness as his legs carried one foot after the other up the hill, skirting the town and following the path between the trees. The sun had made an appearance bathing the fields in a rich golden hue and filtering through the branches of the trees forming dappled patterns on the path. Had David's mind been different he may have noticed the beauty surrounding him and felt the sun on his cheeks but as he strode purposefully on he was unaware of nature gently embracing him as his one thought had captured his mind.

He saw the ghillie in the distance, out checking on the number of grouse, and as a hand was brought up in a wave David returned the gesture but kept on course to his destination. He had worked many a day at Lettoch and knew the daily routine, so as long as he remained vigilant he would be able to get what he needed without being seen.

The farm was one of the biggest in the area and the handsome, stone farmhouse stood proud next to the various outbuildings and sheds. It was a gentleman of a house, strong in foundation and giving in nature, bestowing the onlooker with a sense of courteous honour and good manners. David had always admired it and subconsciously gave a brief nod of his head as if acknowledging an elder.

The hens clucked and pecked at the ground in the far corner as David slowed his pace: his eyes scouring both the fields and the doors to each shed. The cows had been put back out to graze following being milked and the dairymaids had returned to the kitchen and the labourers would be out in the fields til dinner time so he did not expect to be seen or disturbed. The wife of the house had a love of horses and he knew that on weekdays she took one of her horses for a ride at ten o'clock each morning and did not return for at least an hour. With the snow now gone, surely she would be hankering for time with her horse so would maybe be gone a while longer.

Having seen the ghillie out earlier he headed for where he knew the shotguns were kept for the visiting gentry to pursue their love of shooting game. It was a long, low steading set apart behind the farm house with a thick wooden door kept locked, but to those in the know the large key lay on top of the door frame, too big to be kept in a pocket.

With a final look around him, David retrieved the key and inserted it, opening the door with a small creak and entered. Closing the door behind him he breathed a sigh of relief and allowed his eyes to adjust to the dimness of the room. He had never been in there before but faced with rows of shotguns and boxes of ammunition on shelves, no searching was necessary.

The scent of wood lingered in the air from the newly crafted cabinets that held the arms. David had always liked the smell of wood and allowed his fingers to caress the shelving, following the lines and contours of the oak, so like the patterns the current caused in a river. His mind wandered back to when he was a boy helping his father to make a table for their cottage. He had been taught how to plane the wood, cutting away the roughness to leave it silky smooth, the shavings collecting at his feet like ringlets in a bairn's hair. His father had been a patient teacher and David remembered the pride he had felt on hearing words of praise and encouragement.

With the picture of helping his father in his mind, David's fingers moved from the wooden shelves to the row of shotguns and he again felt the smoothness of wood as he walked the length of the first cabinet touching each shotgun in turn until he came to the end of the row. He turned and scanned each one in turn pausing at one near the middle, the hue of its wood darker than the rest. Reaching out, his hand travelled upwards, feeling the coolness of the metal and he made his decision. Taking it down he held it for a second, acknowledging the weight of it before turning to the boxes of shells.

A scratching noise stopped him in his tracks and David stood still and silent, his ears listening for voices outside as four wee legs scurried across the floor. Only a mouse.

His plan had been to take the shotgun to the woodland behind the farm but there was something comforting about the scent of the cabinets which had brought his father back to him and so he changed his mind. He took the twine from his pocket and tied one end tight around the trigger and pulled the barrel down with a click releasing it from the stock and inserted the brass and card shell. Closing the two parts together again he sat himself down with his back to the side of the cabinet. David measured the twine against his leg and tied the other end around his ankle. Flexing and unflexing he tested the distance needed and made the necessary adjustments as his mind succumbed to the relief emerging and trickling through him like the first bubbles of a burn following a drought.

When all was ready David rested his exhausted head against the oak and then with a final breath placed the barrel under his chin and thrust his foot forward.

Willowbank

The train was in its final minutes of its journey to Aberdeen when Annie Clark woke Charlie who immediately sprang to life again as only a child can following a sleep. "We're almost there, loon. The station will be very busy so ye must bide close tae me til we find who is taking us to yer aunt's house."

Annie had only been to Aberdeen twice before and she was wary of the crowds and the busyness of it all but she had a bairn to deliver and a tongue in her head so any nerves would be overcome by thrawn determination.

Charlie nodded and his nose felt the smooth hardness of the window yet again as his eyes drank in the tall buildings.

"We are about to go through a long tunnel and it will be dark for a minute," explained Annie. The train began to slow and entered the tunnel.

"I'm a rabbit in a burrow hiding fae the fox," a wee voice said.

The train slowed to a stop and a throng of folk lined the platform from one end to the other. Charlie had never in his life seen so many people and before the door to their carriage was even open he could hear the throng and urgency of the station. Shouts from conductors, banging and clattering of luggage and goods being removed from the train and the chunterring, metal clanging of other trains, all vied for attention.

Where Annie was nervous of the bustling, crowded city, Charlie was enthralled, but upon alighting from the carriage his nose was met with the stench of boxes and boxes of fish making their own passage to pastures new. Charlie covered his nose with his free hand, the other having been taken by Mrs Clark as he was propelled through the crowd and out through a tall, stone archway. An array of ponies and traps and horses with closed carriages were stationed along the road, some there to deposit folk and others to collect them. Annie made her way along the line enquiring to each man if he was from Willowbank.

"Mrs Clark?"

"Aye," said a relieved Annie, "that is me and this is Charlie to be taken to Mrs Milne."

The Milnes servant took in the dishevelled and filthy child that was Charlie but said nothing. It was not his job to question.

He doffed his cap. "I am Peter Shaw. Come away. Is there any luggage?"

Annie shook her head at Mr Shaw. He was a tall, well built man used to heavy work by the looks of him but his kind eyes softened his bulky demeanor and she decided there was no need to fear him. "He comes wi' nothing but the goodness within him."

Mr Shaw nodded and he helped his passengers into the carriage.

So the two travellers settled themselves on the velvet covered bench and Charlie got his first glimpse of how the wealthy travelled and his first sighting of the streets of a city through the carriage window. Anyone watching him would have thought he was trying to escape a wasp so much did his body move in every direction as his eyes, ears and nose absorbed the sights, sounds and smells of a new life.

Charlie laughed as the movement of the wheels on the cobbles caused him to bounce and Annie was glad that the noise and bustle around them did not seem to frighten him as it did her. Aberdeen was a city with pockets of filth and disease peppered with wealth. Ann herself knew of its brothels, thirty six in number some years previously, which women became prey to as her husband's work as a minister had involved the education of fallen women. She had heard that as many as ninety women a year died as a result of such work so it could not be said to be a lifelong career.

They turned into Don Street with its Georgian houses and Annie took a sharp intake of breath as the horses entered the grounds of Willowbank, through a large wrought iron gate and a sweeping path surrounded by a high wall where a grand, four story house stood. The grey granite sparkled under the afternoon sun and the long windows, the eyes of the dwelling, welcomed them with a softness that mirrored the petals clinging delicately to the centre of the flowers blooming in the garden. Unlike so many others which had failed to bloom in a cold spring, these had been protected and nurtured.

The wide front door opened as they climbed down from their perch and a servant appeared followed by the lady of the house, anxious to see who was to be her son. Rose Milne stood straight backed and composed, her slender frame encased in a gown the colour of the sea on a summer's day. Her fair hair was swept up in regal elegance, a few stray tendrils portraying a softness of heart and framing a heart shaped, bonny face. Her pose belied the rapid beating of her heart which had waited so long for a child.

Rose faltered as her eyes fell on the filthy, barefoot bairn but good manners presided and she extended a welcome to

Annie. "Mrs Clark, please come in for some refreshment. You must be parched and hungry after your journey. Peter will take ye back to the station later."

She knelt down and looked closely at Charlie. "Welcome Charlie, I am to be your mother but first my maid will give you a bath and some clean clothes and then you can come down and meet me properly."

Charlie looked into the eyes of this strange woman that had been his mother's sister and saw a likeness there which frightened him. Tears threatened as a longing for his mama engulfed his wee body and his mind failed to understand what was happening. Annie, sensing his apprehension, lay her hands on his shoulders and led him into the house.

"Now, Charlie," she reassured him, "you go and have yer bath and I'll be here when ye come back down."

He nodded at Mrs Clark, biting his lip, and let himself be led up a wide, winding staircase in a house so foreign to him he may as well have been placed on the Moon.

"I am sorry for the state o' him Mrs Milne. If I had realised beforehand I would have taken him to the rectory and bathed him before leaving. His father is just so bereft from losing his wife and having to disperse his bairns that I think it did not enter his mind to wash Charlie."

"I will admit it was a shock seeing him. I had not realised just how…unfortunate things had become for the family."

"He is a bright and good bairn and I am sure with care and attention bestowed upon him he will do ye proud." Annie faltered, fearing that she had overstepped her mark but she needed to reassure herself that she was leaving Charlie in a home where he would be cared for.

"Rest assured, Mrs Clark, he will receive that and a lot more besides. My husband and I have not been blessed with any children despite being married these past ten years." Her eyes fell upon the small drawer in the bureau where a bottle lay in wait. "This house is in need of a child."

Annie nodded in assent and for the first time since entering, smiled.

Charlie, meanwhile, was refusing to step into his bath which looked nothing like his tin bath at home, which had made a sporadic appearance throughout his life, his bathing usually comprising of a cold dicht in the burn in the summer months and a cloth dipped in warm water in the winter. This bath was huge and white and stood beside a contraption that the maid, Mary, said was the toilet. It had a wooden seat that went up and down and a box hung high above with a long chain dangling from it that Mary said he had to pull when he had finished using the toilet so that water could flush through it. The idea of being indoors and sitting on such a thing was so preposterous that he had laughed for a good three minutes.

"I dinna like baths." He stood with his arms folded and a scowl on his face. Mary stood with her hands on her hips.

"Ye will get into that bath and ye will nae come oot til ye shine like the sun. Ye are as black as the lum and ye smell like a byre."

"Don't care. I dinna want tae hae a bath."

"Do ye want tae eat dinner?"

Charlie's stomach rumbled in answer and he thought of Mrs Clark's words regarding having breakfast, dinner and supper. He already missed his home and the hills but he wouldn't miss an empty belly. He eyed Mary suspiciously, unsure if he could trust her to feed him three times a day.

"Will I hae supper too and breakfast in the mornin'?"

Mary's face softened. "Aye, Charlie. Ye will never be hungry in this hoose. I promise."

Charlie nodded. He would believe it if it happened but he wasn't going to take the risk of not being fed by refusing to bathe, so placing his wee wooden rabbit on the chair he gingerly lifted one leg, then the other over the side of the bath and lowered himself in. "Right ye are. Best get on wi' it then."

Mary stifled a giggle at what sounded like the words from an old man. "I think we are going to get on just fine, Charlie."

FOLLOWING HIS BATH, which Charlie quite enjoyed - although he would never have admitted it- Mary led him to his bedchamber. "This is where ye will sleep and there's some new clothes there on the bed for ye to wear. Mrs Milne didn't ken yer size so hopefully they will fit, but more will be bought for ye now that ye are here and we ken how big ye are."

The loon's eyes darted around the room, unable to decipher the fact that he was to sleep in such a place. The walls were covered in patterned paper of blues and greens and a large dresser filled an entire wall. A rug lay over the polished wooden floor and facing him stood a high, black metal bed which looked like a cage. Charlie stared at the bed. "Who do I sleep wi'?"

"Naebody else. It's yer own bed."

"When my brothers and sisters come they will sleep wi me, just like at home. Papa will maybe sleep on the floor."

"If ye hae any visitors they will sleep in the guestrooms."

Charlie frowned and climbed onto the bed dangling his legs over the side. "It's high up. My mattress at home doesn't hae a bit underneath but Mama's and Papa's does."

"Mine was the same as yours when I was wee, Charlie, now quickly get yersel' dressed and ye can go down and hae yer dinner."

There were many layers to be donned and Charlie was confused with the amount of garments and buttons having only been used to a shirt and a pair of breeks all his life. "I want tae wear my own clothes."

Mary's eyes fell upon the small heap of filthy, ill fitting, worn clothes on the chair knowing that Mrs Milne would surely want them burnt. "They need tae be washed, Charlie. Look at yer new shirt and waistcoat wi' pockets just like a man's." Upon hearing the word 'pockets' Charlie dived off the bed and grabbed his jacket, rummaging till he found his letter and held it tight in his wee hand.

"This is mine. I need tae keep it safe."

Mary glanced at what she thought was probably a picture or some such keepsake.

"Why don't ye keep it in one of the drawers here in the dressing table. Naebody 'ill touch it Charlie. It will be quite safe there."

So the loon opened one of the small drawers at the top and placed his letter there. Mary helped him to dress and combed his unruly hair and the two descended the staircase and entered the dining room.

Charlie eyed the long mahogany table with its white table cloth and an array of patterned dishes. His nose twitched as his brain registered the presence of hot, steaming food that smelled so deliciously different and drew him forward. Mrs Milne and Mrs Clark were seated opposite one another at the far end of the table, their plates now empty and a cup of tea in hand.

"Well now, Charlie, you look like a different child. You are in need of a haircut but we can see to that later in the week. Come away and sit down for your dinner."

Charlie's stomach hurried him up to the table. "Thank ye, Mrs Milne."

"I am not Mrs Milne to you, Charlie. I am to be your mother so you may call me that."

"Aye, Mrs Milne."

Rose opened her mouth as if to speak again but as Charlie tucked into his dinner she let it pass. There was time for the child to adapt. She looked at his face and could see her sister there, around the eyes and nose, and was glad of it for two reasons: a fondness for Grace lingered in her and a likeness to her own face would perhaps make it easier for her husband to accept Charlie as his own. It had been made clear to David that to remain in contact would confuse the child.

Annie smiled to see the change in Charlie. He did indeed look like a different bairn and a bonny one at that. As she looked around at the opulence in the house she knew that he would want for nothing, except perhaps his father and brothers and sisters, but he was only four in age and time would alter that.

"Thank you for yer kind hospitality, Mrs Milne, but it is time for me to leave for the station."

"Of course, I will have Peter come round the front with the carriage, and thank you for being so kind as to accompany Charlie here. He will be taken good care of."

"I don't doubt it." She turned to Charlie, "Well, loon, ye have a fine new home and I'm sure that ye will be very happy here. I will write to ye now and again if Mrs Milne permits it and when ye are older and have learnt to write ye can tell me how ye are."

Charlie bowed his head. So many farewells and folk leaving, and him leaving, and he understood none of it. "Can I go home wi' ye on the train?"

Annie looked into his confused eyes. "Nay, loon. Ye live here now, remember yer father explained it to ye how ye are to stay in Aberdeen."

"Say farewell, Charlie," Rose said, "and I will take you into the garden where you can play for a while. It's a lovely big garden and I have had a tree swing put in just for you."

She took his hand and as Annie left through the front door Charlie was whisked away out the back door to start his new life with his new mother.

*

Andrew Milne returned home to Willowbank from his solicitor's office that evening having yet again been witness to the constant wranglings and battles between Rose's father, Robert, and her brother, Gordon, at the mill. Supposedly retired with his son now in charge but all knew that Gordon was unable to stand up to his tyrant of a father who still very much ruled. Andrew acted as their solicitor and adviser and was supporting Gordon in improving the working conditions and wages of the mill's employees much to the chagrin of Robert. It was Gordon's job to keep the workers working and prevent any insubordination which would be a lot easier if their conditions were safe and they were paid a decent wage. Robert Ross's old ways of bullying and low wages caused nothing but hatred and disrespect.

As he entered his hall he could hear the voice of a child and stopped by the door of the drawing room to collect his thoughts. He knew not why no children had come over the years and he saw the yearning in Rose's eyes which mirrored his own, as he too wished for a son, but to bring up another man's child as his own was another thing altogether even if that child was family. Rose was adamant that the boy take his surname, Milne, but Andrew was unsure of that also.

The door opened. "Andrew, there ye are. Come and meet Charlie." Rose took her husband's arm and led him towards where Charlie was on the floor playing with some marbles, his wee wooden rabbit being used to roll them along the floor.

"Stand up, Charlie." Rose beckoned the loon who did as he was bid and extended his hand as he had seen his father do many times on meeting others. "Charlie Robe'tson," he pronounced slowly, missing out the r in his last name. Andrew took the small hand in his and looked into the eyes so like his wife's, and something gave way inside.

"Pleased to meet ye, Charlie. Can I play with yer marbles too?"

Charlie nodded and Andrew knelt down, and as the two played together Rose let out a long sigh of relief and closed her eyes.

Dinner for Breakfast

Annie Clark returned to Dufftown in the evening to find the rectory empty. When her husband had not been at the station to collect her she had assumed that he had been called out on ministerial business so had walked the mile to their home by the church. She suppered alone, as often happened, and she hoped that whichever parishioner was in need would be comforted.

The old latch creaked and groaned in protest as the door was pushed open some time after eight and Matthew entered his kitchen to find Annie sipping a cup of tea.

"I'm glad to see ye home safe, Annie. I'm sorry I was not able to meet ye but I was called up to Lettoch Farm."

"Everything alright?"

"Nay, quine, I'm afraid that David Robertson has taken his own life."

Annie paled and tears threatened as she thought of his bairns and all that the family had been through. "Oh, how awful. I must have been one o' the last folk to see him. Oh Matthew I should have done something, I could see he wasn't right. Maybe I could have helped and he would still be here."

The tears that had threatened now poured and Matthew held his wife.

"Dinna blame yersel' Annie. He made his own choice."

"Why at Lettoch, I wonder?"

"He had worked there and knew the routine. Let himsel' into the gun shed and…well I dinna need to spell it out. The ghillie found him at dinner time and informed Mr Bruce and I was sent for, among others. Mrs Bruce is in an awful state, hence my lateness."

"Those poor bairns, Matthew."

"Aye. I said I would visit the orphanage and send a telegram to the Milnes in Aberdeen. The manager at Lettoch knows of a brother so he will contact him and I will write to the loons in Canada."

Annie shook her head. "So much tragedy for one family. Their lives were torn apart with the death of their mother and when they wake up tomorrow the poor wee souls will be bereft again."

"Aye."

Husband and wife sat together for a time, each consumed with their own thoughts.

"Will ye bury him? Annie asked. "I ken how ye feel about the new law allowing burials now in sacred ground in daylight."

"Aye, well I believe it to be a sin but if I am forced to by law then I suppose I have no choice.

How did ye get on in Aberdeen? Will Charlie fair well there do you think?"

Annie nodded. "Mrs Milne seemed kind and Charlie was enthralled with his first glimpse of the city. He has a chance in life now and I am glad of it. Tomorrow will bring sad news but also the promise of a better life, one in which he will never go hungry again."

Had Annie been able to see Charlie at that moment she would have witnessed a bairn fast asleep in a warm, clean bed, his belly sated with a nutritious supper and his wee wooden rabbit clasped in his palm. The shutters on his window kept the evening summer sun at bay and softened the city noises of hooves on cobbles.

As the hours passed Charlie slept with little movement and his dreams took him to a far off land in a train. The engine grew wings and flew like a bird over the hills and fields and its whistle blew as the rabbits below scampered and scurried. The metallic clattering and clanking of the train grew louder and Charlie felt the softness of a blanket on his cheek as his eyes opened.

The first thing he was aware of was the comfort and warmth of his bed and the second was the strange clattering sounds outside. He opened his eyes expecting to be in his bed he shared with his siblings with the usual bustle of folk living in one room, but instead he saw a wall with patterned paper and when he turned over his eyes fell upon a large room with dark wooden furniture and a picture of a boat on the wall. A small fire grate nestled in the corner but there was no pot hanging from a hook with porridge bubbling inside, no table and chairs or spinning wheel and no family.

He was quite alone.

Charlie sat up and his train journey the day before seeped into his memory alongside his bath and meeting Mr and Mrs Milne. He remembered his papa saying goodbye to him and not understanding why, and he remembered, as he did every day, that his mama had gone to Heaven, and for the first time in his life Charlie felt what it was like to feel lonely. He had such a longing for his family that he had no words for and had never in his short life woken up alone before.

Confused and frightened, tears began to trickle down his cheeks and he sat in the bed too big for one, and hugged his knees.

Mary found Charlie in that position as she entered his room and opened the shutters. "Oh, Charlie, why are ye greeting?"

Charlie buried his head further into his knees.

Mary sat down on the bed beside him. She could see the ears of his wooden rabbit peeking out from under his thumb. "I like yer rabbit. Are rabbits yer favourite animal?"

Charlie nodded but kept his head down.

"Rabbits are fast runners, aren't they? I see them sometimes when I'm walking by the river. I saw one here in the garden the other day so maybe there's a burrow nearby."

Charlie lifted his head.

"How about we have a look for it after you have eaten yer breakfast?" Mary rose from the bed and fetched his clothes. "Let's get ye dressed and we'll go downstairs. Mrs Milne has told me that ye are to eat breakfast downstairs every day with her and Mr Milne."

Charlie wiped his face and hopped down off the high bed and proceeded to let Mary help him with the array of buttons and layers that constituted his new clothing. With his rabbit firmly in his hand, the two walked down the stairs to the dining room where Mr and Mrs Milne were seated.

"Good morning, Charlie." Rose patted the chair by her. "Come and sit here."

Charlie did as he was bid and Andrew asked what he would like to eat. He noticed that Andrew was eating eggs and meat and wondered why he was having dinner for breakfast. "Porridge please." A bowl was filled and placed in front of him and the three ate their breakfast in unison. The Milnes chatted about their day ahead and Charlie was almost finished eating when the front door bell rang out followed by the appearance of the maid.

"Telegram for you, Mr Milne. The loon is waiting if there is to be a reply."

"Thank you, Elspeth." Andrew tore open the envelope expecting some legal news but his brow furrowed on reading the contents and he glanced at the wee loon eating his porridge. A long sigh emanated from him and he turned to Elspeth. "Ye can send the loon away, no reply for now, and fetch Mary please."

"Yes, sir."

"Everything alright, Andrew?"

Andrew looked at Rose, said nothing, but addressed Charlie. "Mary will be in in a minute to take ye out."

Charlie's eyes lit up. "Am I going home on the train?"

"No, Charlie. Ye are biding with us now, remember?"

The loon's eyes lost their sparkle and he lowered his spoonful of porridge back into his bowl. It was too much anyway: his belly unused to three meals within twenty four hours. Rose was about to speak when there was a small knock on the door and Mary was summoned into the room. "Ah, Mary. Take Charlie out into the garden please and tell Elspeth not to disturb us."

Rose stared at the telegram in her husband's hand knowing that some important news lay in its words. She waited for Andrew to speak when Mary and Charlie had left the room.

"News has come from Dufftown, Rose. Charlie's father is dead."

"Dead?" she exclaimed, but as the word left her mouth her heart rose slightly quickly followed by a dart of guilt. She meant no harm to her brother in law but knowing that there was no threat of him taking Charlie back was relief indeed.

Andrew saw the fleeting mix of emotions on his wife's face and his voice rose, "For pity's sake - a man is dead."

Rose lowered her eyes, chastened. "I'm just confused. Forgive me. How did he die?"

Andrew let out a sigh. "In the worst way possible. No grass will grow over his grave."

Rose took a sharp intake of breath as she whispered, "He murdered himself?"

"Aye."

A few moments of silence passed. Rose waited again, carefully arranging her face and hands as she was unsure how to proceed.

"Well, the wee lad is an orphan now so it's as well he has a home with us. We'll tell him that his father is with his mother now. He's too young to understand anything but he will never know the shame of what his father has done. We can spare him that, at least, throughout his life. Not a word to anyone, Rose."

"Of course."

Her husband rose to leave for work but stopped at the door, a final thought having entered his mind. Without turning he stated, "I'll give Charlie my name," and walked through the door shutting it behind him as Rose lifted her tea cup and smiled. She would not need her laudanum this morning.

The Milnes garden was enclosed by a high hedge which surrounded several mature trees, mainly birch and rowan, along its sides and a selection of bedding plants, roses and large bushes which grew freely. A large grass lawn filled the midsection and a narrow path meandered in an s shape passed the tree swing and down to a small shed.

Mary couldn't help but laugh as she watched Charlie scurrying under the hedge yet again, his body almost disappearing leaving behind a pair of scrawny limbs. "None here," came a muffled cry and he reappeared with dusty breeks and leaves in his long hair only to repeat the process further along the hedge towards the bottom of the garden. "None here," a dejected voice stated.

"Never mind, Charlie. Perhaps there is a burrow next door. I definitely saw a rabbit the other day so they won't be too far away. Come and play on the swing."

Rose had been watching from the drawing room window

and her heart soared as she watched her new child play. He would be everything she needed him to be and perhaps even her father would be proud of her. She shook the thought away. Such thoughts just led to disappointment. She heard voices in the hall and her heart sunk as she noted the end of her time watching Charlie play. Her mother, Ann, had apparently arrived.

Ann had descended from the carriage without thanking her coachman and entered Willowbank as though she owned it, almost colliding with Elspeth who on hearing the arrival of a carriage had made her way to the door. "Where is your mistress?"

"In the drawing room, Mrs Ross."

Ann proceeded along the hall and opened the door to find Rose sitting by the window. "Good morning, Rose," she said, as she positioned herself on the edge of a chair. "I swear that man drove through every hole and rut on the road in taking me here. I shall be bruised for a week."

Rose sighed. "Good morning, Mother. Surely it would be easier to walk, it would take but a few minutes."

"Oh Rose, how many times do I need to tell you, a lady never walks anywhere."

Rose glanced out of the window. She had wanted a few days with Charlie before introducing him to her parents. "I wasn't expecting you today."

"Well, Rose, I must say that I have been hurt by your lack of invitation. The child is my grandchild after all, even if he belonged to Grace. Of course your father will not accept the situation and believes the child must be an idiot like his mother, but I said neither yourself nor Andrew would surely take in an idiot and I know how much you wanted to be a mother. Not entirely sure why though as children rob you of your figure, are very demanding and often cause disappointment."

"Thank you, Mother, I will bear that in mind."

"Does he speak well?" Meaning did he pronounce every word like the Queen as she herself had been made to do.

"He has a country accent but his manners are excellent for his age."

"Hmm, at least he is young enough to train and with both parents gone there will be no interference."

Rose looked sharply at her mother. "You know? Why, we only just heard this morning."

"A friend of mine returned from Dufftown last night having been to visit an elderly aunt and passed on the shameful news to me this morning. Quite excited she was. You have put me in an awkward position Rose as I had to defend this decision of yours amidst a disgraceful situation. I said it was all Andrew's idea, in desperate need of an heir as he is, and as the boy is already here it was already settled."

Rose rang the bell for tea as her mother continued to talk. She had the ability to switch off when in her mother's company, nodding and smiling whilst not listening at all which allowed her mind time to think about what Andrew could say to Charlie. The right words would have to be found to tell him that he wouldn't see his father again.

"Rose!"

"Yes, Mother?"

"Did you hear me? I just asked, am I to meet the child or not?"

"Of course, Mother. Come over to the window and see him play, then I will ask Elspeth to fetch him here."

Ann rose and placed herself by her daughter just as Charlie was diving into the hedgerow once again. "What on Earth is he doing?"

"Looking for rabbits. I think he misses them. His life was quite different to that of the town. Andrew is going to take him along the river tomorrow to look for wildlife and tell him about his father."

Ann looked aghast as Charlie crawled back out from

the undergrowth, his long air dishevelled and covering half of his face.

"Are you sure he's not an imbecile?"

"Quite sure, Mother. Please stop saying that. I will have Mary clean him up and bring him to us."

The two women drank their tea and there came a knock on the door and Mary walked in with Charlie by her side now with clean breeks and a washed face. His hair was still somewhat unruly but Rose quite liked it as somehow it portrayed Charlie himself - thrawn with a mind of its own.

"Charlie, this is your grandmother."

Charlie looked at the woman standing in front of him, staring. She looked like the doll that sat in the glass cupboard, all neat and tidy but with eyes that stared and scared him a little.

Charlie, remembering his manners, extended his hand. "How'd ye do - Charlie Robe'tson."

Ann's tongue was still: its movement halted by the sight of this child, so like Grace at that age. For a second some rare maternal fondness surfaced as she remembered her daughter who, although had disgraced them all by running away with the carter and had been an idiot, she had been a beautiful and kind child. Something akin to guilt accompanied this maternal fondness and Ann found herself reaching out to take the wee hand offered to her and as she felt its warmth a tenderness spread through her and compassion was born.

Charlie witnessed the change in her eyes as Ann again found the use of her tongue. "Pleased to meet you, Charlie. And who might this be?" she asked, pointing to his other hand.

"This is my rabbit. My papa made it for me oot o'an auld piece o' wood." He held it out to Ann. "See his lugs and his tail?"

Rose waited for her mother to correct his speech, sighing

to herself as she wished Charlie to be able to settle in and be himself but to her astonishment her mother smiled - a proper, genuine smile - and she took Charlie by the hand and led him over to the couch.

"Now, Charlie, I want to hear all about you and what you like to do."

Charlie returned the smile and proceeded to tell his grandmother all about trains as Rose looked on, her mouth agape, as she witnessed a mother she had never known and the beginning of what would be a strong bond between her new son and his grandmother.

Pummelling

The River Don ran high and swift, skirting and weaving as it made its way east towards the North Sea. Charlie and Andrew walked north along Don Street leaving the road and finding the track that led to the river which had rounded sharply in the west forming a u shape before again forging its way east. The track became a narrow, well trodden path which ran alongside the river taking them away from where the mill stood proudly, and curtailing the roar of the water pummelling into the giant wheel: its strength turning the wheel and in turn allowing it to create its own power for the machines that lay within.

Andrew had witnessed a child unsure of himself within the house but out by the river Charlie's legs spirited him this way and that as he searched nature for her treasures. It was quieter here away from the constant noise and bustle of the city and Andrew himself felt the wonder of trees and land working its way into his body and calming his mind.

"Do ye like it here, Charlie?"

"Aye, it's like home. There's rabbits here too. I can see burrows so maybe we'll see one in a minute. They're fast though." His eyes scanned his surroundings on the lookout for his favourite animal and, as always, his wooden rabbit was clamped firmly between his fingers.

"Ye are very fond o' your wee wooden rabbit."

"Aye. My papa made it for me." Charlie's wee face fell and his pace slowed.

Andrew saw the change in his demeanour and knew this was the opportunity he needed to speak to Charlie but he was unsure of his words. Without breaking his stride Andrew spoke, "It's good ye have yer rabbit, Charlie, as it will always be something you have that is from yer father."

"He said he would make me a stag when he has time."

Andrew stopped. "Let's sit here a minute by this tree."

The two sat down side by side and watched the river rush by and Andrew glanced at the loon by him who was to be his son. "There's something I need to tell ye."

Charlie looked at Andrew and waited.

Andrew lowered his voice but looked beyond the river as he spoke. "Yer papa won't be able to make ye a stag, Charlie. He's gone now, like yer mother."

Charlie's brow furrowed followed by a look of fear that flashed in his eyes as he raised his voice. "Mama's in heaven. Papa's at home."

"No, Charlie, yer papa is with yer mama. He died and ye won't see him again."

Charlie sprang up and faced Andrew, his face contorted and reddening as his eyes narrowed, "I want my papa! I want my papa!"

Andrew shook his head. "I'm sorry, lad."

Charlie turned and sprinted as fast as his legs could carry him, following the path alongside the river and heading towards the Bridge o' Balgownie, heedless to the rabbits he had been on the lookout for that darted out of his way, or froze in fear, as he sped past. Tears streamed down his cheeks as he tried in vain to make sense of Andrew's words. "Yer papa is with yer mama… ye won't see him again." The words played over and over again in his wee mind, pummelling him in the chest and deafening his ears.

A NDREW CAUGHT UP with Charlie on the other side of the bridge. He was sitting by the edge of the path: his knees pulled up to his chin. He was no longer crying - just silent. Andrew sat down beside him. "Yer father wanted us to look after you and I promise to do that, Charlie, as best I can."

Charlie continued to stare at nothing then scrambled up onto his feet and walked back towards his new home in silence, Andrew walking alongside him, having no words with which to comfort the loon. The whole way back Charlie held so tightly to his wooden rabbit that it dug into his wee palm causing a small bruise to form but the smoothness of the wood gave Charlie comfort as his thumb caressed it.

The Auld Fox

The two young quines walked together towards the mill. The street was busy with the usual folk making their way to their work, some with fuller bellies than others. The sun appeared to slumber still, despite the hour being six, as the haar encroaching from the North Sea imprisoned the light in its dreich greyness. Liza stopped yet again to rub her ankle where her boots dug in.

"Come on, Liza, we dinna want to be late."

"I'm coming. I really hope we get that pay rise as I canna go on wearing these boots. I'm glad to have boots at all but a pair a size bigger would be good."

"Well, hopefully we will hear soon. I think we can trust young Mr Ross. He has certainly improved things in the mill since his father left."

"Aye, he has that, thank the Lord. Getting rid o' that cruel foreman was a good start."

"Aye, and auld Mr Ross is less hands on, so to speak, although I did see him cuff a loon around the lug last week when he came in."

Liza shivered, "The sights we have seen. Poor wee Sandy's lug. I will never forget the sound o' his scream when that nail was driven in."

Maggie drew up her shoulders at the memory. "There's some cruel folk in this world." She threaded her arm through Liza's and the two quines entered the mill to start their day of work followed by their employer, Gordon Ross, who was rushing, as usual, and the angry words of his father still ringing in his ears since the day before.

He darted up the stairs to his office, pausing only to wish the foreman good morning, and sat behind his desk. It had been arranged that Andrew would arrive at the mill at eleven o'clock to go over some legal papers with him and he wanted to have his questions ready. Expanding the mill made sense and even his father could not object to increasing revenue but all legalities needed to be in place and he trusted no one more than Andrew.

The clatter and clangs of the weaving machines had a certain rhythm to them that served to calm Gordon's mind each day, like the rubbing of a newborn's back by its mother: soothing and comforting. He enjoyed his work, and believed himself good at it, despite his father's disparaging comments and interference. He worked steadily and was surprised when the clock struck eleven and Andrew entered the office.

"Good morning to ye, Gordon. What a fine day it is." His smile was wide as he sat himself down at the desk.

Gordon glanced across to the window and saw the dark grey sky and remnants of the sea haar which still lingered. "If you say so. Ye seem very seel."

"I am indeed. Charlie has made a father of me and he is quite a character. I know it's early days and he misses his family but he has a way about him which intrigues me. He is thrawn and speaks as if he was a wise, auld man. This morning, at breakfast, he told me the best place to catch a trout in the river was under a bridge. That's intelligence, Gordon."

Gordon laughed. "It sounds like you yourself have been

caught by a hook, Andrew. Welcome to fatherhood. There is nothing better than watching a bairn grow. Charlie is lucky to have you and Rose as parents and I look forward to meeting him."

Ye will. Your mother has met Charlie and Rose said she was quite charmed by him. I think he will have that effect on all those he meets."

"Even my father?"

Andrew's face grew serious. "Charlie is my son and I will not tolerate any misconduct towards him."

Gordon nodded and talk turned towards work but he wondered if it was possible for his father to be anything but cruel towards a grandson that he did not acknowledge existed.

Half an hour later Robert Ross entered the mill like a sleekit fox on the prowl for any unsuspecting lambs. As he stalked the corridor leading up to the main body of the mill the air before him seemed to thicken and curdle like milk gone sour. The clattering thunder of the rows of a hundred looms each with its own pair of hands deftly moving the shuttles back and forth filled the air and deafened the lugs, but as the fox strolled into the din the curdled air penetrated the workers' noses alerting the lambs to imminent danger.

Eyes spoke to other eyes as the threat signal was sent down the lines announcing the arrival of Mr Ross (senior) no longer proprietor: having handed the gauntlet over to his son but very much still in charge. If he was a fox, his son was a hen.

Although there was an element of fear in the workers' faces it was coupled with a spark of hatred. Every employee young or old, new or longstanding, had heard of, or witnessed Mr Ross's cruelty. He had been brutal in his discipline, and beatings undertaken by either himself or one of his underlings had been administered for lateness or falling asleep and any costly mistakes had found a neck shackled to heavy weights or an ear nailed to a table, no matter the age of its owner.

Fortunately the lambs were to be spared that day as Robert had just been to visit his mistress and his mood was a good one: his ego boosted and petted as he required it to be. There was no doubting his attractive features, despite his advancing years, and he knew how to charm a woman so he sauntered on by the flock and headed towards the steps leading to the office that overlooked the weavers.

Andrew happened to look up from his paperwork just as his father in law came through the downstairs door and saw how he walked with his usual air of self importance but lacking the menace behind it. "Yer father's here, Gordon, and he looks tae be in good humour."

Gordon let out a sigh of both relief and exasperation. "He was only here yesterday, what can he want now? I wish he would just leave me to get on wi' my work."

"Going to tell him that, are ye?"

Gordon sighed again, but louder this time and the ink in his pen dripped and formed a pool over the last word he had written in a letter to one of his buyers. "God damn it," he snapped, just as the door opened and his father pierced the remainder of the calm atmosphere held within the office, with his sharp tongue.

"Efficient as ever, Gordon," he announced on seeing the ruined letter.

"Morning, Father." Gordon answered as he crumpled the page and threw it in the bin by his feet and proceeded to wait as he knew there was no point in asking the reason for this visit. All would become clear only when Mr Ross, senior, chose to disclose it.

Andrew glanced up from his work. "Morning, Robert." His words were direct and lacked the nervousness of Gordon's.

"Andrew," he replied, in the same direct manner with

a nod of his head. He proceeded to walk around the office lifting various papers and ledgers and putting them down again, then going to the window overlooking the River Don, standing for a moment only to walk back to the door and return once again to the window. There was no excitement in his movements, he just ambled about and eventually he sat on a chair opposite Gordon and began to fiddle with the pens lying dormant in their box.

As Gordon continued to wait with his usual expectancy of a tirade over some such thing or other as to how useless he was, Andrew suddenly laughed.

"Yer bored, Robert."

A flash of surprise passed over Robert's face followed by a rush of indignant words. "I am nae such thing. To be bored is to be idle and I have never had an idle day in my life."

"Well we hae work to do so go and not be idle somewhere else."

Gordon's head snapped up and his eyes went between Andrew and his father. There had always seemed some sort of alliance between the two men that Gordon envied and had no understanding of but he was surprised at the words just spoken and the casual manner in which they were said. His father did not do small talk or jokes unless it benefitted him in some way either in business or pleasure, usually when either money or women were involved.

Andrew felt his lips form a small smile, which Robert saw and there followed a bellowed laugh as the old fox jumped up and exited the room. "Me? - Bored?" spouted forth as he descended the stairs and his laughter was swallowed by the booming looms.

"Well, he really is in a good mood," declared Gordon. "He would have eaten me alive with that comment."

"Aye, well, I'm a bit surprised myself but there's yer answer to keeping him away fae here. Find him something to occupy his time elsewhere."

Gordon sucked in his bottom lip, a habit he had when thinking, and decided that Andrew was right indeed.

Cousins at Redwood Manor

Rose had observed Charlie in the two weeks following being told of his father's death. One minute he was a quiet, obedient child and the next he was shouting and refusing any request made of him by either Mary or herself. Terrified that he would not be the child she needed him to be and imagining the gloat in her own father's eyes she decided that action needed to be taken.

"I think Charlie needs friends," she said to Andrew. "He's always asking about his brothers and sisters and he needs to learn to forget about them as no good can come of that. I will call upon my friend Shona and arrange for Charlie to meet wee Fraser. He's a well behaved child and they will start school together so would be a good influence I think."

"Aye, that is a good idea. Ye are right about him needing to be with other bairns but I'm not sure if his cousins are the right ones. This afternoon's gathering at your parent's home may well not be in Charlie's best interest. Gordon's offspring are timid and James's are downright spoilt, conceited and unlikeable - just like their father."

Rose sighed. "Yes, well he has to meet them at some

point so today's as good a time as any."

"I know I usually try to get out of yer family gatherings but I won't have Charlie walking into a lion's den. He's my son now and I will make it known to the Rosses."

"I am glad. You have a way with my father and if anyone can smooth the situation it's you." Rose looked towards the clock. "I will check that Charlie is ready to go. Can you ask for the carriage to be brought round?"

Andrew rose and placed his hands on his wife's waist. "It is a good thing that Charlie is with us. Don't let your family say otherwise."

Rose smiled in answer and within minutes all three were ready to brace both the weather and those in Redwood Manor. The afternoon had brought with it contemptuous weather which alternated between battering the windows with rain and hiding quietly behind corners before launching itself at unsuspecting fellows by taking them off their feet with the power of its wind. The closed carriage stood staunchly outside and the Milne family, in an ungracious manner, ran from the front door and launched themselves into the relative refuge of the carriage. Rose tried to push her hair back under her bonnet. "Mother will have something to say about the state of me." She looked at Charlie. "Oh Heavens above will you look at your hair. I have never known such hair that refuses to behave."

Charlie cocked his head to one side, his curls having been tamed by a comb indoors and a neat parting formed at the side now protruded like the arched tail of a dog. "It's just hair."

Andrew leaned forward and spoke to Charlie, "If anyone ever laughs at how you look or how ye speak, lad, just remember they are no better than you. Some folk are rabbits and some are sly foxes."

"Aye," Charlie answered.

The carriage arrived at Redwood Manor which stood

as if in spite of the world. It appeared to sneer at the stormy weather, its thrawnness apparent: the dark granite and arrogant windows defying the wind and rain. No flowers grew to soften the exterior and Charlie shivered unconsciously as his eyes fell upon the house.

The door was opened and the Milnes poured in, relieving themselves of their coats and hats and Rose positioned herself in front of the hall mirror and proceeded to pin her hair before they were led by the maid to the drawing room. As if sensing danger Charlie placed his wee rabbit into his pocket and glancing at Andrew who nodded in solidarity, they entered the room together, Andrew's hand on Charlie's shoulder.

"Here you are. Goodness, Rose, you are very dishevelled."

Rose acknowledged the expected criticism from her mother with a sigh. "The weather is coorse, Ann," Andrew quipped, "but nothing could detract from the beauty of your daughter."

Easily pleased by any comment pertaining to her looks Ann smiled. "Come in and warm yourselves by the fire and Charlie come and greet your grandmother. Your grandfather is out at the moment but he will be back shortly."

Charlie presented himself as he always did, straight backed and sincere. "Afternoon to ye. I canna say I'm feeling the cauld, nae noo that I wear shoes. Never owned my own pair afore."

There was a second of silence before a loud guffaw erupted from a boy seated at the end of a couch and he spluttered, "He speaks like a coalman."

Charlie thought of young Edward in Dufftown who worked as a coalman delivering it, as others did their wares, and could not see how that was humorous. Andrew stepped up to the boy, looking at him with anger in his eyes but before he could speak Charlie stated matter of factly, "I'm thinking yer maybe a fox. We shoot them in Dufftown."

Now it was Andrew's turn to laugh and he clapped Charlie on the back as the others looked on, unsure of how to react but Gordon smiled. "Welcome, Charlie, I'm pleased to meet you. I'm your Uncle Gordon." Charlie offered his hand, as he was inclined to do, and a proud smile passed Rose's lips.

No such welcome came from his brother, James, whose son was in threat of being shot.

"And I'm yer Aunt Mabel, Charlie," a dark haired woman with a sharp nose and soft eyes said, "And this is our daughter, Victoria. She is thirteen, our eldest." Victoria was looking at her shoes but lifted her eyes on hearing her name and gave her cousin a small smile.

Ann's nose twitched as she noticed the look of disgust that passed her other daughter in law's face. Edith was languishing (un-ladylike in Ann's opinion) on the couch between her husband, James, and their son. Now in days gone past Ann may well have shared her outlook but Ann had a strong feeling of protectiveness towards her newly found grandson and as flighty and uncaring as she could sometimes be, when she got the bit between her teeth over something, she was not inclined to let it go.

Andrew, having expected an unwelcome response from James and Edith, interjected, "This is your Aunt Edith and Uncle James and their son, Archie, now I wonder, Ann, if it's maybe time for Charlie to be allowed to go up and play with his other cousins."

"Yes, of course. I'll have the maid take him up."

Young Archie was quick to comment, "I'll take him up. We can get to know one another better and I'll make sure the twins are kind to him."

"Well that is kind of you, Archie," his mother said. "Considering his earlier rudeness," she added, her tone barbed.

Rose faltered and looked to Andrew who in turn looked

at Charlie. Charlie knew to expect to meet several older quines and a loon his own age, whom Andrew had said was a nice loon like himself, so he feared nothing in meeting them but he was aware of the fox waiting to lead him upstairs. "Right ye are, thank you," he said, and as he followed his older cousin out of the room he secretly passed his wooden rabbit into Andrew's hand on his way past.

A moment of trust that did not go unnoticed by Andrew.

As the door closed, Victoria, naturally quiet by nature, stood up and addressed her grandmother. "Please may I be excused? I wish to go upstairs also."

"Why, of course, Victoria. You are the eldest and can keep an eye on things and do come down if Charlie is in need of anything."

Rose smiled and whispered to her husband, "She's a tell tale and not keen on her cousin so we will know if anything untoward happens."

Andrew could feel the rabbit in his pocket and smiled. "He'll be fine. Don't you worry."

CHARLIE FOLLOWED ARCHIE up the stairs. Charlie wasn't sure why he had given Andrew his rabbit, some small voice in his head had made him do it. They reached the landing and voices could be heard; some loud, some soft. Archie opened a door and waltzed in. "Well now bairns look at the surprise I have brought for you to play with. Our own wee urchin - wait till you hear him speak."

Charlie looked around the large room full of toys. There was a shelf with board games and a great pile of books and the most marbles Charlie had ever seen in an open tin box. In a corner a huge dolls house full of tiny furniture took up what seemed like half the room and two bairns were squabbling over a musical toy, the likes of which Charlie had never seen. Standing proudly in the middle of the room was a rocking horse which was mounted and rocked quite ferociously by a loon holding on to the long, brown mane with one hand and slapping the horse with the other.

A quine put down her book and approached Charlie. "Are you Charlie? My mother said you were coming today. I'm Ruth and I'm eleven." She pointed to two other quines who were drawing at a small table. That's Agnes and Ann, they're my sisters. The loon on the horse is our brother, Joseph."

Charlie nodded. "I'm Charlie."

Archie sat on a stool by the window and beckoned his own siblings, the twins who were bickering over the music box. "Ian. Eleanor. Come over here and meet Charlie. He has his own pair of shoes. Never had a pair before, can you believe that?"

Ian laughed. "Only newborns have bare feet. Are you a newborn? You look small enough. How old are you? Two?"

Charlie was used to being called small. He had always been small. "I'm nearly five and I'm nae a newborn. I'm awa tae school shortly."

"He speaks funny." Eleanor said.

"Aye, Eleanor, that's because he's an idiot like his mother. I heard Father say so."

Something altered in Charlie's chest and his hand went to his pocket for his rabbit but of course it was gone.

Archie saw him reach into his pocket. "What's in there then? What does a country loon carry in his pocket?" He launched himself at Charlie, picking him up by his legs and shaking him upside down in the hope of tipping any possessions out of his pockets. The others watched, some laughing, some biting their lips, their eyes uncertain.

"Let me doon," Charlie shouted just as Victoria entered the room and although quiet by nature she had some of her grandfather in her.

"Put him down!" she roared.

Archie laughed and continued to shake Charlie but nothing fell from his pockets and he stopped, roughly releasing his cousin and laughing again as he stumbled to right himself.

Victoria addressed her brother as if his mother, "Joseph, go and get the marbles and play with Charlie. Ruth, go down to the kitchen and ask the cook for a treat. She never says no to you." Joseph lowered himself from his horse and fetched the large tin of marbles and Charlie, a little unsure, peeked into the tin and took out a large, blue marble and followed Joseph to the other corner of the room to roll their marbles along the wooden floor.

The twins were still giggling and pointing but the taking of the music box by Victoria's hands silenced them. Archie had seated himself again on the stool, a grin on his face that would have been handsome if not for the hard eyes. Victoria walked slowly over to her cousin, younger by a year but whom had always antagonised her and she whispered in his ear. "I know what you stole and I will tell Grandfather."

Archie's grin disappeared. He looked at Victoria who merely raised her eyebrows and gave a slight nod of her head. "Now be a good loon and be kind to our new cousin."

*

Down in the drawing room the conversation went as it always did. James lorded over everyone, Edith ignored Mabel, and Gordon and Rose tried to please their mother. Andrew sat back and watched the theatre that was his in laws. Robert was still to appear, probably on a visit to a mistress disguised as a visit to an old friend. He was unsure if the family were fully aware of his indiscretions. He waited for the comments on Charlie to begin and he didn't have to wait long.

"Well, Andrew, how does it feel to be a father to another man's bairn?"

Andrew looked his brother in law in the eye. He had expected that question. "Well, James, I can tell ye that it's an honour. To be entrusted with another man's bairn is a privilege."

James scowled at the unexpected answer. "You are not worried he is an idiot? He seemed a bit aggressive to me the way he spoke to Archie."

Andrew did not rise to the bait. "He replied to rudeness as I, his father, would instruct him to. He is no idiot, James, as time will show."

"Charlie is a part of this family and here to stay," Ann said. "Andrew and Rose have graciously taken the child in to be cared for and brought up as a gentleman. And a gentleman is exactly what he will turn out to be. Now I will have Beatrice bring in some tea."

Rose looked at her mother and husband grateful for their words and chose to ignore the tut that emitted from Edith's tongue followed by the low words, "On your head be it."

Just as tea was being served young James returned to the drawing room to join his elders and sat down with a look of irritation.

"Is Charlie alright, Archie?" asked Rose.

"He's playing marbles with Joseph and Victoria is making sure everyone is behaving."

His dejected tone told Rose everything she needed to know and she smiled and sent up a thank you to Victoria.

The door opened and Rose's father strode into the room with a jubilant step until he saw his entire family gathered round a table of cups and saucers. "Oh, I forgot you were coming."

Ann looked embarrassed and Andrew laughed. "We aim to please with our good looks and witty conversation, Robert."

Robert smiled despite himself. He tolerated Andrew, perhaps even liked him, not that he would have admitted it.

"Tea, Robert?" asked Ann.

"Aye, and some cake. I'm starved."

"Did you not eat at the Grants?" his wife enquired. Andrew waited in interest for that answer as he knew that Findlay Grant was out of town on business and not due back till Wednesday. Gordon was privy to the same information and he noticed the frown appear on his face.

"Their portions are somewhat meagre, Ann. No one compares to you as a host."

Ann blushed and smiled at the compliment that came so easily from her husband's lips as she passed him a large slice of cake.

Edith leaned forward. "Young Archie did very well in his Latin exam last week. First in his class." Mabel felt a pang of envy at how easily Edith spoke. She was far more confident than she as Robert had always made it known that women should only speak if spoken to.

"And what about mathematics, Archie?"

Archie faltered. "I came second in the class, Grandfather."

"Make sure ye are first next time, lad. No one gets ahead by being second best."

Young Archie thrust out his chin. "Yes Grandfather, I won't be beaten again."

"You never quite grasped mathematics, did you, Gordon?"

Gordon sighed as the thought, *Here we go*, entered his mind, followed by, *Well I haven't put the Mill in debt yet so I must have some grasp o' it*, but merely said, "No, Father."

Ann cleared her throat. "Charlie is upstairs, Robert. Shall I call for Beatrice to take him down?"

Robert had forgotten that distasteful fact and his eyes hardened as he turned to Andrew. "I do not wish to have that imbecile in my home. I am surprised that you have allowed Rose to persuade you of such foolery."

"Father." Rose exclaimed as tears threatened.

Andrew was prepared for his father in law's reaction. "I will not explain myself to you, Robert. Charlie is our son now and that is that. You do not have to meet him but as we were invited here today he has naturally joined us and is currently playing with his cousins. If you do decide to meet him I will not tolerate any rudeness or cruel comments directed at him."

Robert rose and positioned himself in front of the fire facing Andrew. "How dare you. This is my house and I will damn well speak as I please."

"Aye, it is your house and I respect that just as I'm sure Findlay Grant respects those who are loyal to him in his household."

Robert heard the veiled threat.

A look of thunder passed over his eyes but he recovered himself and turned to his wife. "Fetch Beatrice, Ann. Let me see this precious bairn."

The bell was rung and Andrew touched Rose's hand, a gesture of reassurance.

"What, pray is your opinion on this new addition to my family, James?"

"Well, Father, I wouldn't want to offend my dear sister by my answer. Best ye make up your own mind."

"How very diplomatic."

Victoria entered with Charlie behind her and it did not go unnoticed by her parents how determined and grown up she looked. She rushed over to Robert smiling a wide, genuine smile that was returned. "Good afternoon, Grandfather."

Robert took his granddaughter's hand and the walls sighed as the air in the room was freshened as if the windows had been opened and the scent of flowers had danced inside. As ruthless and cruel as Robert Ross could be, his eldest grandchild had spun her way to his heart with golden thread and in his eyes a no more perfect human being existed.

"Victoria, how delightful."

"Grandfather, you must meet Charlie. It must be difficult for you but he is a mere bairn and deserves our kindness. You are a kind man are you not?"

Now Robert, although he could not see it, was similar to his wife in that he liked to be seen in a certain light and he wanted with all his might for Victoria to approve of and look up to him.

Robert conjured up a friendly voice, "Of course. Let me see him."

Andrew rose. "Charlie, meet yer grandfather. Robert, this is my son, Charlie."

The loon's hand went out and was shaken too firmly by Robert. Charlie winced, but looked him in the eye. "Pleased tae meet ye."

Robert's eyes penetrated; the blueness of them darkening and judging as he looked the boy up and down but his words remained light. "Well, I wish you well in the Milne house, now you must excuse me as I have some letters to write."

Ann released the breath that she had been unaware of holding and busied herself with the offering of more tea. It was declined and one by one the party departed Redwood Manor. The rain and wind had dissipated allowing for a more elegant ascent into the carriage and as the Milnes rode away Rose asked her son what she thought of the visit. An element of fear sparked in his eyes but his words came strong and sure, "When I'm a stag - I'll hae antlers."

Alice

Charlie walked with Rose along Don Street and down High Street towards the magnificent King's College, the cobbles beneath their feet worn smooth and uneven. The houses, some inline with the road and others set back standing proud behind wrought iron gates and high walls, were grand and grey, the austerity of the granite broken only by plants or glimpses of sun which turned the dreich grey a sparkling silver. The Autumn leaves lay along the side of the road, the wind having blown them the day before forming a river of red, orange and yellow which they followed and Charlie kicked at the crisp leaves that lay in mounds by doorways, trapped in corners awaiting the return of a different wind to release them.

"Don't scuff your shoes, Charlie. You need to be smart when visiting folk. Mrs Buchan will think terrible of me if you arrive all dishevelled with dirty shoes. Maybe we should have taken the carriage after all."

Charlie stuck out his bottom lip. "I like kicking the leaves."

"You can kick as many as you like on the way home as long as you behave when we are there. I'm sure you will have a fine time playing with Fraser."

Charlie eyed the countless leaves as a cat would a ball of wool, but kept his feet walking, albeit reluctantly. "I'd rather play wi' my brothers and sisters. When are they coming?" Tears threatened in his eyes and a rush of panic passed over Rose's face. The Buchan's home was only three doors away so she quickly took Charlie's hand and stopped, turning to him and adopting what she hoped was a reassuring tone to ward off any tears.

"Charlie, I have told you this already. They need to settle into their new homes, same as you. They are well and happy so come on let's go and you can have a fun afternoon with Fraser and there will be cake. I know how much you like cake."

Charlie burrowed his feelings of loss into a deep corner of his heart that sometimes caused his chest to feel heavy and made his breathing go all strange. He had no understanding of the whys and wherefores of not seeing his siblings or parents: he just knew that he missed them.

Charlie nodded in response but did not speak and they continued on to the house named Elmgrove where once again Charlie was swallowed up by the grandness of the Aberdeen wealthy.

FOLLOWING THE USUAL polite introductions Mrs Buchan called for her maid to bring Fraser down to meet Charlie. Within a minute a boy his own age entered, taller and broader than Charlie with an open face and well behaved straight hair as light as barley. He was holding a small wooden horse in his hand mirroring Charlie's own clutching of his wooden rabbit. They each eyed the others toy with approval and just as Fraser was about to speak there exploded into the room a creature: all layers of petticoats and bows with the longest fairest hair Charlie had ever seen, who after careering into her brother stopped suddenly and curtseyed.

"Goodness, Alice, is that any way to enter a room?" her mother chided.

"Sorry, Mama. I wanted to see Charlie." She looked straight at Charlie and announced in a mother's tone, "I'm Alice and you can play with me too."

Fraser recognised his sister's tone and sighed. She was a mere fifteen minutes older but Fraser was no match for his bossy, boisterous, twin sister.

Charlie looked back at the angel before him for that is what he believed her to be. The sun reflected off her almost white hair and her large blue eyes sparkled with humour and warmth. For once his tongue remained still until nudged by Rose. "Afternoon to ye," he stumbled and before he knew what was happening Alice had grabbed his hand and was pulling him out the door, "Come on, Fraser, we'll go outside to play."

The two ladies laughed. "I don't know where she gets her ways from, Rose. I try my best to instruct her but a part of me hopes she holds onto that confidence when she grows up."

"Yes, Shona, I wish I had half her confidence. I was too wary as a child." She did not continue but the two women had been friends for a long time and Shona knew Rose's parents well.

Charlie felt the warmth of Alice's hand as she pulled him out through the door and into the garden. "Come and see our den, Charlie. Our uncle helped us make it. He says all bairns should have a den in their garden."

"We can play in it even if it rains," added Fraser as he crawled into the opening beneath a large oak tree.

Charlie followed suit and found himself cocooned in a low den with walls and a roof made from a mixture of old planks of wood and long branches covered with fern. The lower branches of the tree provided more shelter and it was a dry and comfortable hideaway. The three bairns sat crossed legged, in a semicircle, their knees touching.

"Can I see yer rabbit, Charlie?" asked Fraser.

"Aye. My papa made it fir me." Charlie's voice faltered as he handed over his wee wooden toy.

"It's good. Here, ye can hold my horse. I got it from the shop."

"Mama says yer papa died," Alice said as Charlie took the horse from Fraser.

"Shoosh. Alice. Mama said not to say that."

"It's ok, Fraser, I know all about dying. Remember when Pepper died? He was our dog, Charlie, and he got ill and so did our Granda. He died at Christmas and it felt funny in here." Alice put her hand on her chest. "Kind of sore and achy."

Charlie looked at Alice. "It feels like that in there for me too."

"Do you think hearts cry? I think mine cries sometimes," she added.

Charlie thought about that for a minute. "Aye. I do."

"Papa always says that Mama has a big heart. She cried lots when Granda died so maybe your heart grows bigger when someone dies."

"Is that bad?" Charlie asked.

Alice shook her head. "No. Papa says folk with big hearts are kind. Mama is kind so we will be kind too as we have achy hearts that cry."

Charlie thought again. "So unkind folk must hae wee hearts."

"Old Mr Duncan next door is always angry and grumpy so he must have a wee heart," added Fraser.

"Oh yes, his heart must be the size of a marble. I think yours is as big as a ball, Charlie." said Alice. "I knowed you were kind soon as I saw you."

Charlie smiled at Alice and felt something in his chest again but it wasn't the same feeling he had when he thought of his kin. She smiled back and Charlie recognised the feeling of happiness.

Fraser reached behind himself and lifted a small tin and handed it to Charlie.

"You can play with these if you want to."

Charlie opened the lid and found himself looking at four wooden animals. A fox, a cow, a pig and another animal that he did not recognise had a long nose like a snake and large ears. They were exquisitely made and Charlie turned them in his wee hand, smiling as he did so. "What's this?" he asked, picking up the one he didn't recognise.

"That's an efant." said Alice.

"No, Alice, it's an el- e- phant."

"Do they live in Aberdeen? I've never seen one in Dufftown." asked Charlie.

Fraser shook his head. "Uncle George went to In-dee-a and he saw lots. In-dee-a is far away. He says they are huge, much bigger than horses and they are really strong."

"They have these long things here, see?" Alice pointed to its trunk. "They can pick up trees."

Charlie's eyes widened and his mouth opened in awe. "I'd like to see an el-e-phant."

"Uncle George has animal heads in his house that he shot in In-dee-a. One's called a tiger and it has huge teeth. You can come with us one day and see it, Charlie. There are lots of heads in a big room and they are all different. I'm not scared of them at all."

"I'd like tae see them, Alice."

"We have to go on the train to visit Uncle George." Alice continued.

"I love trains. I came tae Aberdeen on the train and I'm gaan tae drive one when I grow up."

"We go on the train every Saturday to visit our granny."

Charlie stared at Alice. "Every Saturday? Ye are so lucky."

Alice jumped up and grabbed Charlie's hand again.

"Come on Charlie, Fraser has a train set you can play with. He never plays with it."

Charlie found himself being hauled out of the den as fast as he had been hauled out of the parlour and it caused him to giggle. As the three bairns played with hoops and balls and trains and wooden animals Charlie forgot for an afternoon to miss his family. The tight, heavy feeling in his chest dissipated and he found himself running and laughing and rolling on the grass, his mind filled with fun and the excitement of having new found friends. He liked Fraser very much.

He was in awe of Alice.

School

As soon as Charlie opened his eyes excitement flowed through his veins as he remembered what day it was. Monday the fifth was here at last. The talk within the walls of Willowbank had centred around commencing school for some weeks now, and outwith it too, as Charlie spoke of nothing else, and although glad that he was looking forward to going, the household were eager for him to start just to have a reprieve from the subject.

Mary had laid out Charlie's clothes the night before following his bath and Charlie had even acquiesced to having a haircut on Friday with no girning or boosy lip in sight, which was an unusual occurrence indeed.

Mary combed Charlie's unruly hair that matched Charlie's legs which also seemed to have a life of their own as he jumped and twitched, so eager was he to leave. "Hold still, Charlie, for heaven's sake. I'm trying to tame your hair so yer mother will be satisfied you leave this house looking respectable."

"I don't ken what 'spectable is but I need tae go, I can hear Peter outside wi' the carriage."

Mary gave up the fight and let the loon go watching him dart down the stairs as though he were on fire. Rose was in the hall and met Charlie at the foot of the stairs almost colliding with him. "Well, Charlie, I can see you are keen to go. Now remember your manners and sit still and listen well so as not to get into trouble and for goodness sake hold your tongue. You ask too many questions. You are there to listen, not talk."

"Aye, Mrs - Mother."

Rose sighed but she also smiled at her son. It would take time, she knew, for Charlie to see her as his mother but she could be patient. She followed him outside to where their smaller Brougham carriage was waiting and Peter held open the door for Charlie to enter but the loon shook his head. "I want to sit beside you so that I can see everything."

"That wouldn't be proper, Charlie." His mother said.

Charlie's eyebrows sprung together and his arms folded as if a timber hitch knot. Thrawnness emanated from him like heat from a roaring fire and Rose had a choice to make. She could hear her mother's voice in her mind condemning any such improper behaviour and smiled. "Very well."

Charlie flung his arms around her waist causing Rose to startle and the hug was over before she had the chance to return it as Charlie scrambled up onto the carriage seat with a push up from Peter. As the wee traveller waved, Rose could feel the warmth of where his hands had touched her and swallowed her emotions as she returned his wave.

Peter pulled on the reins leading the horse through the cobbled streets and Charlie witnessed the comings and goings of folk going about their early morning business from his vantage point high up at the front of the carriage. The reek was already belching from the factory chimneys adding to the smell of fish making its way from the harbour to the train station or various shops throughout the city. They passed cart after cart carrying merchant wares to and from factories, mills, shops and grand houses, filling King Street in both directions with the noise of hooves and wheels on cobbles and shouts of 'morning' or warnings of 'watch yersel' to folk on foot.

The women on the street were working women, wrapped in their shawls to ward off the bitter wind that plagued Aberdeen, their feet trying to avoid the horse manure that forever clung to the road, the steaming piles lying in wait for any running loon or quine late for their place of work, whose eyes and feet were not in sync.

The ladies of Aberdeen were either eating their breakfast and drinking tea from china cups or still languishing in bed - an unheard of concept for a working quine except perhaps those who serviced paying men in the brothels and public houses. As Peter turned off King Street and weaved his way through the smaller roads heading towards the Grammar School, they travelled up a stretch of Broad Street, renowned for its brothels. Charlie, of course, was oblivious to the dens of iniquity, now in slumber, as he passed by.

The hustle and bustle of city life excited Charlie and enveloped his senses with unfamiliar sights, sounds and scents that piqued his curiosity and invigorated his mind. Even the unpleasant ones which were present as they travelled along smaller streets of squalor intrigued him, and his tongue, rarely quiet, constantly blethered to Peter.

"I dinna like fish. They hae starey eyes. Even when they're on my plate they still stare at me. It's fun fishing for them. I've been fishing wi' my papa but I dinna like them. How come they smell so bad here all piled up in boxes on the carts? I hae to hold my nose every time one goes past. Do ye think they know they hae starey eyes? Auld Mr Thompson fae the farm has starey eyes like a fish but Mama said I shouldn't tell him that."

Before Peter could answer Charlie's tongue was moving again. "I have tae sit still all day at school and listen and learn. I'm nae sure if I can sit all day but I will try my best as I want tae learn and be a scholar. I want tae learn how tae drive a train. I love trains, they're the best things in the world next tae rabbits. Nothing beats rabbits but trains are better than coos and sheep. My dad said I need tae be like a stag. Are they good at keeping still all day?"

Peter shook his head and smiled. He didn't have much time for bairns and their bletherings but the wee loon beside him was such a bundle of energy and so curious about the world that Peter couldn't help but take a liking to him despite the constant stream of words and questions that were forever flowing from his mouth.

"Stags can stand like statues of rock, Charlie. Proud creatures they are and very clever too. I grew up in Braemar and saw many a deer."

Charlie liked the sound of that and for a minute at least, Peter's ears got a break from the constant blethering as Charlie thought of stags being proud and clever.

The buggy pulled up outside the Grammar School on Skene Street and Charlie was out of his seat and on the ground before Peter had a chance to fully pull on the reins. Charlie barely heard Peter telling him he would pick him up later as he stood at the foot of the school looking up at the tall granite stone building with its turrets and long windows. The roundness of the turrets softened the hard, grey edges lightening the austere mood, and the windows, like eyes, allowed the light to penetrate bringing a sense of life to the stern character of the school. He had been to visit only once when his new father had taken him to be enrolled and he had been in awe of it then as he was now. Dwarfed as he was by its heftiness, Charlie felt a shiver run through him: not of fear but of excitement.

The grounds were busy with loons between the ages of five and fifteen all dressed in their dark uniforms like miniatures of their fathers who wore the uniforms of the gentry. Charlie was pressed and starched and even his unruly hair had been temporarily tamed by some potion that Mary had procured on instruction from his new mother. He carried a leather satchel for which to take books to and from school and his young mind ached to be taught. He knew the importance of school and Andrew's words stuck in his mind, "Education gives you power, Charlie. If you work hard you will do well and have a good life with money and a home. It gives you choices, Charlie, always remember that."

The scholars had to enter through the side door - the front door reserved for masters and visitors only- and on the stroke of half past eight Charlie walked through the door and followed his peers along the labyrinth of corridors till he reached his classroom. Rows of desks were laid out each with a slate laying in wait for a hand to scratch on its surface with a sharpened piece of lead as he learned and mastered the subjects taught. The master, Mr Moir, positioned himself at the front, cane in hand, a large piece of slate on the wall behind him on which he had written his name and the date. There was a map of the world to his left and the right hand wall was home to two tall windows facing east which provided both heat and light in the warmer months but come winter the scholars would feel little warmth and the open fire that lay to the right sent its heat up to the high ceiling or was absorbed by the master who would take up residence there. Had Charlie attended the school in Dufftown he would have noticed how different the two were. In Dufftown he would have sat bare footed, his feet scuffing the earth floor wearing his one set of thin clothes and breathing in the smoke from a lumless fire.

As the school master began to speak, imparting his knowledge to the young minds in front of him - some hungrier for knowledge than others - Charlie felt a deep sense of excitement rise up from his toes which pulled at the corners of his mouth and widened his eyes. He drank in every word, as a drouth would whisky, and savoured each letter that touched the palate of his mind.

Fraser sat beside Charlie, quiet as a lamb, absorbing the teachings in much the same way as his friend. The difference between them being the questions put forward by Charlie. Fraser dared not speak as once or twice some of the older boys had been punished for asking foolish questions or giving wrong answers. The master had not appeared disgruntled at Charlie's enquiries but Fraser knew he himself would not risk making any of his own.

The midday break had allowed freedom of both legs and tongues as the scholars ran and played in the grounds following eating their meal in the dining room containing rows and rows of the longest tables either had ever seen. Their first experience of school life was etched, as if in stone, onto each loon's brain and Charlie knew that he would remember it forever.

HAVING BEEN RELEASED by the master at the end of the day Charlie careered across the school grounds towards Peter waiting with the carriage but stopped short when he saw Fraser just ahead and about to climb into his own one. Veering off to the left he caught up with Fraser and clutched his arm preventing him from entering. Sticking his head through the door he announced a steady stream of questions with a wide grin, "Afternoon, Alice. Did ye like school? What did ye learn? What's yer master called? Are ye hungry, I'm starving?"

Alice started to laugh. "You're funny, Charlie. I liked it a wee bit. The master is Mr Drummond and he's very strict. He's a bit like cook."

"Oh," said Fraser. "He must be very strict."

Charlie reddened. "He didna cane ye did he?"

"Oh no, Charlie. No one got the cane."

Charlie's face returned to its normal colour as his anger receded. "Will ye be here everyday to pick up Fraser fae school?"

"Aye. My school is just round the corner."

Charlie's face lit up again. "I'll see ye the morn' then. You too Fraser." He ran off to his own carriage with his chest bursting not only from a day of learning but with the knowledge that he would see Alice every single school day.

The Photograph

Andrew took a moment to savour the change in his wife as she sat at her dressing table brushing her long, fair hair. He saw the clearness of her skin and the brightness in her eyes and a smile was never far away from her lips. "Ye were right, Rose, to persuade me to take in Charlie. You were in need of a bairn and I must admit, I was too."

Rose turned from the mirror to face her husband and smiled. "He's a fine child and so clever, Andrew. When I think back to his arrival six months ago and he entered the house looking as black as the lum and speaking like a servant, I thought I had made a grave mistake."

Andrew spoke with tenderness in his voice, "He has cured ye, Rose."

Rose turned back to the mirror and let her eyes fall for a second. "I am ashamed, Andrew. It helped so much at first when I was sick with grief over not having a child and my spirit was so depressed but it seemed to take hold of me and I know that sometimes my behaviour…" The tears spilled as her throat tightened and Andrew stood up from the edge of their bed and went to kneel by his wife.

"It's in the past and ye are happy now. We are both happy. There is no need to mention it again. We have a good life ahead with a son to be proud o'."

Rose let herself be held and comforted and her smile returned as she knew that his words were indeed true. Her eyes turned towards the small drawer in her dresser where the bottle of laudanum lay untouched. "It will never pass my lips again," she whispered in his ear.

"I know. You no longer have any need of it. Now let's get ourselves down to breakfast before Charlie has eaten us out of house and home. I swear I have never seen a bairn eat so much food."

Rose laughed. "And no doubt he will eat a ton of cake that mother offers him this afternoon. She does like to spoil him every Sunday."

Charlie was indeed on his way to breakfast. Nurtured with kindness, knowledge and food both his mind and limbs had grown stronger. The fawn had begun to grow.

Mary looked at the loon as he appeared downstairs. "Well, Charlie, ye seem tae hae outgrown another pair o' breeks. I'm sure all yer food goes straight into yer legs."

Charlie grinned as he looked at his bare ankles. "Aye. I'm the same height as Fraser now. No one can call me the smallest in class anymore. I'm the fastest runner too. Naebody can catch me."

"Well just you run awa' up stairs and put on the other breeks in the bottom drawer. They should fit ye fine." Mary noted the desperate look Charlie gave the bowl of steaming porridge on the table. "Yer breakfast will still be here when ye get back down."

Charlie sprinted off at a rate of knots. Sunday's were a mixed blessing as he missed seeing Alice but he enjoyed parts of his weekly Sunday visits to his grandparents home. Being surrounded by his cousins gave him a sense of belonging but he was aware of an air of dislike that came from both his grandfather and his cousin, Archie. His mind remembered his cousin's words from the previous Sunday.

"When you fail at school everyone will know you are an idiot and send you away to the lunatic asylum. No one comes out of there again."

Archie had sneered and laughed in his face and Charlie was frightened in case he was indeed sent away. He had grown used to a full belly and a warm bed and although his chest still ached sometimes for his parents and siblings, he liked the Milnes. The thought of never seeing Alice and Fraser again made his breath come quicker and reminded him of the day Andrew had told him his father had died. He had swallowed hard and determined not to let Archie see his fear he had spat, "I'll show ye."

Archie had merely laughed again before leaving to rejoin the adults.

As he quickly changed into another pair of breeks, Charlie made the decision that he would do whatever it took to stay at Willowbank and on returning to the breakfast table he addressed Andrew and Rose, "Morning, Mother. Morning, Father."

Rose and Andrew shared a look and smiled.

*

The residents of Redwood Manor were readying themselves for the arrival of their brood. Ann demanded their presence every Sunday, which came wrapped in an invitation, but no refusal was expected. Robert allowed the gathering but would be hard pushed as to explain why.

Robert stood in his bedchamber half dressed, a whisky already in his hand despite the hour being before midday. His brood were about to descend which meant a wife overly fussing and a house full of folk he bragged about in public but had little interest in in person. He shouted through to Ann's bedchamber, "Why do we have these insufferable afternoons?"

Ann soothed as she always did. "It is the way of the gentry, and we are gentry, are we not?"

Robert threw back his drink and did not reply. If one of his mistresses were free he would make his excuses to leave but of course having family themselves they too were occupied. His latest acquisition, the daughter of an old business acquaintance, would provide some pleasure later. He had already made arrangements to meet and she would not disappoint him. She was a feisty one and he liked feisty. His wife had always been too amiable but of course that was her role. The thought of his latest mistress, combined with the whisky now flowing through his veins, sedated his impatience and he crossed the hall to where his wife was readying herself for her guests. He entered without knocking and found Ann being dressed by her maid. "Leave us," he ordered.

"Yes, sir."

Ann turned. "Robert, I must get dressed, the family will be here in half an hour."

Robert stood and looked at his wife standing in her undergarments, the thought of his later meeting in his mind. "We have time," he answered and knowing what he meant, removed her bloomers and lay on the bed.

"You do choose such awkward times, husband."

*

ANN ENTERED THE parlour just as her family began to arrive. Thankfully Robert had been quick and her hair was still in place. Her new dress fitted elegantly to her curves and she was pleased. Robert would be as polite as Robert ever could be, with his kin, so hopefully any arguments would be avoided thanks to her. She knew how to please her husband. She had been doing it for forty years.

Gordon and Mabel were the first to arrive with their children which was both a blessing and a curse. Young Victoria greeted them with her usual warmth and Robert, following welcoming her in with open arms whispered to his eldest son. "How you managed to sire such a wonderful creature is beyond me. Perhaps she doesn't belong to you at all."

Gordon did not rise to the bait. His father's words though cruel did not contain the usual venom in them so he concluded that he must be in a good mood. He had been racking his brain for ideas to keep his father entertained and out of the mill but nothing had come to him yet. "Will you be coming by the mill tomorrow, Father?"

Robert glared at him. "Why?"

"No reason. Just wondered." Gordon was already regretting the question and wished Andrew was there to deflect any blows.

"I don't yet know, Gordon, but you will be the first to know if I turn up."

Gordon nodded and breathed a sigh of relief as the door opened and in trundled the rest of his family having arrived at the same time in their respective coaches. The twins, Eleanor and Ian were bickering as usual and their brother, young Archie, marched in behind, his chin up higher than looked comfortable which gave him a comical appearance which was surely the opposite of what he was trying to portray. He kissed his grandmother's cheek and shook his grandfather's hand. Ann turned from him. "Well, Charlie, I'm sure you have grown an inch since last week. You will be a gentleman before we know it. Come and tell us all about your week. What have you been learning at school?"

She steered Charlie over to one of the couches and sat beside him, her full attention on his words. Archie seated himself opposite and glowered at Charlie.

"Ann, we are all hungry," Robert barked. "It is time for the younger ones to go through and we will make our way to the dining room."

Ann stood. "Of course. We can see the children later. I have a surprise for us all."

Andrew nodded to Charlie who followed his cousins out of the room leaving the two eldest, Victoria and Archie to dine with the adults.

"What surprise, Ann?" asked Edith as she swilled her already half empty glass in a bored fashion.

"You will have to wait and see but I promise that you will love it."

The party filed out the door towards the dining room, Ann ensuring that she was second last and just before she entered the room she stopped for a moment, her hand going behind her and she stroked the front of her husband's trousers. Robert coughed and the couple moved forward to take their seats at opposite ends of the table. *That should keep you well behaved,* thought Ann.

Andrew was seated next to his father in law, "Do you have plans, Robert, now that hunting season is over?"

Robert leant forward. "The Hallé Orchestra is playing in the Music Hall next week. It's the first concert of the new season so we will attend on opening night."

"An excellent choice, Robert. Rose and I attended one o' their concerts last year. Quite magnificent they were."

"So I've heard. Not my thing of course."

"And yet you are going."

"One must be seen, Andrew, one must be seen."

Rose smiled, and whispered, "He is like Mr Tremenheere in Margaret Oliphant's book, *An Odd Couple.*"

Mabel gasped beside her and Rose faltered. She had not meant to say that out loud. She stole a glance at Mabel who let out a small giggle which went unheard by the others. Rose smiled back and continued to eat her soup. Mr Tremenheere was a man who lived by the edicts of the gentry, forming all his opinions through them. Margaret Oliphant had a way of portraying the plight of women under such men.

"There is to be a Shakespeare play in Her Majesty's Theatre and an author reading in the Music Hall but I have forgotten who," Ann interjected.

"Oh heaven's," Robert added. "I remember falling asleep years ago listening to Dickens reading. Couldn't hear a word he said from my seat."

"Oh, but dear, we have much better seats these days."

"Yes indeed. I have come far in life. Nothing handed to me unlike you, Gordon."

Young Victoria looked up from her soup. "I would very much like to know who the author will be." Her comment distracted her grandfather away from her father.

"Well, Victoria, your grandmother will find out for you and you shall accompany us. Perhaps it will be a more enjoyable evening if you are there."

"Thank you, Grandfather. I would like that very much. I know you are not keen on reading but perhaps this author will be of interest."

"Perhaps. For you I will listen."

"May I join you that evening, Grandfather?" Archie asked.

"No, you may not. Stories are for women. You need to be able to read legal documents and ledgers. They are what drive this country."

"Of course." Archie said. "We are studying a new subject at school, Economics, which determines the most effective use of resources."

"Well your father will be glad to know that. The banking business needs to keep ahead."

"It does indeed," Archie's father replied. "Archie will make a fine banker, no doubt."

Of course Archie as the eldest was expected to follow

in his father's footsteps.

"There was mention of the subject in last week's newspaper. An article concerning the university. There seems to be more choice of subjects to study these days," Gordon said.

"Aye, Gordon, I feel we would enjoy it more nowadays. Some of our learning was rather dry was it not? Remember old Mr Chalmers? He had the ability to put a whole class to sleep within a matter of minutes."

Gordon chuckled. "Aye, Andrew, and he never even noticed. He was quite mad, I'm sure. He would have conversations with himself and often you would see him in the grounds talking away with no one beside him."

"Talking of madmen," Edith interrupted, "I wonder if Queen Victoria will be at Balmoral for longer this year following yet another assassination attempt last year. Surely it is safer there than in London. My father is expected to be invited to Balmoral on some business."

Robert bristled and Ann intervened, knowing her husband's jealousy of those in higher circles than himself, and she wanted nothing to spoil the afternoon ahead. "Seemingly the Queen herself takes few visitors and all business matters are dealt with elsewhere and, Robert, I forgot to mention that we have been invited to the Fraser's Easter Ball."

Robert smiled. "I will look forward to that." He would also look forward to a private get together with Mrs Fraser who had long since been in his debt over a delicate matter.

The rest of dinner passed quite amiably, as Ann had intended, and on hearing the bell she jumped from her seat and announced, "The surprise is here everyone. We need to make our way to the drawing room where the seats have been arranged." She hurried to her husband's side, her face beaming. "Robert, I have taken the liberty of hiring a photographer to come to the house. People always have to attend a studio but I thought we could be the first in Aberdeen to pose in our own home in front of a real fireplace and not some cloth picture. We will be the talk of the town."

"That is a surprise indeed, Ann. The talk of the town. Let us go now, we mustn't keep the man waiting."

The family, both intrigued and excited, made their way to the drawing room and the maid was sent to fetch the children. The photographer, Mr Fiddes, was in the process of setting up his equipment and the party sat in awe watching him arrange everything. He held each piece as if it were a newborn and arranged the camera towards the back of the room quietly talking to himself as he did so, or perhaps, as it looked, he was actually speaking to his camera in a caressing tone.

"It is clear now, Ann, why you said to dress in something befitting a royal visit. Thankfully I listened and have worn my green gown which I know compliments me."

"You look perfect, as always, Edith." she replied, taking in what was a beautiful gown but did not mention the lifeless hair that always hung from Edith like pokers and no amount of curling irons could take hold of the rats' tails and transform them. Ann scanned Mabel and Rose. Mabel was a sweet but plain girl so no competition there, but Rose, she noticed, was looking particularly bonny these days with clear eyes and fair skin. *I will have to make a point of seating her at the other side of the fireplace,* she thought.

The children were ushered in and, for once, even the twins behaved themselves. The air of feverish enthusiasm and expectation enveloped each one in turn, animating the words and thrilling the eyes. Charlie had seen the painted portraits of his ancestors on the walls but now he was being told that there would be something called a photograph of him taken and it too would go on the wall. He leant in to Andrew. "I've seen my face in the mirror but canna imagine what it will look like on the wall."

Andrew laughed and whispered, "You are lucky, Charlie, because ye are a handsome boy. Look at him there," he said pointing to an unfortunate painting of a man on the far wall, "he was yer mother's great uncle. Beards hide a multitude of sins."

Mr Fiddes cleared his throat. "Ladies and gentleman, she is now ready to take your portrait."

"She?" Robert asked.

"Yes, Mr Ross. I call the camera a she as she is a wonder of beauty and as slick as any vessel."

Robert had no reply for that so merely sat where he was ordered to, and presently with all in their rightful place each man, woman and child stood or sat as still as a statue and tried their very best to portray an image of either elegance, beauty, pride or eminence. Charlie sat on the floor in front of his parents, a wide smile on his face as he thought about telling Alice all about cameras.

Various different photographs were taken, some of family groups and some as individuals. Robert was enthralled and watched Mr Fiddes intently, keen to learn about the workings of the camera. He had not fully appreciated the magnitude of the invention before and had dismissed it as a fad but Mr Fiddes had brought examples of his work and he was impressed. The last time he had visited the billiard room in the Music Hall he had seen a certain type of photograph that women posed for. An idea began to form in his mind as he again asked Mr Fiddes to show him how the camera worked.

*

Later in the evening Robert sat in the same drawing room, whisky in hand. Ann had impressed him that afternoon, in more than one way, and looking out onto the street, the heavy rain battering against the window pane, he decided against his meeting with his latest mistress. Perhaps he would call late if Ann did not satisfy him. It had been an entertaining day and the idea that was playing in his mind since the afternoon had excited him. He rang the bell by the fireplace and his servant entered. "Simpson, stoke up the fire and send Ann to me. We are not to be disturbed." Having retired early for the evening Ann arrived wearing a dressing gown and demanded to know why she had been called from her bed.

"I wish to see you, Ann."
"Well, I am here. What is wrong?"
"Nothing is wrong, dear. I wish to *see* you."

*

ANN HAD ARRANGED the recently taken photographs in the parlour and was delighted with the results. She had expressed to Mr Fiddes that she be made to look perfect or no money would cross his palm, and he had not disappointed her. There was a painted portrait of her that she liked very much hanging in another room and she had been concerned that perhaps the lack of colour in a photograph would not be flattering but that was not the case at all and she was quite satisfied. Her friends and acquaintances would be quite envious. Unbeknownst to Ann, Mr Feddes employed the technique of making tiny scratches on a glass negative which resulted in the smoothing out of wrinkles and any other blemishes on a person's face. The effect was transformational and his clients were indeed impressed with what they believed to be a true likeness. Robert had been keen to learn this trick from him and Gordon was to be the one who benefitted although oblivious to the fact.

The mill was functioning at full pace with orders both coming in and going out at record speed. The new machines were working well and as long as the River Don did not run dry the wheel would continue to turn and cloth be made. Gordon was keeping a close eye on all orders, as well as the bank balance, and for once everything seemed to be running smoothly. The workers were no longer up in arms over pay, Gordon having listened to Andrew and upped wages. His father was unaware and would no doubt find out next time he poked his nose into a ledger but till then Gordon was happy to keep him in blissful ignorance. As long as Robert received a good share of the profits he would hopefully be satisfied.

Andrew arrived at the mill on Wednesday afternoon. "I have drawn up the legal document you asked for. Peter Coutts should be happy enough with the terms as both companies benefit."

"Thank you. I will sign it and have it sent to him immediately. It is, as always, a relief to have a trustworthy friend as my solicitor. I don't think I would have fully trusted my father when I took over if you hadn't been the one to draw up the papers."

Andrew sat down at the desk. The photograph taken at Redwood Manor of Gordon's family sat in a small frame beside the inkwell. "Ye needn't have worried. I know he badgers you and watches you like a hawk but at the end of the day he wants the mill to thrive and continue to be a profitable business."

"I can't quite believe that Father has not set foot through that door for nearly three weeks. I dared not mention his absence at dinner on Sunday lest he took it as an invitation."

"Aye, I saw him in the card room on Saturday. He asked if everything was as it should be with the mill and when I said yes he merely nodded and carried on playing. It was not the usual Spanish inquisition. Perhaps he has found something to relieve his boredom after all."

"Well whatever the reason, I am glad of it and long may it continue. Did you win yer game of cards?"

"No I did not, so I visited the billiard room before returning home to cheer myself up. I am much better at billiards than cards."

Gordon laughed. "It's fortunate that the Music Hall houses both, and for those of us with talent for neither there is always the parlour or the supper room in which to drown one's sorrows in a dram or two."

"I hear that a certain Sir acquired himself another's wife on Saturday. Her husband was away on business and they were seen having supper in the Music Hall. Seemingly she was extremely polite towards him."

Andrew let out a small laugh. "Well it is the meeting place for polite society."

"Some houses have open evenings and hers has been mentioned," Gordon added.

"Aye, I have heard of such things." Andrew got up and crossed the room, stopping to look out of the window.

"Fine if you are unmarried perhaps. I have never strayed from Mabel and never will. I know a man of your standing would never betray my sister."

Andrew had his back to Gordon. "Of course."

A Time of Blossom

Time spun like the weft being drawn through cloth, pulled over and under the warp thread. Two springs had passed since Charlie's arrival at Willowbank and as he played with Alice and Fraser outside Rose turned from the drawing room window overlooking the garden and sat opposite Andrew whose head was bowed low over a book.

"Charlie is such an interesting child. He is so headstrong and thrawn with certain things, yet so patient and kind with others. One minute he is horsing around and giggling and the next he is delicately holding some insect or other and teaching his friends all about it. Fraser listens half heartedly but Alice stares at him adoringly. It's quite sweet."

Andrew chuckled. "He told me the other day that Alice is the only quine he knows who isn't scared of anything."

"Well I know this much, whoever marries Alice will have to be able to stand up for himself. Her mother despairs at her forthright confidence and prays she will outgrow it."

"I certainly hope Charlie doesn't lose his. When he sets his mind on something there's no changing it and that may well stand him in good stead as a man."

The sound of laughter and skirls could be heard and as Andrew and Rose looked out of the window Charlie caught a glimpse of them and waved with such force that his entire body shook and his wide grin portrayed a loon full of innocent happiness.

The previous afternoon he had come out of school and ran with Fraser towards the carriage because Charlie knew not how to walk. It had been arranged for him to visit Fraser's house and he was to stay for supper. This had become something of a habit encouraged by Rose who could see the positive effect Fraser had on Charlie, and encouraged by Charlie who could see the positive effect of Alice.

Alice, as usual, was already seated in the carriage when her brother and Charlie charged in.

"I am going to marry ye, Alice, and I will own my own train and we can travel wherever we want. You can come too, Fraser."

"We will be brothers. I have always wanted a brother," Fraser replied.

"I was going to tell you next week that I had decided to marry you. I've already told Mama what kind of dress I want to wear to the wedding," Alice added.

"Who will you marry, Fraser?" Charlie asked.

"I don't want to get married. Quine's are too bossy."

"Oh but you have to marry, Fraser. It's the law. Don't worry I will find you a wife. Dorothy in my class is lovely and quiet and not at all bossy. She will do just fine."

Charlie recounted the conversation in his head as he ran and jumped and played with his friends. His heart was full and it mainly belonged to Alice.

His time spent with his kin in Dufftown was a distant memory and as time passed it became harder for Charlie to remember their faces but his chest still ached sometimes when he thought of them. He had learned not to ask about his siblings anymore and calling Rose and Andrew mother and father came easily to his tongue now.

School achieved its aim of not just educating, but thanks

to a skilled master who believed that learning should be made interesting, it accomplished the aspiration of the need to learn. Charlie loved everything about being a scholar. He sat, as he had on his very first day, enthralled and wide eyed allowing his mind to absorb learning like the roots of a plant soaks up water. His inquisitive mind caused him to ask many questions which may have displeased certain masters who did not wish to be interrupted but Charlie's questions were so pertinent and asked so intently that no master could refuse to answer fully and enthusiastically.

He recounted his learning to his parents in the evenings and his excitement was evident.

"Today we learnt all about the Jacobites and Bonnie Prince Charlie. Imagine him ha'ing the same name as me and he wisna… wasn't very tall. I dinna mind now if I din… don't grow very tall. Ye can be a great man and nae be tall."

"Yes, indeed. I think you will be a great man, Charlie, and the way you are growing you may well be tall," his mother replied.

"Fraser says that when he grows up he has tae study medicine like his father. Will I have tae do what you do, Father?"

Andrew thought for a second. "I would be proud if ye chose to study law like me, Charlie, but I will not insist on it. Ye can choose yer own path."

"I'd like to drive a train but John's father is a banker and he says banks run countries so I might run the country instead."

Andrew chuckled. "I'm sure ye would make a fine job o' running the country."

*

It was a cool autumn afternoon in October and the Balgownie Links golf course was dotted with the distinctive red jackets of the golfers' uniform. James Ross was playing against two fellow competitive bankers whilst teaching his son, Archie, the intricacies of the game. Each man had his own caddie, loons of around twelve in age, of working class. Archie was not overly keen on learning how to golf as it was not a sport that interested him but of course that was not a reason not to play as it was all about being seen in the right circles.

Mr Thompson and Mr Anderson were close acquaintances of James, and Archie had met them several times before. The game started quite amiably but it became apparent that Mr Anderson was not at all in good humour. With every misdirected putt his temper flared. The forecaddie, whose job it was to stand near the hole and watch where expensive *Gutty* golf balls landed so they would not be lost, had an awful time retrieving Mr Anderson's golf balls far from their desired destination. The undulating sand dunes and prevailing sea breeze were enough to test the best golfer but add in a bad temper and it became a game of wits for his opponents.

Having no way of winning his game he roughly grabbed his club from his caddie to take his turn to tee off at the last hole. The ball soared into the air veering left away from the flag and the forecaddie, a young loon, kept his eye on the ball until he saw it coming straight for him and with nothing but a second to react ducked his head into his hands but was violently struck on the back of his head.

The men stopped, their movements frozen as their minds deciphered what their eyes had just witnessed. The forecaddie lay on the ground half hidden by the bushes that edged the green. Archie was the first to move, his legs carrying him along the grass till he reached the loon who was lying motionless. He knelt down with no idea what to do as his hands went from reaching out to touch the loon and back to cradle his own head. James appeared at his side and put his ear to the boy's mouth. "He's breathing. Help me sit him up, Archie." Together they levered the loon up and he gave a grunt as his eyes slowly opened.

"Thank God," said Archie.

"Aye." He spoke to the young forecaddie, "Ye are going to be alright, lad."

Mr Thompson had now arrived and together they carried the barely conscious loon across the course to the club house where they laid him on a bench. Mr Anderson was already there standing stony faced watching proceedings.

"Has someone been sent to fetch a doctor?" James asked.

A fellow golfer replied, "Aye. I heard Mr Thompson shout for one before he ran to where the lad was. I sent my caddie."

The loon groaned again and his hand went up to the back of his head. James knelt beside the bench. "Doctor's on his way, loon. Ye have had a nasty bump. There's nae blood though," he added as he looked at the back of the lad's head.

"Damned fool was standing in the wrong place." Mr Anderson stated.

Archie looked at Mr Anderson and felt his concern turn into anger. "Ye slammed that ball without caring where it went, so angry were ye at losing. He was standing well away from the green."

Mr Anderson faced Archie. "And just what are ye implying?"

"Enough." James intervened. "No one is implying anything. Archie, go and get something for the loon to drink."

Archie glowered at Mr Anderson but did not say any more. The loon groaned again and attempted to sit up. "Where am I?"

"Ye are in the club house," James answered. "Ye were

hit by a golf ball."

"My head hurts."

"Aye, lad, I'm sure it does. What's yer name?"

The loon looked vacant for a second before slowly answering, "...Duncan."

Archie returned with a cup of tea and handed it to his father.

"Here, Duncan, take a wee sip o' a drink. The doctor will be here soon."

Thankfully the caddie that was sent to fetch a doctor knew that one was just a few minutes away at the ninth hole. His friend caddied for Dr Reid occasionally and today was one of those days.

Dr Reid entered the clubhouse somewhat out of breath and had the caddie bring him his bag which he had left in his carriage. "Well now, laddie, let's have a wee look at you." He proceeded to examine his patient asking questions as he went and Duncan responded as best as he could. After a time Duncan appeared less groggy and confused to the relief of all bystanders. "Ye have been very lucky, Duncan. Ye are concussed but the dizziness will pass with plenty o' rest. I will take ye home in my carriage." He turned to the men, "Perhaps one of you would accompany him in the carriage?"

"I will come with you, doctor," Archie said. He then turned to James. "I'll make my way home afterwards, Father."

James hesitated but could see the determination and worry on his loon's face. "Alright, Archie. Take a Hansom cab home and I'll be there when ye get back." He pressed some money into Archie's palm.

James and Mr Thompson wished the lad well but Mr Anderson uttered not a word which did not go unnoticed.

Duncan gave the doctor his address and the horse pulled the carriage south towards Exchequer Row. Young Duncan groaned occasionally but spoke when spoken to and before long the doctor had turned his carriage into a short, narrow street of high tenements. It was a busy street which led onto Shiprow which served as a thoroughfare to and from the harbour.

As the carriage stopped it was eyed with interest by folk. Being a poor area gentlemen's carriages did not tend to stop there. Some scurried past with urgency fearing some retribution for some demeanour or another, others looked on with trepidation, ready to defend their home if need be. No one wanted to be evicted onto the street for not having paid their rent.

Some bairns who had been playing flocked around the doctor. "I like yer coat, mister. Are ye a soldier?"

Dr Reid was surprised at the question until he realised that he was wearing his red coat: the uniform of the golf club. "Nay." He smiled. "I am a doctor."

Duncan was helped from the carriage and Dr Reid knocked on the tenement door. A bairn of about nine in years appeared, very thin and pale looking with a shawl wrapped tightly about her. Dr Reid looked down at the quine. "We are looking for Duncan Ogilvie's family."

"They live upstairs. Second floor. Door on the right." She scurried away and disappeared into her home on the ground floor.

Dr Reid looked behind him. "In we go then. Take yer time, Duncan, and hold my arm if ye need to."

The three of them entered into the shared building and the first thing to hit Archie was the stench. It was nothing that had ever pervaded his nose before and he found himself trying not to breathe as they ascended the stone staircase. Duncan managed the climb and opened his door alerting his mother to his presence. On seeing Duncan her hand went to her chest and she jumped from her chair dropping the garment she had been sewing onto the dirty wooden floor. "My loon. Are ye hurt?"

"Aye, Mother."

The doctor stepped forward. "I am Dr Reid. Duncan has been in an accident but he will be alright after a good rest. May we come in?"

"Aye, aye, come away. What happened?" she asked as Duncan lay himself on a bed in the corner.

"He was hit on the back of the head by a stray golf ball. He has some concussion so needs to rest for a few days until he recovers. He might feel dizzy and a bit sick for a while but that should pass soon."

"A few days? So he canna work then?" her voice rose in panic. "And ye'll need paying doctor."

"Nay, Mrs Ogilvie. No payment is required but ye must let the loon rest for a few days."

Archie looked around the cramped room which had a scent similar to the hallway. Two very young bairns were on the floor playing with a rag of material and a spoon. Their clothes were threadbare and their hair matted but they were happy bairns: quick to smile and babbling in the way bairns who cannot yet speak, do. One crawled over to Duncan and lay his head on his brother's arm and Duncan rubbed the top of his head. The room was cold and the air foetid.

"Is yer husband in work, Mrs Ogilvie?" asked Dr Reid.

She shook her head. "He died last winter. Duncan is my oldest loon and provides for us alongside my sewing money." She turned to pull a blanket over Duncan. "Did he get paid today or did the accident happen before he was finished?"

Archie knew that Mr Anderson would have no intention of paying Duncan and on seeing the living conditions of the home, for the first time in his life he had come face-to-face with poverty. Stepping forward he reached into his pocket. "I have his wages here." He placed the coins his father had given him into her hand. "It all happened rather fast but if it is not enough I will make sure he gets what is due him." Archie had no idea what Duncan would have been paid and hoped it was enough. He would walk home.

Duncan's mother took the money with obvious relief. "Thank you…oh but this is too much surely?"

"Duncan worked hard today, Mrs Ogilvie."

"Well thank ye, Mr…?"

"Ross. My name is Archie Ross."

"Thank you to ye both for helping my loon. I will see that he rests."

"Ye are welcome. Good day to you."

Archie took a final look around and left with the doctor. Outside he breathed in some air and asked Dr Reid, "Do many folk live as they do?"

"Aye, lad. I'm afraid so. There is a world of poverty in our streets. That smell is a mixture of

defective sewers, damp crowded conditions and unwashed bodies."

Archie shook his head and had no words for such information. He realised that he had lived a privileged existence for sixteen years without any idea as to how little some folk had.

He knew there to be one hundred and fifty thousand people in the city of Aberdeen and he shuddered to think how many lived like Duncan.

HAVING WALKED HOME from Exchequer Row, Archie was in sombre mood. He found his father in the drawing room and sat heavily on a fireside chair. "Ye were a long while, Archie. Is Duncan home safe?"

"Aye, Father, but what a home he has. I have never seen

the like. Duncan is head of his house as his father died last winter and his mother has younger bairns to feed." Archie's voice began to rise. "I very much doubt that Mr Anderson will be caring. Did ye see him today, Father? He has some temper and did not seem concerned for Duncan at all. The loon could have been killed."

"He has a temper indeed and I must admit that I was unimpressed with his behaviour towards the lad but it was an accident all the same. He didn't deliberately hit him with the ball."

"I wouldn't be so sure and he owes Duncan his wage. I gave Mrs Ogilvie the money ye gave me for a carriage."

"Don't you be getting involved. It is not your place. There are charities to help the poor."

Archie got up, thunder in his eyes but calmness on his tongue. "I'm going to study. I have work to do for tomorrow."

*

Come Sunday the family gathered at Redwood Manor as was the habit. Charlie had grown to know his cousins, as they did him, and having lost some of his country brogue and proved himself intelligent in his learnings he was no longer deemed an idiot. Even Archie no longer bothered him. His grandfather's opinion, however, remained unchanged and Charlie was acutely aware of his threatening presence. He rarely spoke to Charlie but he prowled around him like the sleekit fox he was.

Ann always had all of her grandchildren join the adults in the parlour which irritated Robert but he had long since realised the importance of family news to impart in polite conversation with his peers, so sought first hand knowledge of their achievements. He liked to boast with the best of them.

"So Ian, are you top o' your class like yer brother, Archie?"

"Not quite, Grandfather. Maybe second," he lied.

"Well, it's less important with ye being the second born but ye must try harder. Ye cannot be an embarrassment to yer kin."

"No, Grandfather."

James bristled at his father's comments, being the second born son himself, but said nothing. It was Archie who spoke, "We have been studying recent Parliamentary Acts and I find the Entail Act of 1882 very interesting."

"Ah, yes, that ruffled a few feathers," replied Andrew. "I have had clients who wish to fight it in court as they wish to bequeath their land to someone out with their family."

"Forgive my ignorance but what is the Act about?" asked Ann.

"Land must be kept in the family. An heir can no longer sell it or bequeath it to an illegitimate child." Andrew replied.

"It hardly seems fair. Surely ye should have the right to do whatever you wish with your own land."

"I agree, Uncle Gordon. What is your opinion, Grandfather?" Archie looked straight at Robert.

Robert's eyes betrayed his anger but he kept his words light. "It does not affect me. My land will be passed down to my first born and that's that."

The room stalled as all knew that his first born had been Grace, Charlie's mother, but even had she lived no inheritance would have gone to her, being female. Gordon would be the sole heir of the land that Robert received on his marriage to Ann.

Edith, was acutely aware of tension in the air which she saw as being inadvertently caused by her son, and strived to alter it. "I hear that Sir Muir was commending you on your great shooting last season, Robert."

Robert's self importance was raised by the compliment

and his internal anger gave way to pride. The conversation turned towards leisurely pursuits but it was Archie, yet again, who created tension.

"Did Father tell ye of our game of golf the other day, Grandfather?"

"No. Did ye finally beat him?"

"Unfortunately the game was interrupted when Mr Anderson, in a fit of temper, struck and badly injured the forecaddie." The anger was evident in Archie's words.

"It was an accident," James said. "Archie here helped the loon and assisted the doctor in taking him home."

"That was very kind, Archie," added Rose.

"It's hardly a home. I had not realised the extent of poverty in Aberdeen. I have been ignorant of it till now." He looked at Charlie and thought for the first time what his start in life may well have been like.

Robert showed his annoyance once again. "Do not be fooled. The poor choose to live as they do. They blight our streets and want sympathy for it. They always have some sob story or another."

Mabel found her often quiet voice. "I don't think that's fair, Robert, I myself am involved in charity work and there are indeed folk in need."

Ann could see that her afternoon of family time together was quickly degenerating and Robert would either say something that she would regret or storm out altogether. "Let us play some parlour games. Robert, why don't you pour yourself a whisky and play some cards with Victoria."

"Yes, Grandfather, I would like that very much."

Robert acquiesced as he could never refuse Victoria anything and the afternoon was saved. Andrew observed Archie and was impressed with his convictions. The lad was growing up. He watched him playing with Charlie for the first time in two years. *Despite your parentage you might well turn out to be a man of morals and one who wishes to improve the lot of others.*

*

ARCHIE DECIDED TO return to Duncan's home a week after the incident. He had been unable to get him out of his mind and felt compelled to visit. He had the cook make up a hamper of cold meats, scones and cake (swearing her to secrecy) and jumped into a Hansom cab. It was a freezing cold day, November having brought with it the obvious beginnings of winter and he huddled into the back of the cab as it swiftly manoeuvred through the streets.

Alighting on Exchequer Row he braced himself for the onslaught of stench and poverty to his senses and proceeded up the stairs to the second floor where he deftly knocked on Mrs Ogilvie's door. He could hear the sound of a bairn crying and had to wait a while before the door was opened. Mrs Ogilvie stood in front of him, her eyes blank and dark, her hair dishevelled and her clothes unwashed. Archie stumbled, "Good afternoon, Mrs Ogilvie, I have come to see how Duncan is."

Duncan's mother shook her head.

"I am Archie Ross, I helped to take him home the day he was injured. I have brought a hamper with me." He held out the basket and Mrs Ogilvie turned and went back to her crying bairn but she did not shut the door. Archie hesitantly followed and entered the room. The two bairns that he had seen before were both there but there was no sign of Duncan.

"Is Duncan out working?" he enquired.

"My loon is dead."

Archie blanched as if a spark from the fire had landed on bare skin. He placed the food on the wee table and sat himself down slowly on the edge of a wooden chair. "How?...When?..."

Mrs Ogilvie sat with her bairn on her lap rocking him

slowly and plucking at a thread on her sleeve. "Two days ago. Had some kind of fit, right here in front o' me. Nothing I could do. Hadn't been right since the accident. Kept forgetting things and feeling dizzy."

Archie lowered his head.

"How will ye manage?"

"We'll manage."

Archie rose, sensing he was not wanted. "I am so sorry, Mrs Ogilvie."

She did not reply and Archie left, closing the door behind him. He staggered back down the steps and into the street, his heart hammering in his chest.

Duncan had been twelve years old.

A Birthday

THE DAY OF Charlie's seventh birthday dawned and true to form he was out of bed and dressing before his eyes were fully open. Mary no longer helped him with his layers and shoes as he had learned long ago how to dress as a young gentleman. She did however lay his clothes out each morning in readiness and although it was a thankless task persisted in trying to tame his unruly curls with a comb each morning.

Mary entered to make his bed and tidy away his bedclothes. "Many happy returns to ye Charlie. Cook has made yer breakfast and there's strawberry jam for yer bread tae go wi' it."

Charlie licked his lips. "My favourite. She said there would be an extra thick layer in my cake too. Have ye been into the parlour? Are there presents there? I tried to take a peek last night but the door was kept firmly shut."

"Aye, I have been in and I can promise ye, ye will not be disappointed."

Charlie popped his wee wooden rabbit into his pocket, as usual, and sprinted down the staircase launching himself into the dining room, whereupon he careered round the table and landed his bottom firmly on his chair. "Good morning, Mother. Good morning, Father," he said followed by his usual cheeky, infectious grin.

His parents laughed where others may have scolded. "Many happy returns of the day to ye Charlie," was echoed by them both and Charlie tucked into his cooked breakfast.

Rose decided that Charlie had waited long enough to see his presents and led him to the parlour. "Close your eyes, Charlie and I will lead you in."

Charlie squeezed his eyes tightly together grinning from ear-to-ear as his mother led him to the wee table in the corner of the room. Andrew stood to the right of the table and he himself waited eagerly for Charlie's reaction as he had suggested one of the gifts to Rose.

"Ye can open yer eyes now, loon," Andrew said and Charlie's eyes sprung open and feasted on what lay before him. He saw a board game called *Snakes and Ladders* that he had played at Fraser's house and remembered telling his mother how much fun it was and his hand touched the cover of a new book but his eyes lit up even more on seeing a magnifying glass and his fingers reached out and touched the handle made of part of a stag's antler. He picked it up and stroked the handle feeling the contours of the antler and the coldness of the decorative silver tip. Bringing it up to his face he held it over his new book and peered through the glass. Charlie looked at his father, "Oh thank you, Father, this is the one we saw in the shop isn't it?"

"Aye, Charlie, it is. I knew ye would like one for looking at yer beloved insects and anything else that intrigues ye in the garden or elsewhere."

"Please may I go out now and use it?"

"Yes but keep your clothes clean as your guests will be arriving shortly."

"Yes, Mother. I will be careful," he replied as he walked - for once- out of the room holding his magnifying glass as if it were a newborn chick.

Charlie went straight to where the geraniums grew and used his magnifying glass to look closely at the petals and was delighted when a bee landed on one of the flowers and he was able to get a good look at it as it gathered the nectar. He marvelled at the delicate see through wings and the tiny hairs on its legs. Before long his guests arrived and Charlie was summoned to greet them formally before they were ushered into the sunny garden to play.

Charlie had chosen to invite Fraser and Alice only, being his closest friends, and the three played as they always did with each making the other laugh and Alice imparting her worldly knowledge on everything. Fraser held the magnifying glass close to the bark of the tree where the swing hung from its ropes and Alice was perched there commenting on the state of the country that her father had been discussing at breakfast. "Papa says the country is falling apart and we need a lection, whatever that is. I think it might be like thread as thread holds cotton together."

"The country is not made o' cotton, Alice." her brother stated.

"I am quite aware of that, Fraser, that is why I said it might be *like* thread. I don't know what keeps a whole country together."

"Our country is very small on the map of the world that is in school so I don't think it will need much, of whatever it is, to keep it together." Charlie said.

"Charlie, look at this beetle climbing the tree."

Charlie scrambled off the grass and joined Fraser who handed him the magnifying glass. He followed the beetle as it moved upwards but before long it was too high for him to see it through his magnifying glass. "I want to see where it's going." Charlie began to climb the tree putting his new present in his pocket so he could safely clamber up the branches. About halfway up the oak tree there was a thick branch that grew horizontally where Charlie had sat many times before. A small hollowed area nestled there where the two parts of the tree joined and often creatures gathered inside. "There's loads today," he shouted down and proceeded to take his magnifying glass out of his pocket and survey the delights before him. Another insect that wasn't a beetle scuttled into the hollow and disappeared. It was not one that Charlie had seen before and he was eager to see it again so manoeuvred his body round twisting and turning to try and see deeper into the hollow. So intent was he on the insect that he forgot to hold on properly and without warning Charlie suddenly found himself falling.

A scream left Alice as Charlie landed at her feet with his arm wedged under him at a funny angle. Fraser ran inside for help and Andrew and Rose appeared in the garden seconds later shocked to find Charlie laying on his side, whimpering. "Have Peter fetch the doctor, Rose. It's obvious his arm is broken."

Rose did as directed and Andrew proceeded to lift Charlie up causing a scream of pain to be emitted. "I'm sorry, loon, I know it's painful but I need to get ye inside and the doctor will sort ye out, good as new." As Andrew held his son he breathed a sigh of relief to see no blood on him.

Mary was charged with escorting Alice and Fraser home who had been reassured that Charlie would be well, a piece of birthday cake having been given to them by the cook as they went out the door. The doctor arrived to examine Charlie who lay white as a sheet in his bed, Rose holding his hand and offering words of comfort. "Oh doctor, please give him something for the pain. He is so young and it must hurt him so very much."

"Don't you worry, Mrs Milne, I will see to it. Now then, Charlie, let's take a look at you."

The doctor administered some laudanum. "The arm is definitely broken but easily set and he has bruising down his side and abdomen but apart from that I would say that he has had a lucky escape. Once I have bandaged his arm he must rest it till it heals which will take several weeks."

Rose breathed a sigh of relief. "Thank you, doctor." She remained by Charlie's side as he slept, having placed his wee rabbit by him on his pillow.

Charlie slept on and off for the rest of the day, the tincture providing some relief from his pain. The following morning when he opened his eyes the pain had gone and he looked upon two faces, their smiles soft and loving as they embraced him.

Alice was not allowed to visit him the next day no matter how much she protested. She stomped and raged at her mother but to no avail. She thought perhaps it was because she was a girl but Fraser wasn't allowed to visit him either. The two were packed off to school with the promise of cake on their return and that was that.

On hearing the news of Charlie's fall, his grandfather reacted with his usual thoughtlessness, "Of course he fell out o' a tree. What else would ye expect from an idiot."

Part Two

The March of Time
1899

THE FAMILY BIRTHDAYS that followed as the years went by in Aberdeen were far less memorable than Charlie's seventh, unless you counted the gathering for his cousin Ian, James and Edith's loon and younger brother to Archie, whose twenty first birthday was reported in the newspaper as being of such debauchery that surely he would never be permitted to enter a certain hotel again. Ian had been a classmate of Charlie's but had not had the fortune of either Charlie's brains or common sense.

On finishing his university education - much to the

relief of his masters - Ian had been ready to celebrate. He had considered himself a man and sought to do what men did: consort with women, drink whisky and be the master of his own fate. With money in his pocket and a thirst for life alongside his fellow newly graduated scholars he had gone in search of some fun.

One of the young loons had taken charge and led the group of young gentlemen to a tavern, of a certain ilk, on Flour Mill Lane. There existed different brothels throughout Aberdeen, and indeed Scotland, that served each class within society, therefore a landowner, a clerk or a sailor could find himself a place in which to commandeer a woman for his own needs.

The evening had consisted of the losing of virginity, the drinking of much whisky and a brawl involving two bankers, a solicitor, four students and a woman's garter, but not necessarily in that order, which had thankfully not ended with a report in the following day's newspaper otherwise several fledgling careers may have been derailed, not to mention the minds of certain mothers.

Robert had laughed and slapped his grandson on the back having heard of the event from some acquaintance with the words, "Ye will never forget yer first sight o' a woman."

The era, such as it was, was like a penny: it had two sides, each one quite different from the other. Some folk were oblivious as to what lay on the other side believing their lives to be more linear. The poor were still poor and the rich were still rich, men had mistresses and women could not vote, sons followed in their father's footsteps and corsets still squeezed tight on waists.

Men gathered in the billiard and card rooms and spoke of women and life with the air of superiority handed to them at birth. Whisky flowed and loosened tongues as it had a habit of doing and opinions were aired.

Andrew was in the billiard room and believed himself to be in good company, when the conversation turned to wives. He was in a philosophical mood. "Of course we are badly behaved creatures, or ill-gatit as my mother is prone to saying. Our lives consist o' a set o' scales with good manners and propriety on one side and debauchery and deceit on the other. We flit through life with each side forging an unlikely alliance and our conscience lies somewhere in the middle, often untouched by either."

"There is no need for a conscience as far as a wife is concerned, Mr Milne. A man has needs and that's all there is to it. There is a need for discreteness, aye, so as not to appear vulgar about it but that is all."

Andrew sighed. "I am undecided."

Mr Yule continued, "I have had only one mistress and for the past ten years she has been my companion. I consider myself loyal to both her and my wife. I am not one of those who changes mistresses frequently or has more than one at a time."

Another acquaintance joined the conversation. "Each generation since the beginning of time thinks that they are better, more worldly, than the last and that they have invented the concept of modernism or sex but of course that is not the case at all. History repeats itself and will continue to do so. We are approaching a new century but nothing will really change. Some will have more money, some less. Some will fail in life, some will succeed. Some will be born and some will die."

Mr Yule took his shot at the table. "How very enlightening, Mr Simpson, I will be sure to raise my glass to the year 1900 and toast more money and success."

Andrew missed potting his next ball. "You are right about history, Mr Simpson, it does seem to repeat itself. We keep on making the same mistakes."

"Ye are very maudlin this evening, Mr Milne, which is

not like ye at all."

"Aye, I'm sorry. I think I will head away now. Goodnight all."

As Andrew walked out the main door of the Music Hall onto Union Street he found himself turning right instead of left towards home. Already feeling disturbed, home meant a wife who needed laudanum more than a husband so he headed towards the comfort of another to soothe his troubled soul, if not his conscience.

*

Alice Buchan, meanwhile, had become the lady she was destined to be, much to her mother's exasperation. She had not grown out of a strong minded, confident disposition but her saving grace, according to her mother, was her beauty that often prompted the words, "Surely her face will save her from maidenhood." Her second thought, which she never allowed to become spoken words, was, *I wonder if her brother could give her some tincture to calm her thrawn spirit.*

Fraser of course had followed his father's footsteps and studied medicine, a profession which suited his quieter nature. Having never forgotten the sight of Charlie's broken arm all those years ago, he had taken a particular interest in the skeleton and opted to specialise in osteology. He was fascinated by the structure and strength of bone and what happened to it when it broke. A part of him was somewhat disappointed that he had never broken a bone of his own, without having to endure any serious pain or injury, just so that he could lend personal experience to his studies. He had received a strange look from his tutor on voicing this regret and had never repeated it.

Their mother, Shona, concerned herself with two things: the charities relating to the welfare of the poor and the marrying of her children. Alice no longer erupted into a room but her presence had the same effect on those within it.

Thursday morning found Mrs Buchan being called upon by a visitor and she called for her maid to fetch Alice.

"Ah, Alice, Miss Barclay has come to visit and we were just discussing the latest fashion."

"Good morning, Miss Barclay. I am sure that you would much rather discuss my brother."

"Alice. What a thing to say," her mother admonished.

"Mother, you know perfectly well that Fraser is too shy in making his intentions clear and a lady has little time to waste on waiting. Now, Miss Barclay, let us come up with a plan to make it easy for my brother to propose. The sooner he is settled the better."

Alice's mother sank into her chair, defeated, but as the corners of Miss Barclay's mouth began to twitch and the twitching became laughter, soon the room was filled with the giggling of three quines, one middle aged and two young, all who loved Fraser.

"I think, Alice, that the sooner you are settled the better too. Surely only one man will put up with your forthrightness so let us hope that he proposes soon before he changes his mind and decides to find himself a quiet, amiable quine."

"I do believe that he will propose soon, Mother. I have already told him that I wish to be married in the spring."

Ann Ross had been thinking of her own wedding that day. She tried not to acknowledge how many years had passed since she had walked down the aisle, a young and radiant bride. Her mind was discomfited and as she looked upon the muddled laces of her corset lying on the chair she had some sympathy with them.

She entered the parlour dressed in all her finery. She

and Robert had been invited to dine at Sir Muir's home situated on a large estate on the outskirts of Aberdeen. Of course it was an honour to be invited to such occasions but if truth be told Ann would rather have stayed at home. As she waited for her husband to appear her eyes observed the portraits that adorned the walls. Ignoring the old oil paintings of long since dead ancestors she allowed them to settle on the photographs taken of her and her family and felt something akin to regret.

"What are ye doing staring at the walls?" barked Robert as he marched into the room.

Ann bristled. "I was looking at the photographs and lamenting the passage of time. I am no longer young and beautiful and our children have at times been somewhat of a disappointment."

"You were far too soft on them, Ann, especially Gordon. He has no gumption in him at all and he married such a pathetic woman who is scared of her own shadow."

"He has succeeded with the mill though, has he not?"

Robert snorted. "Only thanks to my keeping an eye on him and Andrew's influence."

"James is very like you in many ways."

Robert took this as a compliment. "Aye, it's just a pity he was not my first born son."

"I suppose that's my fault."

"Nay, but ye have interfered too much with the raising of grandchildren and now look what's happening. Half of them act like degenerates and as for political affiliations go, well I needn't tell you how embarrassing that is."

"Andrew is in favour -"

"Andrew should know better than to side with the working class."

"But Charlie -"

"Do not mention that name in this house."

Ann remained silent and Robert leaned forward to take

a closer look at one of the photographs. "Ye are old now indeed. That is why I no longer visit yer bedchamber. Come, it is time we were away."

*

Sir and Lady Muir's parlour was a throng of conversation where guests partook in drinks and pleasantries and introductions prevailed before being led into the dining room. The party consisted of twenty people of various rank and status within the middle and upper classes, some of whom were friends and others who served the purpose of beneficial acquaintances. It was impossible to tell whether conversations were genuine or manipulative, so used were folk to having to keep up appearances and get on in life successfully.

Ann herself had been attending such occasions for so long that she herself was no longer sure if she meant the words that she uttered or if they sprang from the desire to keep her status as a devoted wife and mother who knew her place and was an excellent hostess. Robert was adept at charming both sexes and had the ability to sound sincere in all his conversations. It was an act that she quite admired and had never been embarrassed by his behaviour in society.

Sir Muir and his wife floated around the room welcoming their guests. He, a tall man with skinny legs and a portly belly of advancing years and she, a voluptuous, much younger wife who had married for money. Lady Muir's delicate laugh was smothered by her husband's loud bellow which reverberated around the room.

Presently Ann and Robert were greeted. "Good evening, Mr Ross, Mrs Ross. We are so glad that you could come. You are looking very well Mrs Ross."

Ann bristled for the second time that evening. Now

people referred to her as looking well - in her younger years she looked 'exquisite,' or 'beautiful.'

"I am very well, thank you, Sir Muir."

Lady Muir added, "Yes you do look well and you, Mr Ross, look as dapper as ever and will no doubt regale us with some witty tale at the table."

"I will try my best to please you, Lady Muir."

As the conversation continued Ann couldn't help but compare herself to Lady Muir. Seeing the photographs earlier had disturbed her mind and in front of her was a woman twenty five years her junior wearing a low cut velvet dress which barely encased her ample bosom. Her raven hair was pinned in the latest fashion and her perfume was heady, almost sultry.

Ann recognised it. She looked at Robert and his earlier words came back to her.

The room was filled with guests of middle age bar three couples whose years tallied up as much as her own but thankfully both herself and Robert had aged better. Of course, men were forgiven for growing older and became 'distinguished' but a woman was not so fortunate no matter how much care she took in her appearance.

When it was time to dine, the hostess, as was the custom, instructed each gentleman which lady he would be accompanying to the dinner table. The order by which each couple entered the dining room was established according to status and with this gathering being held by the upper class Ann was aware that they would be somewhere in the middle. Ann had been born into the upper class but on marrying Robert things were now different.

Each man accepted his partner for the evening whom he would serve at the table and converse with. Lady Muir continued, "Mr Ross you shall accompany Mrs Norman MacDonald." Robert bowed and offered his arm. His partner for the evening was attractive and fairly interesting to converse with from memory. Lady Muir had pleased him and he would please her in return the next time they met. "Mr Scott you shall accompany Mrs Robert Ross." Ann smiled. Mr Scott was extremely affable and handsome. He was exactly what her fragile ego required.

The ten courses were delicious but etiquette prevented that fact from being commented on. The meal passed, as did the after dinner drinks in the drawing room, and the Rosses left in better spirits than when they had arrived.

In the carriage home Ann was in a thoughtful mood. "Have I been a satisfactory wife to you all these years?"

Robert appeared surprised. "Ye have. I believe I chose well. Ye provided me with money and heirs and performed your duties well. Ye were beautiful and amiable and I have not regretted the marriage."

Ann did not reply and retired immediately on returning home. Robert, having spent an enjoyable evening, sat in his drawing room with a whisky and congratulated himself on his choice of wife and mistresses.

THE FOLLOWING MORNING Charlie listened as Alice read out the letter she had just written, ...*The only way to change legislation with regards to women and children is to have women sitting in Parliament. Desperate living conditions and lack of money force women into desperate choices. We need to stand together as one and I urge each and everyone of you to pick up your pen and write to our Government to demand change. Further meetings are planned and again I urge you all to attend....*

"It's a good letter, Alice, concise and well informed, as always. Ye are a great asset to yer cause and I am confident that the Independent Labour Party will gain more momentum this year and be firmly established as the party of the future. A new century is dawning and I feel it in my bones that great things will be achieved. I intend to become more involved with the party and fight for the working class. Living and working conditions need to change for the better and I want to be at the forefront of those changes."

"It gladdens my heart to hear that. Now, I must send this before Mother sees it. She is all for women's rights but wants nothing to do with the process of achieving it, seeing it as immoral somehow. I have tried to explain to her that nothing will change without women fighting for it but she thinks it vulgar and unladylike to protest and stand up against men in Parliament. I do not wish to upset her, I know she already thinks me too stubborn and independent but I am the way I am."

"And I would have ye no other way, Alice." He reached out and took her hand whereupon a discreet cough came from Alice's maid, who was of course present, as no man could visit an unmarried woman unaccompanied. Eliza was a new maid and too fastidious in her duties as far as Alice was concerned.

Charlie turned to leave as Alice spoke, "I wish ye luck with telling yer grandfather yer political plans tomorrow."

"Thank you, but ye needn't worry. I know how to handle him."

Aspirations

"THE POOR?" ROBERT shouted. "My God, man, has yer education taught ye nothing? By all means go into politics but not for the sake of the poor who choose to live in squalor and taint the land."

Robert was seated in his study and faced his grandson who stood before him. The study walls were adorned with art and Robert's desk was clear of papers but a leather bound album lay closed by his right hand. His whisky cowped as Robert thumped the glass down.

"Being poor is not a choice, Grandfather. The government does not do enough to help them and I intend to change that. The Public Health Act was welcomed but a lot more needs to be done. I have been corresponding with Keir Hardie and I agree with much of what he stands for." He stood facing Robert, his words strong and confident. He would not be bullied by his grandfather again.

Robert laughed. "You will be a laughing stock in Aberdeen and an embarrassment to yer kin. For God's sake if you must have a cause make it a worthwhile one. Help the country's economy, don't squander its money on those not deserving of it. Hardie lost his seat, and for good reason. The Independent Labour Party will not gain ground and Hardie is all but forgotten already."

"I disagree. The party is gaining momentum and I wish to be a part o' it. My mind is set. I am determined to help the plight o' the poor and provide them with healthy homes and work for the unemployed. I also believe that women should have more rights and I support their right to have a say in the world of politics." Charlie himself was surprised at those last words. Fighting talk indeed.

Robert's face contorted and he rose from his chair and walked around his desk. His nose was but an inch away from the loon's face. "Ye will not make a fool out o' me. I am head of this family and you will do as you are told. Drop this dumbfounded idea and go back to being the pathetic loon ye always were."

A chin was raised. "I may well have been pathetic as a loon but no more. You taught me how to stand up to others by your own ill treatment of me. Do you think I have forgotten your hatred so thinly disguised? Or the reason why?"

Robert stepped back. "I don't know what ye are talking about."

"Oh I think ye do, Grandfather. I may have been young but I have never forgotten."

"Ye are full o' lies. Leave the poor to their chosen fate or you will regret it."

Now it was the loon's turn to laugh as he left the room.

Charlie was not surprised to hear such words and as the door closed a smile passed his lips and he thought to himself, *Ignorant fool.* Charlie returned to the parlour where the rest of his family were seated. Now that all the grandchildren were grown, Sunday dinner had become evening drinks.

Edith was the first to speak. "Well, what did he say?"

"Nothing that I had not expected. My mind is set and I will continue in the bank till I am hopefully elected into

Government. I am young yet but politics needs young blood."

"Well I am proud of ye." Andrew said.

James looked on. "You know that I agree with your grandfather but if you are planning on staying on in the bank then that at least is sensible. Ye are doing well there and are making sound decisions so surely ye can see where money should be invested. Perhaps time will change yer mind."

Rose rose from her seat somewhat unsteadily and embraced the loon. "You were brave to tell your grandfather and I know you will do us proud. I just wish…"

Andrew went to his wife's side. "Time we were off. Good evening all. Gordon, I will be in by the mill at some point tomorrow." He led Rose out of the house and into their carriage.

No conversation took place on the ten minute journey from Redwood Manor to Willowbank as the carriage made its way through the Aberdeen streets. On alighting at their home Andrew escorted Rose through the door and upstairs to her bedchamber where she immediately took her wee bottle from its drawer and drank.

"Was the wine not enough? That poison will not help ye Rose." Andrew's voice was hard.

"Leave me be," she uttered.

Andrew turned from her and left the room, descending the stairs and back out into the streets in search of some comfort of his own.

*

Robert too was in need of some comfort as he sauntered into the Music Hall's parlour where he made his usual rounds of talking confidently with the men and complimenting the ladies. He may have been in his seventies but his looks had not deserted him and women of a certain age found him attractive, and of course were softened by his compliments and his ways of pleasing them. His arrogance was his saving grace for had he been obsequious he would have been despised. Instead his openness with both sexes allowed for amiable business with gentlemen and amiable pleasure with women. That night he intended to acquire both.

"Good evening, Sir Muir, Lady Muir. Are ye both well?"

"We are indeed, Mr Ross. We have just been to the Opera House and thought we would drop in for a nightcap," replied Sir Muir.

"Very good." Robert lowered his voice. "I am glad to see you both here as I would welcome your advice on a family matter."

"Why, of course. How can we be of assistance?" Sir Muir replied, his ego plumped up as was his belly.

"None of us need reminding of the anarchist group here and the trouble caused, although things appear quiet at the moment, but my young, ill informed, grandson is of the mind that the poor are in need of help and wishes to pursue that aim through politics." He leaned in towards Sir Muir. "I am sorry to say that he is in agreement with the Independent Labour Party. Our economy, land and businesses must be protected."

Sir Muir's face was serious. "I understand, Mr Ross. Best to nip anything like that in the bud. I will do my utmost to deter his progress for all our sakes."

Lady Muir leaned in, her large bosom barely contained in its velvet casing. "I will call upon his mother. Do not worry, Mr Ross."

"Thank you, kindly. I knew you would both understand."

Sir Muir turned to his wife. "Elizabeth, would you mind if I conducted a little business? I will have you taken home in the carriage."

"Not at all, dear, and no need for me to return home as I will stay in town with aunt Dorothy. I have some belongings there so you can return home late without fear of disturbing me."

"Excellent." Sir Muir replied, and he kissed his wife's cheek who promptly left the parlour.

Meanwhile in the card room three gentlemen were conversing.

"Wives have to be amiable and serve their husbands which makes them convenient but extremely boring most of the time."

"Aye, a bit of feistiness is good. I have two mistresses at the moment and one in particular tells me exactly what she wants me to do. I'm not sure where she learnt such things but it is intriguing. Her father is a Lord so perhaps the upper class women have a different education."

"I'm not sure about that but I introduced my house maid to my mistress and the three of us had a very pleasant evening."

A low laugh was emitted as a hand slid into a pocket. "Have you seen these photographs?"

ROBERT TOOK A carriage and alighted a few houses away from where Lady Muir's aunt resided. Walking purposely he looked right and left before climbing the steps and entering through the unlocked door. All was dark as the household had been told to retire but he knew the way to the guest wing and climbed the stairs. A light shining beneath the door signalled his destination and he entered without knocking. The fire burned brightly and Elizabeth lay on the chaise lounge covered only in a silk dressing gown, her raven hair loose on her shoulders. She looked him in the eye.

"I wasn't sure what you would want, as this was

unplanned, but as you have a family problem I suspect you are in need of some comfort."

Robert laughed. "How considerate of you."

Strong Quines

Rose awoke late the following morning to a pounding headache. Her hand went to the drawer by her bed and she withdrew her medicine, swallowing a mouthful straight from the bottle as she did most mornings. It was the best cure to having drunk too much wine the evening before. She no longer hid her need for laudanum. The years had embedded its hold on her and Rose almost welcomed it now.

Andrew, she knew, would have left some time before for work, so there would be neither angry or pitying looks for her over the breakfast table. She was accustomed to both. She had not forgotten her promise made to him when Charlie had arrived in their home but it had proven too difficult and now it was just how life was.

On descending the stairs Rose was surprised to see her husband in the hall. "Good morning, Rose. I have forgotten some papers."

He did not comment on the fact that she was not yet dressed as he sped into his study and returned a few seconds later with his papers. He kissed her cheek and left through the door as quickly as he had entered it. Rose raised her hand and touched her cheek where the feel of the kiss lingered.

Mary appeared from the kitchen. "Did my husband

sleep in his bed last night?"

Mary hesitated. "No, madam."

The feel of the kiss now felt like a slap. "I wish to have a bath after breakfast and tell Cook that we will have roast beef tonight - my husband's favourite."

"Yes, madam."

"And send word to my mother that I will be calling in at eleven o'clock."

At eleven o'clock on the dot, Rose's carriage drew into the driveway at Redwood Manor and she alighted.

Ann received her daughter in the drawing room. "I had to change my plans for you this morning, Rose, so please enlighten me as to the urgency."

Rose sat down on a couch. "Mother, I am determined to hold onto my husband but in order to do that I need to be free of laudanum. I have relied on it for far too long and it is time to relieve myself of it. I believe you to be the only person firm enough to be able to help me."

Ann smiled. "There is strength in you, after all, quine."

*

Gordon was going through the week's orders for the mill when his father appeared. Robert had formed a habit of visiting, with his usual condescending manner in tow, every Monday afternoon. It was reassuring for Gordon to know exactly when his father would come. When he had first handed over the reins, Robert had visited and interfered every other day but thankfully retirement from the mill had settled into a routine although Gordon was unaware of whom his father tortured with his presence the rest of the time. Andrew usually made himself available on these days but for some reason Robert was early and Andrew had not yet arrived.

Robert walked around the desk and stood behind Gordon looking over his shoulder at the ledger in front of him. "Orders are up this week, that's good."

"Aye, Father, a large order came in this morning."

"I see it's from Parker's. Make sure they pay ye on time. I don't trust them."

"Well, Father, they haven't been late wi' a payment in ten years."

"Still, ye can't be too sure so keep a close eye."

Gordon could feel his father's breath on the back of his neck and rubbed it. He was aware of sweat forming in his armpits and berated himself for the effect that his own father had on him. With Andrew's absence Gordon felt more exposed and sought for a way out of the inquisition that would follow with regards to business. "Victoria mentioned last night that she is planning to visit ye tomorrow if ye are free."

Robert leaned back and went to stand by the window, "She is an angel of a child. Always has time for her grandfather. I will make a point of being in tomorrow."

"She dotes on ye, Father." *God knows why*, he thought to himself.

"She respects me, unlike the rest. If she had been a loon she would have gone far in life with my support."

"Women these days intend to go far in life despite being women." Gordon regretted the words as soon as they left his lips.

Robert's good humour dissipated immediately and his voice rose with each word, "I suppose a man with no backbone like yerself is in support of women's rights and no doubt wants to give yer workers here a pot o' gold as wages with a mansion to live in besides."

Gordon sighed. "I just think that the world could be a

fairer place, that's all."

Robert placed his hands on the desk in front of his son and glared at him. "Ye think it's fair to be handed things on a plate? Ye think it fair that I worked my fingers to the bone to get where I am today for it to be taken away and given to the working class? Are ye telling me that ye wish Victoria to be out working? She is about to marry a wealthy man. Would you have her give that life up and serve others?"

"There is no point discussing this, Father."

Robert's anger grew. "Aye, because ye know that ye are wrong just like that ignorant nephew of yours. All that money paid on a gentleman's education and he throws it back in his family's face."

"He has principles and beliefs that are as strong as yours, Robert." Andrew stated as he walked through the office door.

Robert's eyes narrowed as he turned away from the desk. "Principles and beliefs instilled by you. Ye have gone against the grain o' yer class and should be ashamed. I will make sure that loon never gets into politics."

Andrew took a step forward. "And I will make sure that he does."

"Ye will not embarrass me."

"Oh, Robert, I think ye can do that all by yourself. Give my regards to Lady Muir."

Robert stepped back and left the office slamming the door behind him.

"Lady Muir?" asked Gordon.

Andrew shrugged. "Oh nothing ye need concern yerself wi', Gordon. Is there any tea on the go?"

Gordon looked at Andrew and not for the first time wondered at the relationship between his friend and his father.

Later that evening Robert had installed himself in the guest wing of aunt Dorothy's house. The weekly arrangement worked well. Lady Muir always visited on a Monday and stayed the night and insisted, because she was of generous heart, that the staff prepare a tray for her supper and have the evening off. The only other presence in the large house was old aunt Dorothy tucked up safely in bed and her nurse who never left her side at night.

Robert was caressing a breast. "Have you been indiscrete about our arrangement, Elizabeth?"

Lady Muir was somewhat surprised by both the question and its tone. "I have not, Robert, and I resent the insinuation. What do you mean?"

"Someone hinted to me today that they knew of us and I know that I have not told a soul."

Elizabeth sat up. "Who hinted?"

"It is irrelevant. I merely need to know who might have spoken so that I can protect you."

"Protect me?" She laughed. "Oh, Robert, I think you know that it would be me who protects you. My husband believes me to be the perfect wife and any hint of a scandal would be quashed by him to protect my name. You on the other hand could be made out to be a liar, spreading vicious gossip relating to a tryst with me, Lady Muir, which of course no one would believe. You are a class below me. You would be banished from society and I would be forced to find another lover."

Robert left the bed still half dressed as he had not long arrived and Lady Muir spoke with authority. "Get back into bed, Robert. Ye have not finished what ye started and I will not be dismissed. This is your problem, not mine."

Robert hesitated, but looking upon the voluptuous woman who had been his mistress for quite some time he realised that he didn't want to give her up and by the sounds of it she would not let him anyway. He sidled back into bed. "There now, Robert, no more talk of boring things."

Robin Hood

Charlie looked at the messy desk. Papers were strewn everywhere: half written letters lay crumpled on the floor and several speeches with words crossed out and ink smudged onto the pages lay in wait for a fountain pen to finish them.

A knock on the door disturbed his thoughts. "Mr Buchan to see you, Sir."

"Thank you, Brown, send him in, please."

Fraser entered the study and shook his friend's hand as he spied the desk. "Speech not going well?"

"You could say that. I am trying to convey that the Public Health Scotland Act of '97 was only the beginning of much needed change in the poor's living conditions. Folk are still living in squalor. Unemployment is still too high with the result that the new poor house at Fonthill is bursting at the seams. The trade unionists are up in arms which stands us in good stead as we continue to work alongside them but I feel we need to be more organised. I haven't even begun to write anything on the brothel situation and I have to leave in two hours." Panic was rising in his face.

"First of all stop pacing and sit yourself down. Let's go through each point separately and I will help you to put it all together as a speech. It might be a good start to choose which areas are of most concern to you and focus on them. Best to talk passionately about a few things rather than fleetingly list a load of points."

Charlie nodded in agreement and was glad that his old friend was there to help.

The two men sat together for the next hour and a speech was written that would hopefully convince the listeners that they were right to follow the Independent Labour Party and that a wealthy young gentleman was on their side.

Brown was asked to bring two whiskies in and a toast was made. "Thank you, my friend, I fear I would still be pacing the floor with a blank piece of paper in my hand had you not come."

"It was a pleasure. I will be there to cheer you on. Alice desperately wants to attend but of course Mother will never allow it."

"It's probably for the best seen as I intend to talk of brothels. As wordly as Alice perceives herself to be I do not believe she has any notion of what a brothel actually is."

Fraser's brow furrowed. "I am not so sure. Considering she is not yet married Alice seems to be aware of many things since joining the Union of Women's Suffrage. I understand that you support her belief in women's rights, and she would never marry a man who did not, but Mother will be a lot happier when she is no longer responsible for her so perhaps put her out of her misery and marry Alice sooner rather than later."

"I very much intend to marry Alice, as you well know, but I need to secure my place in politics first. I am doing well in the bank but it is not where my heart lies."

"I have a feeling that Alice will not be kept waiting."

*

Fraser stood by Andrew at the front of the hall and Charlie appeared just as a hush descended on the crowd. Some two hundred folk had made their way to listen to the speeches made by the party they hoped would bring about major change for the working class and they were not disappointed. Several notable men of the time stood up and pledged their allegiance to Scotland, the Independent Labour Party and its people and great thundering applause erupted throughout the hall as the final words were spoken. *"The poor have but a ghost of a chance in life. Together we will change that, giving all people an equal chance in life for a good education, a decent wage and a healthy home."*

Fraser clapped and cheered, proud of his friend's success. He clasped Andrew's shoulder in comradeship as they each remembered Charlie's start in life and how he had instilled in them both a need to help those less fortunate.

The following day the newspapers were full of the previous night's speeches and particular mention was made of the term '*a ghost of a chance*' with a cartoon of a ghost frightening the upper classes and stealing their wealth in *The Worker's Herald*, a Socialist newspaper. It lauded the Party's progress but it also posed the question, '*Can a gentleman be a social reformer?*' for there were those who distrusted the grandson of Robert Ross. Memories were long and his treatment of his workers in years gone by had not been forgotten.

The Evening Gazette portrayed a cartoon of *Robin Hood* and asked its audience, '*The young gentleman is proving himself to be an asset to his party and a thorn in the side of his peers. What does his family make of his political leanings? What are his motives? Is he a Robin Hood?*'

Charlie laughed to himself as he read the article in the newspaper. He remembered re-enacting the story of Robin Hood with Fraser and Alice in his back garden. Fraser had played the part of Robin Hood and of course Alice had been Maid Marion. He had been Will Scarlet until Alice remembered that Maid Marion fell in love with Robin Hood so had suddenly bellowed, "Fraser you will have to play someone else. I cannot fall in love with my brother." Fraser had reluctantly given up his part and the game had continued at Alice's bequest.

Others whose followers were Conservatives, had not been so kind with talk of '*defying his class*' and being '*a man of weak constitution: soft on those who do not help themselves.*'

And the *Aberdeen Journal* wrote, '*Mr Robert Ross - humiliated by his own blood.*'

Robert read in earnest before lashing out at Ann. "I am sick of reading about your grandson and his follies. He is slandering my good name." He stormed out of Redwood Manor. He could not simply call upon Sir Muir - even Robert knew his place. He made his way to the art gallery which always had the effect of soothing his mind. Neither a lover of music or reading, Robert found solace in art which would perhaps have come as a surprise to some had they known. As he sauntered around the magnificent granite building allowing his mind to think of cruel ways in which to stop his kin from embarrassing him he quite by chance fell upon Sir Muir sitting admiring a particular Claude Monet painting. Seizing the opportunity Robert approached him. "Good morning, Sir Muir. It is a work of greatness is it not?"

"Ah, Mr Ross, it is indeed. I find myself becoming lost in each brushstroke and the colours are breathtaking."

The two gentlemen sat in silence for a moment allowing the painting to envelop and soothe before Sir Muir spoke.

"I have spoken to the editor of *The Aberdeen Journal* and have his assurance of a decimation of character. That should suffice, I hope, to derail this political situation. I cannot get rid of the Party but I can perhaps get rid of certain up and coming leaders."

"I do not wish to appear ungrateful but is there no other way? I feel that my family is reflected badly in the newspapers by association."

Sir Muir turned to face Robert. "You asked for my help and I agreed as I do not wish Labour to gain momentum any more than you do. I cannot see how else it could be achieved."

Robert looked behind him to see if anyone was within earshot. "Perhaps a spot of blackmail?"

"I will give it some thought. Meanwhile it could be arranged that the next political meeting goes unattended. An unfortunate incident which prevents him from turning up."

Robert smiled, "A good beating would do the trick."

Sir Muir stood up. "I will not condone violence, Mr Ross. That is not what I meant at all."

Robert felt panic in his chest. "Forgive me, Sir Muir, it is the stress of the situation making me say such things. Mrs Ross is beside herself with worry and embarrassment and I wish to protect her."

Sir Muir sat down again and lowered his voice. "I quite understand. A wife needs protecting and there is nothing worse than a wife who is upset. It is not at all good for them. They are too often consumed with worry over something or other. Lady Muir is often upset, being of a delicate nature, so I know exactly what you mean."

Robert smiled to himself as he had never known Elizabeth to be upset over anything. She was wiley indeed to have her husband believe she was of a delicate nature. He made to leave. "I thank you again, Sir Muir, and I leave things in your capable hands."

"I will see you at the club, Mr Ross. Good day to you."

Robert left the gallery with an idea circling in his head as a hunter would its prey. *Sir Muir may have influence in government and with certain newspaper proprietors but he is clearly weak in nature. If the pen does not stop this slurring of my name then fists will, but I may need to bide my time.*

His little studio lay in wait and he had two women arriving at nine o'clock that evening. Today was turning out to be a good day after all.

Success

Ann had taken Rose to their country house, Talla Cluaran, near Inverness, ascertaining it to be the best place for her to wean herself off laudanum with no distractions or temptations and plenty of fresh air. It was arranged, discreetly of course, for the local doctor to oversee the process and Ann's most trusted maid accompanied them.

The house stood on a hill just outside the town of Inverness overlooking the Inverness Firth towards the Black Isle. Although somewhat larger than Redwood Manor it had a softer, more welcoming appearance, lacking the austerity of the Manor. Made from warm coloured sandstone instead of the grey granite used in Aberdeen lended a gentle warmth that invited visitors, imbued by the bonny gardens that enveloped it. It had belonged to Ann, having been inherited as she had no brothers, but on marrying had, by law, become her husband's property.

Once Rose had been settled into her room, Ann spent her days either walking in the countryside, in the garden or by Rose's bed. She took no visitors, having deliberately failed to inform any acquaintances of her arrival. Rose needed complete privacy and staff were not informed of her illness. Ann wrote to Robert every few days but received only infrequent, short replies relaying his social visits. He had attended many dinners and functions without her and she was somewhat miffed.

The weeks were passing excruciatingly slowly for Rose as her body rid itself of the laudanum but the measures the doctor put in place were working and her mind was clearer than it had been in years. She began to feel less dread on waking as to what lay ahead. The nights had been long and interspersed with chills and vomiting but now she slept steadily.

Sitting in the garden one afternoon mother and daughter enjoyed some tea and cake.

"You look better, Rose. A little too thin but definitely better."

"I feel better, Mother. It has been a painful experience in many ways and I don't think I have ever felt so physically ill but the worst has passed and I feel stronger."

Ann looked about her. "This is a healing place. I came here after my mother died, before I married. She designed this garden, you know. She had a great love of plants and flowers and spent a lot of time out here. Talla Cluaran is Gaelic for Thistle Hall, aptly named as so many bonny thistles grow all around here."

"It is beautiful. What was she like?"

Ann thought for a second. "I think she preferred plants to humans. I was her only child but I rarely saw her or my father until I was about twelve when I presume I was old enough to know how to behave. I spent my time with my governess."

Rose straightened her back and swallowed. "Were you close to your parents when you were older?"

"I tried my very best to be the daughter they wanted. Mother made sure that I spoke like an English woman even though we lived between here and Aberdeen. She herself was English you see and wanted me to speak like her. Somehow I never quite lived up to her expectations. I was always too quiet or too loud, or too fat or too thin. I don't think they really wanted children at all."

Ann went quiet and Rose scrambled to find the right words to speak to her mother. "Have you enjoyed being a mother?"

Ann looked at her daughter. "I don't think I knew how to be a mother but I have enjoyed the idea of it."

Rose absorbed her mother's words. It explained much of her own upbringing. She took her mother's hand. "Bringing me here was a motherly thing to do."

Tears sprang to Ann's eyes on hearing those words but the tears turned to laughter when Rose proclaimed, "I don't think I knew how to be a daughter but I have enjoyed the idea of it."

Mother and daughter sat in silence for a while enjoying the peace of the garden.

"I have spoken to the doctor. I think it's time we went home and the doctor agrees. The rest is up to you now."

Rose bit her bottom lip and tears threatened. "Do you think he will want me, Mother?"

Ann clasped her daughter's hand in a rare show of affection. "Rose, I have watched you vomit and shake and cry as you rid yourself of that poison and I have seen how strong you truly are. Andrew will see the change in you too."

Rose released a pent up breath.

"You will need to put some flesh on those bones though. No man wants to hold a skeleton. Now, I will have the maids pack our things in preparation for travelling tomorrow and I will send word to Andrew informing him of your return."

"And Father too?"

"No, I think I will surprise him."

"But father doesn't like surprises."

"Exactly."

*

Rose arrived home in the early evening before Andrew had yet returned from his office and was ushered in out of the cold to sit by the fire in the parlour.

"Welcome home, madam."

"Thank you. It is good to be home," she replied, and realised that she meant it. Her eyes moved around the room and she looked upon Andrew's pipe and the photograph of Charlie on the bureau. The books and trinkets and various paintings that were all around were each a part of home and her memories intermingled with these items and photographs like wisps of mist in the trees. Rose leaned back and closed her eyes, allowing her mind to remember fond memories of happy times spent in the house that she had lived in since the day she had married.

"Enough," she said out loud and she rose from her chair and called for her maid.

Following a bath and dressing in her burgundy gown which accentuated the return of colour in her cheeks, Rose sat at her dressing table whilst Catherine styled her hair. "I am glad that the fashion has changed. It suits my figure better."

"Ye look lovely, madam."

Satisfied with her appearance, albeit a little too thin, she descended the stairs just as Andrew returned home.

Andrew hesitated and Rose felt his eyes penetrate as he tried to ascertain her level of consciousness. "It has been a long time since we had supper together."

Andrew nodded. "It is. Let us eat together then."

Rose threaded her arm through her husband's. "And we will not talk of politics or Charlie or anyone else. We will talk of things relating to us only and perhaps plan a visit to Edinburgh. It's been a while since we visited."

Husband and wife sat down together and for the first time in a long time the conversation flowed.

*

The momentum of the Labour movement's success rose as the months passed. Working with the Trade Unionists to meet the same end, their power strengthened and the Government was beginning to realise that it had no choice but to listen. Women's voices too grew stronger as they demanded radical change to society. Many believed that a new century would bring with it unprecedented change for the better and excitement was rising.

Robert, and those like him, were fearful of change which threatened their standing. Servants appeared restless and wordlessly insolent at times and even Ann was confused at times. Upon visiting Rose one morning, she had commented as such. "My maid acts as if she no longer cares if my hair is in place or my clothes suitably pressed and I was dumbfounded the other day when she asked if I thought she should have the right to vote. I mean, whatever could she vote on - she knows nothing of the world of business or politics? I myself would not know of such things. Your father has always said that women have no place in either."

Rose hesitated. "There is so much talk these days of women's rights as well as the plight of the working class. You are perhaps right about the vote as what does a servant know of the world but I must admit to being in agreement with some changes needed in poor living conditions."

"Well, you would I suppose considering Charlie's start in life but I agree with your father in that how they live is a choice. He is unbearable to live with these days with all the newspaper articles. I cannot remember the last time we had breakfast without him storming out. Despite all the negative press the lad is becoming ever more popular. Of course I get the blame for having a grandson who goes against his class. Is it absolutely necessary for all these political affiliations, Rose? Could Andrew not have a word and put a stop to it as he is the one who encourages him the most. James is as angry as Robert and working in the bank alongside him is not helping. I am even beginning to feel sorry for Edith and you know I loathe the woman."

Rose gasped. "Do you really, Mother? I always thought that you liked her the best."

"Neither of my daughters in law are what I would have chosen but at least Mabel is a genuine soul if somewhat insipid. Edith is sly and I don't like sly."

"Well I never. You surprise me sometimes, Mother."

"And you me, quine. You are strong and you must stay that way. Do not be bullied by anyone - not even by me."

Rose laughed. "I'm not sure how to respond to that comment. But I will say that I will not ask Andrew to say anything of the sort."

Ann harrumphed. "I suppose I asked for that. I will just have to start having my breakfast in bed. That will infuriate my staff even more, no doubt, but I don't care. I am too old to care."

Rose's face softened. "You will never be old, Mother. Your spirit is too strong."

Rose smiled at her daughter but did not answer her. Her spirit had been thrawn and held up by the society in which she belonged but age and Robert had dampened it and she no longer felt supported by her class.

"I have been naive in life," she whispered to herself.

*

As Charlie arrived in Willowbank his father was

pouring the whisky.

"A toast to celebrate yer success, loon. Ye are growing in popularity and the party is growing in numbers. Sláinte Mháth."

"Thank you. Sláinte Mháth."

"Yer grandfather is trying his best to thwart your progress but to no avail it seems. Society knows that family name and reputation are everything. He cannot speak ill of you publicly without disparaging himself. He continues to excuse you as young and naive in his club and of no threat to the upper class."

Both gentlemen took a drink from their glass. "Gentleman have been known to openly disown their kin for less but I think ye are right, my grandfather would not risk his name and reputation. He likes the idea of appearing as a family man. As to me being a threat I do not wish to take anything from the wealthy that we cannot afford. Grandfather is scared of losing a single penny or a yard of land."

His mind returned to his last confrontation with his grandfather, *Ye are an idiot and soon society will have had enough of yer embarrassment. I have contacts and their patience is wearing thin, as is mine. I will not intervene if they see fit to throw you into the lunatic asylum.*

"I do wonder though what he will do if pushed too far."

"You leave yer grandfather to me. You will have a career in politics and I have more influence than he. By the way, I looked into your suspicion of your mail being intercepted but have not as yet found a perpetrator. I feel that it must be a post office employee who is being paid handsomely. It would be prudent to personally hand me your correspondence and I will post it on your behalf."

"In that case, please have this delivered to Alice. It is of a very personal nature and I am keen for her to receive it without delay."

Andrew chuckled. "Aye, Robin Hood, I will ensure that Maid Marion receives it first thing."

Charlie withdrew leaving his father to his promise of delivering the letter.

*

A NDREW KEPT HIS promise and Alice did indeed receive her letter the following morning. She carried it in her pocket of her dress the entire day and by bedtime had read it so many times that it was now crumpled. Mother always said she would frighten any man away with her over confidence and forthright ways but here she had proof of the opposite.

Her maid bustled around her. "Do ye wish tae wear yer blue gown the morn'?"

"Oh no, Liza, I will need the burgundy one. I have a feeling tomorrow may be a special day." She twirled around the room in her nightgown as Liza looked on. "Well I dinna need two guesses as to who that letter is from. There is only one man could put such a smile on yer face."

"Mother will be pleased to see me marry."

"Of course. He is a gentleman and has a bright future ahead o' him, has he not? And he clearly dotes on ye so I'm sure yer mother will be reassured that he will make a fine husband."

Alice jumped into bed and Liza snuffed out the candle as she left. As the darkness descended around her Alice allowed herself to imagine a wedding and a gown and a feast and a home of her own and a family. She remembered telling her mother all those years ago that she was going to marry Charlie and what kind of dress she wanted to wear. As she cuddled down she whispered into the air as she did every night, "Goodnight, Charlie."

An Unfortunate Incident

Charlie looked into the mirror and observed the cut of the tailor made suit that portrayed the man in its reflection to be the gentleman that he was. The silver pocket watch was placed into his pocket, a collar was adjusted and he left his house.

Tonight was to be an important meeting and the largest one to date. He had been asked to speak as the main speaker and he hoped to persuade the crowd that he was indeed a man who had the tenacity to bring about change for the working class by supporting the Independent Labour Party and following on from Keir Hardie's pledges a decade before. His previous contributions had gone down well but he knew there was still some way to go to persuade the working class that he was on their side so folk were expecting great words followed by great actions from him. He hoped that nerves wouldn't get the better of him as he pulled at his collar for the umpteenth time.

A large audience had gathered in the concert hall and as this was not expected to be a night to bring trouble few policemen were in attendance. Andrew had decided to accompany him,

"I am proud o' ye, loon, and I hope ye succeed tonight."
Charlie stood by the entrance.

"Thank you. You go ahead, I want a minute out here to steady my nerves and go over my speech again."

Andrew clapped him on the back. "Right ye are. I wish ye luck."

It was a fair evening and only the prevailing south west breeze could be felt, cooling the back of the neck. A small group of latecomers hurried past him and disappeared into the hall and he allowed his eyes to close for a second to calm his heart. This was the night he had been waiting for and could well be the turning point in his political career. With a final breath he raised his chin and straightened his back and grasped the door handle. As he was about to enter a hand was thrust over his mouth as two strong pairs of arms dragged him into a waiting carriage.

Charlie was helpless as hands were bound by rope and the carriage lurched as it sped through the streets.

"Who are you? What do you want with me?"

His questions went unanswered and no amount of struggling could undo the rope from his hands which had been thrust behind his back. The curtains were drawn in the carriage so any passersby could not see a man struggling, held down by two others: legs pinned firmly to the floor to prevent any stray kicks.

"Nae point in trying tae fight. We are just takin' ye for a wee ride into the countryside." The voice was matter of fact as if announcing some everyday happening.

Charlie was unable to discern whether the men were violent or ill-trickit. He was praying for the latter.

"I don't know what this is about but I have to attend my meeting." He continued to struggle against his captors but his words were ignored and their grip did not loosen. He could smell their sweat, or perhaps it was his own that penetrated his nostrils. No fists struck him but he was held fast to his seat. He could tell by the lessening of noise that the carriage had left the city but he had no idea in which direction it travelled or indeed its destination. His body tired of struggling and he allowed himself to sit still. The hands that held him loosened but remained where they were and thoughts raced as to the whys and wherefores of the situation and if he was to be harmed at the end of his journey. As the minutes passed his thoughts alternated between the words of his speech, that in all likelihood would not be spoken that night, and words he had not yet spoken to Alice and the loon wondered if fate would allow her to hear them.

The horses ploughed on, pulling the carriage onwards, and the sound of their hooves battering the road became rhythmic as they slowed to a steadier pace and the wheels rumbled below him as the carriage swayed. No conversation took place between the men and he did not know them nor did he recognise the carriage, although it was an elegant one. The seats were padded and he could feel the softness of velvet under his hands. The ornate lamps shone and the curtains were trimmed with lace. His kidnappers wore the attire and leather boots of the working class so were likely servants to the owner of the carriage. *Who might that owner be? I know my grandfather's carriages and this is not one of them. I am unsure if that makes me feel easier or more unsettled.*

An instruction was given and the horses slowed their pace. The carriage turned full circle and came to a stop.

"Out," he was instructed. He stumbled out of the carriage into the darkness.

"Gee up," a voice commanded and the carriage pulled away without him.

"Where am I?" he shouted to the retreating carriage.

"Peterculter. Only two hours walk," the driver shouted

over his shoulder as the horses began to gallop.

Left bewildered, but unharmed, he made his way back slowly on foot with the knowledge that no speech would be made by him that night.

Inside the concert hall the crowd were jeering at the no show. Many had travelled far and felt hard done by, "Untrustworthy!" "Lacks conviction!" were words bandied about. A rumour spread like wildfire, started by a spark placed at the back of the hall, telling of having seen Robin Hood running away from the concert hall. Andrew and Fraser were at a loss as to what had happened and surrounded by anger their concern was sheathed.

THE MORNING NEWSPAPERS were full of Robin Hood's change of heart. Charlie was silent as he watched the newspaper being flung across the room. "Ye look like a fool. The circumstances are irrelevant. No one is likely to believe that you were grabbed and dumped miles away and those that do believe it will think ye an even bigger fool for letting it happen."

He did not answer and as Charlie left the room the words, "God knows what yer grandfather is going to say," rang in his ears.

Today was the day that he had intended to propose to Alice but with the embarrassment of last night and the morning's newspapers he quickly wrote a note of apology that he would not be calling on her today and had his servant deliver it.

ROBERT SAT AT his breakfast with Ann and read the words beneath the cartoon of Robin Hood cowering behind a lady's skirt, alongside the words, *Is the Ross blood yellow?*

He felt a mixture of both relief and anger. Muir had

proved worthy of stopping his grandson, as surely this would be the end of it, but this reflected badly on Robert himself as he too looked foolish by association. He would have to spin a line or two at the gentlemens club this evening, berating his kin but at the same time talking of young blood and foolish notions in the hope of acquiring sympathy and support.

Support was welcomed but he loathed sympathy.

Ann looked on anxiously as she observed the thoughts whirling in her husband's mind. "Robert, I…"

"Do not speak, Ann. I am going out. You produced an idiot of a child and now a grandson of the same ilk." He left the table and made his way to a mistress in Queen Street where his demands would be met without question.

*

ALICE READ THE short note handed to her by her maid informing her of the change of plan. "How dare he not come. Father was consumed with anger at breakfast but by not coming speaks of cowardice and guilt and will only fuel Father's anger. He will never consent to marriage now." She paced the floor as her mind tried to think of a solution then grabbing her pen frantically wrote a note and thrust it into her maid's hand. "Have this delivered immediately and do not tell Father anything. Today will go ahead as planned."

CHARLIE SMILED AS he read the words in the hastily written note demanding pride, bravery and a call to action. They were her own qualities that she demanded from her future husband. The note was pocketed and a return letter addressed to Alice's father,

…Further to the attempt to slur my good name I wish to

state to you, sir, that I intend to stand firm by my political convictions and defy those who threaten to curtail my voice and slur my good name. I shall continue with my work with renewed vigour and in doing so hope to make both my country and those in my life proud. I intend to call upon Alice this evening and hope you have no objection….

*

ANDREW WAS PACING the floor, his mind absorbed. This was an unfortunate embarrassment but he had contacts of his own and so would find out who Robert was using to help prevent his grandson's political advancement. Meanwhile a counter attack was required by a rival newspaper to dampen the damage done. Some palms would be oiled and plans put in motion.

DAVID BUCHAN SAT in his study later that day and addressed his daughter's suitor. Charlie was relieved to hear Alice's father talk of conviction and having a backbone, "I must admit that on reading this morning's newspaper I believed ye to be doomed and unworthy of my daughter's hand but your letter to me and the words ye have just spoken have convinced me of your strength of character."

"I am very glad to hear it, sir. If anything, I am now more determined than ever to stand up for what I feel is right and will pursue a life in politics with fervour. I have made sound decisions in the bank and have sufficient funds with which to marry."

Alice was surreptitiously listening at the door and knew for certain that she would marry the right man on hearing his next words. "It has become fashionable in recent years to ask the father's permission for his daughter's hand in marriage. Knowing Alice, as we do, we both know that she will make up her own mind and will not tolerate any decision being made for her. With that in mind I respectfully ask for your blessing as opposed to your permission. I do not wish to scupper my chances."

Alice's father bellowed a long, hearty laugh. "Ye are right indeed and truth be told Alice's forthright, thrawn character could well have scuppered her own chance of marriage but I see that you admire it and for that I am glad. Ye have my blessing, lad, and I do not think ye need worry. I am sure that Alice will accept yer proposal."

Alice did a little dance and scurried away unseen when Charlie left her father's study. She would be called shortly to go to the drawing room and the word 'yes' was already on the tip of her tongue.

*

THE FOLLOWING MORNING, thanks to Andrew, the newspapers talked of underhand goings on in politics and how freedom of speech should prevail. Robert's relief at the end of his grandson's political career had been brief to the point of non-existence, so fast was the turn around. By the time the evening papers were printed it was the Conservatives who were looking shamefaced. The whole thing was a sham and Sir Muir had proved unworthy of his word. Robert avoided his club that evening and instead put into motion his long awaited idea.

It was time to end this embarrassment.

Celebration

Alice's mother sighed with relief on seeing her daughter's engagement in the newspaper. Now that it was official, surely it would go ahead as planned. She would sigh an even bigger one when she saw her married. "Ye worry too much, Shona," her husband said on hearing a second sigh.

"It's just that she was always such a strong willed bairn and I worried that no man would want her as a wife."

"Well, she is wanted and more importantly she is happy."

"Aye. Ye are right. I was looking through some things yesterday and I came across a scrapbook that Alice made when she was wee. She used to cut out favourite pictures from magazines and newspapers and one of them was of a dress and I remember her saying to me that that was the dress she was going to wear when she married Charlie. It brought a tear to my eye. Sometimes I wish they could all have just stayed as bairns."

David patted Shona's hand. "We have been lucky to have had two bairns who have grown into clever and caring folk. Both will be settled soon and for that we can be thankful."

Shona smiled. "Aye, and when our grandchildren come along it will be you who will spoil them the most. Ye never could resist a cheeky smile."

David finished the last of his tea. "Right, wife, enough reminiscing. I have calls to make - the sick won't wait, not even if I give them my own cheeky smile." He kissed Shona's cheek and left their dining room to attend to his patients.

Alice appeared for her breakfast just as her father left. "Morning, Mother. Sorry I overslept. I was too excited to sleep last night as I kept thinking about the wedding."

"That is understandable. I remember being the same but ye must hurry, quine, as we need to leave for our appointment with the dressmakers soon. By the way the announcement is in this morning's newspaper Alice. I am going to cut it out as a keepsake."

"Ooh let me see it, Mother. It will seem more believable when I see the words in print. Is that daft of me?"

"No, lass, I thought the same," she replied and mother and daughter laughed - their thoughts in sync.

*

A SELECT FEW had gathered in the Grand Hotel on Union Terrace. The guest of honour was touched by the presence of his close friends alongside several political and banking acquaintances who were there to help celebrate his engagement to Alice as well as his rise in political popularity. Charlie was glad to hear both the congratulations and the encouraging words regarding the Independent Labour Party's growth.

Fraser was in attendance, as was Charlie's father, and the all male consort of gentlemen enjoyed an evening of good food and drink. The opulent surroundings of Aberdeen's newest and most fashionable hotel with its stained glass windows and glass dome was a place of sophistication. The irony of the surrounding opulence and wealth against the backdrop of the nearby squalor appeared to go unseen.

Charlie's uncle James was also there despite not being in agreement with the politics of some of the guests but, like his father, Robert, always made himself visible at important events. Andrew approached him with a whisky in his hand. "I am glad to see ye here, James. I wasn't sure if ye would come."

"Despite what ye might think, Andrew, I don't always agree with my father."

A Beating

Ann had been invited to call upon an old friend the next morning and alighting from her carriage onto Deemount Terrace she took a moment to breathe before ringing the doorbell. Agnes Grant had moved into her new house following the marriage of her son. He had inherited his father's property and wealth but she had been well provided for and chose to move to the smaller abode beside Duthie Park, with limited but adequate staff, and her son now occupied Balfour Hall, the family home nestled on the banks of the River Dee.

Agnes welcomed Ann and the two women sat down to a cup of tea. The teapot was lifted and tea poured into two fine, porcelain cups whereupon both ladies poured a small amount of tea into their saucers and sipped from the rims.

"I am glad to see you back in Aberdeen, Ann. I know you enjoy being up in Inverness but you left so abruptly and I must admit that I find some of my other friends tedious company and I have missed you."

Ann smiled but the smile did not quite meet her eyes. "It was a spur of the moment trip. Rose and I had a restful break and I think that the country air did us both good."

"I think that perhaps ye are not being quite truthful with

me, Ann, but I will respect yer privacy and will not pry. You should know by now that I am here if needed."

Ann nodded. "I do know that, Agnes, thank you. There was a delicate matter that needed to be dealt with and I have done just that."

"And yet ye appear unsettled?"

Ann drew in two consecutive short breaths, an Aberdeen way of breathing which had the sound of the words, 'Aye, Aye', being spoken quickly on an in breath. It was a common behaviour used unconsciously with no particular reference, but one which Aberdonians employed.

"Do you ever feel that nothing really matters anymore? I used to be so adamant about the right way to host a party or sending my children to the right school and wearing the right dress to the right function."

Agnes moved from her chair to sit by her oldest friend. "Do ye remember my granny at my wedding? She floated around commenting loudly on the inappropriateness of the flowers and the food and whispered, for all to hear, on guests' attire, occupations and manners. I was black affronted but a tiny part of me envied her her confidence and forthrightness and I hoped that when I was old I would have that same strength of character and conviction in my words. We worry so much about conforming."

Ann laughed. "Oh I remember your granny well and she was hilarious. I can mind trying so hard not to laugh in front of my mother who was tut tutting."

"Well," Agnes continued, "I am a widow, therefore respected, but also independent, single and sexually experienced. Our society is a little afraid of widows, especially young ones. I am past the age of being a danger to a wife whose husband may stray but I think that we have reached the age where we can get away with many things. Age is a marvellous excuse to misbehave."

"But I don't think I have ever misbehaved, Agnes. That is

why I feel so unsettled. Life is passing by so fast and I have lived the life of a wife and mother but don't actually think I have really lived at all. Our class has so many rules and to have strayed beyond those would have meant disgrace. I am not sure if I have truly known fun, even as a child, and now it's too late."

Agnes clasped her friend's hand. "I don't believe it's ever too late for anything. Granny wrote me a letter once which I have kept all these years telling me how to misbehave. I will give it to you to read later. What do you think would be a fun thing to do? We could do it together if ye would like that."

Ann sighed. "That's just it. I don't know what would be fun. I don't have the first idea."

"If ye were twenty years younger I would suggest taking a lover but I don't suppose ye want one now."

"Agnes." Ann's hands went to her cheeks. "What a thing to say. I have never taken a lover in my life."

"Never? Really? But how on earth have ye gotten through fifty years of marriage without one?"

Ann stared at Agnes, her mouth open. "Have you had a lover?"

"Goodness me, yes. Findlay was a good husband in many ways but once I had provided an heir he rarely visited my bedchamber so I had dalliances over the years. All very discrete of course. And ye must remember that I was widowed relatively young so had needs of my own. I never wished to remarry so having lovers has suited me perfectly."

Ann shook her head. "Well I never. All these years we have been close friends and I never knew."

"I thought ye wouldn't approve so I didn't tell you. Ye were right about rules and I would never have wanted any scandal. I chose carefully."

"Did you love these men?"

"There was one," Agnes hesitated. "He was married so

it was an impossible situation. He would never have left his wife. I was quite heartbroken."

The two quines sat in silence for a few moments, each lost in their own thoughts.

Ann stirred and turned to Agnes. "I… Do…Do you regret them?"

"Oh no. Definitely not. Husbands have lovers all the time so why can't we?" She saw the look on her friend's face. "I believe I have shocked you, Ann."

Ann looked at Agnes. "I believe I am a little bit jealous." The corners of her mouth twitched.

Agnes burst into laughter and Ann snorted in a very loud and unladylike way which caused both to giggle more and before they knew it one was clutching the other for support as they gasped for air. Corsets pinched and sides were held but eventually the mirth subsided and the ladies, that they were, returned to their sober selves.

Agnes left Ann in the parlour for a moment whilst she went to fetch her granny's letter. Ann looked across at the photographs on the table and she spotted a small portrait taken of Agnes's grandmother. Wanting to take a closer look she rose from her chair and crossed the room to the where a collection of frames, both large and small, sat. Picking up the portrait she smiled at the face that she remembered had held so much mischief. Lowering it again she placed it back where it belonged beside a picture of Agnes's daughter, Isabella. Several years lay between her and her older brother and she was the spit of her mother. Another photograph was of Isabella with her husband on their wedding day. They had moved to London following marriage and Ann had not met their family but knew that Isabella had borne a son and three daughters, all grown up now of course. Agnes talked frequently of her grandchildren and was always boasting of how successful John was in his business. A further photograph of all the family, a recent addition by the look of it, caught Ann's eye and she picked it up. Her eyes moved from one face to the next and stopped as she looked at Isabella's son.

She replaced the photograph and returned to her seat.

Agnes came in with the letter and Ann, with a great show of hustle and bustle, and promises of lunch, took her leave and ascended the comfort and reassurance of her carriage.

*

Sunday evening came around and went as it always did with the family descending upon Redwood Manor. There had been a blissful month with Ann away in Inverness with Rose that Robert had not had to endure his kin for an entire evening. He had found a pleasurable activity to occupy his time and had been loath to return to the habits of old but it was easier to acquiesce to one's wife at times.

Tonight's gathering was somewhat different though as Robert was in high spirits. He even managed to refrain from ridiculing Gordon. Only three of his grandchildren attended as most were now married with families of their own but the important ones were there. Charlie's cousin, Victoria, the eldest of the Rosses grandchildren, and still very much the only one that Robert truly cared for, had just married a gentleman from England. This fact was only tolerated by her grandfather as her betrothed was of great wealth and status and Robert could claim him as family to his social peers and be lauded for it. The wedding had been held in St Machar's Cathedral and was nothing if not grand. Victoria sat by Robert and charmed him with anecdotes and excitement of her new life as a married woman.

"I am delighted that ye could come tonight, Victoria. Ye are looking well so I think married life must suit you."

"It does, Grandfather. It is a pity that Philip is away on

business but he knows how much I enjoy our Sunday's that he insisted I come without him."

"Well I am glad that he did."

Charlie was standing by the fireplace and took a moment to survey this family of his. He marvelled at how things had not really changed in all the years they had been gathering at Redwood Manor. It was the same act of pretending to tolerate one another sprinkled with a fluttering of dislike or jealousy and topped with a dollop of genuine care. If the evening were a pudding it would be a trifle: so mixed was it in character.

Gordon and Mabel sat as they always did: close together, one bolstering the other, united against any negative remarks or tirades passed over as family banter. Politeness prevented them from standing up for themselves or perhaps it was fear. Occasionally one would pat the other on a knee and when one was speaking the other would nod and smile. There was such an air of innocence about them which was perhaps why they were ridiculed.

Charles observed James and Edith. They rarely sat together, each languished nonchalantly and acted as if in their own parlour. James agreed with everything his father said and Edith rolled her eyes a lot. They had always seemed an odd couple to Charlie as knowing genuine love between his parents, Charlie often wondered whether his aunt and uncle even liked one another.

Edith commented to Rose, "This summer has been so uninteresting. I haven't been to a decent play or concert."

"I attended a poetry reading last week at Duthie Park. I cannot remember the poet's name which is terrible of me as he was extremely good. I found his reading quite moving."

"Oh I cannot stand poetry but I did hear of some scandal in Duthie Park the other day involving Mrs George Baird. Only been widowed a month and was seen walking along Lovers Lane in the park with a man almost half her age. He was rumoured to be Mr Simpson, her late husband's business associate, who has just returned from America."

Ann laughed. "Well, I hope it is true."

"Mother." a shocked Rose replied. "That is very unlike you to say such a thing."

"Her husband was a brute. Her reputation will not suffer. The walk will be passed over as a lapse in thinking following her devastating loss."

Andrew was being particularly attentive to Rose all evening which had not gone unnoticed. Charlie was glad that his parents appeared much happier than of late.

Victoria turned towards the fireplace where Charlie still stood. "Tell me, cousin, will you be marrying shortly? I can highly recommend a short engagement."

"Alice recommends it too," he replied which caused a ripple of laughter within the room.

Robert was overly generous with his whisky which James commented on as his glass was refilled. "It's not like you, Father, to be so free with yer whisky."

"The mill's yearly profit was up substantially from last year so I think a wee celebration is in order."

Charlie thought of those with empty bellies and purses.

"Will ye be offering some of those profits to the poor, Grandfather?"

The walls closed in as the room held its breath.

Robert did not rise to the bait. "Let us not spoil this family gathering with talk of politics. I propose a toast to Alice, in her absence, who will be a welcome addition to our family. To Alice."

The others raised their glasses, "To Alice."

The rest of the evening was perhaps one of the most pleasant there had ever been in Redwood Manor and no one seemed in a hurry to leave. Edith was the only one to comment on it whilst waiting for her coat.

"Perhaps we should meet less often as we appear to

have got along so much better having not been here for a month."

For the second time that night the room held its breath. To comment on the regularity of an invitation was the height of rudeness, family or otherwise. Ann had issued these invitations for nearly thirty years and to suggest a change was indeed an insult. It was Robert, again, who rescued the room from awkwardness. "Edith, I do believe you forget yourself but we all have lapses of manners at times so as soon as you have sincerely apologised to my wife you will be forgiven and no more will ever be said."

A deep flush crept up Edith's cheeks and she swallowed hard before speaking. "Please forgive me, Ann. I did not mean to speak out of turn."

Ann observed Edith's discomfort but took no pleasure in it. "You are forgiven, Edith, now Mabel, tell me where you found the material for your beautiful dress. I will be in need of a new dress for the wedding."

Mabel beamed under the compliment and the room once again restored its equilibrium.

As always, the group left together much to the chagrin of the staff having to run and fetch the right coats and escort each one to their carriage simultaneously. It was such a rushed and somehow undignified fare to have them leave en masse, something which Ann had frequently commented on, but she was tired these days so no longer fought it. Being a wet night no one tarried and all carriages left swiftly to deliver their passengers to their prospective abodes.

When the family had departed Ann decided to retire to her room but before ascending the stairs she commented to Robert, "I have rarely known you to be so amiable at our family gatherings. Perhaps you are mellowing with age, Robert."

Her husband chuckled, "Perhaps."

*

THREE MEN HAD positioned themselves strategically in Golden Square. Under the cover of darkness they approached only when the carriage began to move onwards. Charlie was powerless as rough hands smothered and grabbed, dragging their prey along Lindsay Street and into the nearby alley that led to St Mary's Cathedral. Fists and feet pummelled into a head, a chest and a stomach, the sickening sound of boots striking flesh desecrating the holy grounds of the church. The beating was quick and effective and a threat was issued, "Get out o' politics or Alice gets hurt." He was left bleeding and barely conscious and Charlie had never felt so helpless.

*

JAMES WAS FURIOUS the next morning when the loon had not appeared for work. The bank did not take kindly to tardiness and James was embarrassed. He sent word to Andrew asking him to call in at his son's apartment, which was not far from the solicitor's office, to see if he was there.

Andrew read the note handed to him by a messenger and immediately left his office. He knew by the tone of the message that James was angry rather than worried, but he himself was somewhat concerned. There had been many attempts at decimation of character and Andrew still had not found out who Robert had on his side. He made his way to Golden Square on foot.

Situated behind the Music Hall, in the centre of town, it was an elegant square of modest town houses with a circular garden in the centre. Andrew had imagined his son as a gentleman living in such a place.

He hoped that he would find the lad recovering from too much whisky the night before but a sense of foreboding crept into his blood. He had not before thought of any risks where politics were concerned.

*

CHARLIE'S MIND WAS whirring. Alice had to be protected at all costs. He knew the injuries would heal and the bruises would fade but the threat against Alice had been real and that terrified him. Andrew's arrival calmed the whirring of his mind. "My God, who did this? Ye need to see a doctor."

"Nae doctor. I will heal. Listen to me. They threatened Alice. Whoever sent those men to beat me sent a message. I am to stay out o' politics."

Andrew's face, which had paled on seeing the injuries now rose in colour as anger pricked then coursed through his body like lightning. "I will find out who is behind this. Yer grandfather is against ye but even I don't believe he did this."

"Either way, I must concede. I will not put Alice in danger."

Andrew knelt down and touched his shoulder. "Ye will stay here and rest. I will send someone to help ye and I will tell the bank that ye have taken ill. Do nothing about yer role in politics. Promise me ye will not write any letters or notes to anyone in that regard. I promise you that I will sort this sorry business and I will make sure that Alice is safe."

Charlie closed his eyes in thanks. He knew his father would keep his word and that Alice would be protected.

Andrew made his way to the bank and informed James of what had happened. "He didn't want a doctor but I have sent mine along to make sure he will be alright. I am going to see the editor of *The Aberdeen Journal* to see if someone has been putting pressure on him. It may well be the same person who instructed the beating."

James shook Andrew's hand. "Thank you for letting me know. It's a shameful business." He went to a drawer in his desk and handed Andrew some banknotes. "Do what ye need to do to find answers. I will see to it that Alice is safe."

Andrew hesitated. He was not in need of money but appreciated that this was a family problem. "Thank you, James. I will use it wisely." He turned to leave when a thought struck him, "Best keep this between us for now. No mention of a beating."

James nodded and Andrew left the bank.

*

ANDREW ENTERED THE building of *The Aberdeen Journal* and was shown to the editors office. Mr Murray was a man in his forties, clean shaven, as was the new fashion, and of slim build. He had been editor for five years and was a man of ambition both professionally and personally. "Good morning, Mr Milne. What do I owe this pleasure? I take it ye have been satisfied with the paper's influence on your family's situation?"

The smirk did not go unnoticed by Andrew and he felt his anger rising. *Steady now, Andrew. Remember why ye are here,* he thought to himself.

"Ye have certainly been thorough in your efforts, Mr Murray. My father in law must have paid ye well?"

Mr Murray's brow furrowed. "I have no dealings with Robert Ross."

"And yet ye carry out his orders?"

The editor rose from his seat, all traces of the smirk gone. He glowered at Andrew, holding up his left arm where a mangled hand lay, and spat the words. "I will never take orders from that man. He is responsible for this."

That was the last thing that Andrew had expected to hear and his thoughts tripped over one another. "I am slightly confused, Mr Murray, as I had assumed ye were being paid to-"

"Oh I am being paid, Mr Milne," he interrupted, "although I would do it for free. I take great pleasure in mocking yer family in my newspaper. When I was approached and offered a great deal of money to do just that I was somewhat delighted." He had a mixture of challenge and defiance on his face.

Andrew's eyes narrowed. "I am assuming that yer hand was injured in the mill as a boy and if that is the case why do ye run a newspaper that errs on the side of the upper classes?"

Mr Murray could tell by Andrew's tone that it was a genuine question and his face softened. "When my hand was injured I was eight years old and I could no longer do any type of manual work and it was only by luck and good fortune that I was taken on as a messenger by Mr Christie who was editor of this very newspaper. As time went by he took me under his wing and eventually he himself became the proprietor of the newspaper. Having no sons he trained me up, bettered my education and here I am. I will always be grateful to him which is why I remain here but it is my newspaper and I will use it as I see fit. I am a gentleman but I am working class at heart."

"I don't suppose ye will tell me who pays you?"

"Nae need to as far I can see. I do my best to ridicule Robert Ross's grandson and humiliate him in the process and that's that."

Andrew leaned forward. "And ye condone violence too, Mr Murray? Ye are happy to see the loon badly beaten and left in an alley?"

The editor's eyes widened and he shook his head. "I

know nothing of that, Mr Milne, and I certainly do not condone violence." He held up his mangled hand once more. "I wish no man, pain or injury."

"I believe ye, Mr Murray. Do ye think the man who pays ye may be responsible?"

"I doubt it. I am a shrewd man, Mr Milne. I refrain from having dealings with cruel folk and do not regard him as such. It is purely a financial arrangement although he does seem to take pleasure in seeing Mr Ross humiliated. Perhaps that is personal but that is none of my business."

Andrew rose to leave. "Thank you for your time."

"I have no ill will against yourself, Mr Milne, which is why I have spoken freely. Ye have a good name and it is spoken of that ye have had some influence in the better working conditions in the mill. It is only Robert Ross I dislike."

Andrew nodded. "I understand."

Standing outside the newspaper office Andrew let out a long sigh. The bundle of notes still lay in his breast pocket. There had been no point in offering Mr Murray money to reveal who was paying him as he could tell that he was a man of principle. He hated Robert and justly so. Andrew knew only too well how Robert had handled accidents in his mill and had at times been the cause of them. He was no nearer in finding out who was responsible for the beating though.

*

CHARLIE SAT IN his uncle James's drawing room opposite his father and his uncle Gordon. Whisky was poured into four glasses and the fire crackled steadily, its red and orange flames flickering and dancing along the walls and reflecting off the glass in the window that was smothered with the black of dark outside. The cuts had been treated but the skin was badly swollen and the bruises were a dark purple, obscuring the eyes.

James started proceedings. "Were these the same men that kidnapped you a few months ago?"

"No. These were rough, violent men. A different breed altogether."

Could this just have been a couple of under class men acting on their own and full of empty threats?" Gordon asked.

Andrew spoke up, "But it makes no sense for them to beat up someone who is on their side. Money would override allegiance in men with no principles."

Charlie nodded in agreement.

"I agree and I believe their threat against Alice was real."

"I wonder if this is more than political. Perhaps someone has a personal grudge against ye." added Gordon. "Are ye aware of any enemies?"

"No. I know, being a gentleman, I was not trusted in the beginning by many to fulfil Labour's policies but I think I have come a long way over the past few years and in the last year in particular to convince them otherwise. This is not the work of the working class. This is one of our own or from the upper class who see me as a real threat to their way of life."

"Political wranglings have always happened through speeches and newspapers. I do not know of any man who has been beaten for representing a particular party. It is the way of the world to have different viewpoints and we vote accordingly. I think ye are right, Gordon, this has to be personal."

"Can ye think of no-one who would wish ye hurt?"

"No. I have many friends and acquaintances and as far as I am aware I have never been cruel or hurtful to anyone. I know that my political leanings have brought embarrassment at times to your doors and for that I am sorry but I also know that you support me." He looked at James as he spoke.

"Aye, loon. I didn't in the beginning but ye have done yerself proud."

"So we are no further on in our thinking," stated Andrew.

Gordon spoke up. "I have asked the foreman in the mill to ask around to see if anyone knows anything. I like to think that my employees are satisfied in their work these days and hold no grudge against me as they did my father. Sometimes men boast of beatings so perhaps some information will turn up."

"That was good thinking, Gordon. Meantime what do we do?" asked James.

"I must protect Alice at all costs. I see no alternative but to leave politics." The words were strong but resigned.

"I told ye before not to be too hasty. We will find out who is behind your beating and meantime perhaps ye can suggest that Alice visit a relative away from Aberdeen."

"But, Andrew, he has a point. If the threat against Alice is real is it not too risky?"

"If no one knows where Alice is then she will be safe."

Charlie shook his head.

"Ye are forgetting how thrawn Alice is. I have not told her of my beating as I do not wish her to see me like this or worry her in any way. I have already lied to her by sending a note saying that I am out of town on business. Any hint of the threat will make her determined for me to stay in politics as she will not be bullied into feeling scared."

"I will speak to her father. We have kept him out of this but he has a right to know that Alice may be in danger so he will succeed in getting her away. He is happy about the forthcoming marriage so will want things to go ahead as planned."

Gordon interjected, "Would it be prudent to use the newspapers to help find out who did this? A reward perhaps?"

"No." Andrew answered, "We cannot risk infuriating whoever is behind this. It may make things ten times worse. We need to each make discreet enquiries within our circles as to who may be an enemy."

Charlie rose and circled the room.

"Some sort of announcement will be needed in the newspaper though. We need whoever is behind this to think that they have won. Perhaps some sort of illness hinted at which may prevent my working. That should buy us some time. I cannot go out in public looking like this and I certainly cannot have Alice seeing me."

"We can ask Dr Buchan to come up with an illness that would suffice and I will inform the newspapers."

"Aye, that is a good plan and with him aware of how things stand he too will be an asset in both protecting his daughter and in making his own discreet enquiries."

Charlie sat down again relieved that Alice's father would be a part of the plan.

Gordon turned to him. "As hard as it may be, lad, ye have no choice but to hide out. Better to stay here I think. Any suspecting newspapers will attempt to commandeer ye at home. We'll make sure Alice leaves Aberdeen too and before any newspaper announcements are made."

"Alright, Gordon, thank you."

"So, gentleman, we have a plan at least. I suggest we go out this evening and start to make our enquiries."

"I will go immediately to see David Buchan and with any luck he will have Alice out of Aberdeen first thing tomorrow," James said. "Then I will visit my club."

"One more thing," Andrew announced as all eyes turned to him. "We have no idea who is behind this so we must not trust no-one. So no sharing with our wives or closest confidants in case they inadvertently say something. If everyone believes what appears in tomorrow's newspapers then the man responsible for the beating will hopefully be convinced that he has succeeded in his quest. Outside of us, David Buchan will be the only man we can trust."

"Are ye including my father on that list? He may be an asset to us in making enquiries."

James' tone was neutral but Andrew was wary.

"I honestly believe that the fewer who know what has happened the better. This has to be contained. We cannot put Alice at risk."

James nodded. "Right ye are."

Charlie had no choice but to let others do what needed to be done.

James went directly to the Buchan's residence and David Buchan sat quietly as James spoke, having been asked to listen and not react hastily to what he was about to hear. When James had finished speaking David looked him in the eye. "Alice will not be here tomorrow. I will not inform ye of her whereabouts. I trust ye to sort out this situation and I too shall make my own discreet enquiries."

James shook David's hand. "Thank you for understanding."

Enquiries

The following morning, a Tuesday, bloomed delicately as the sun's warmth slowly unfurled. Rose was only half conscious of Andrew leaving her bed as sleep slowly left her and she awakened. A small smile surfaced as her eyes opened and she watched her husband ready himself for his day ahead. Since returning from Inverness life had changed immensely and no longer imprisoned by the hold of laudanum, her mind and body was unconfined. Hesitant at first, Andrew had been unsure of Rose's recovery but over the weeks, as he became accustomed to the change in her, he became more confident in his observations and began to see the woman he had married all those years ago, allowing himself to return to her bed.

"Good morning, husband."

Andrew turned from the mirror, comb in hand. "Good morning, Rose. Did ye sleep well?" he asked as he moved across the room and kissed her on the mouth as he sat on the edge of the bed.

"I did. Ye are up early this morning."

"Aye, I have much work to do today so may well be late this evening."

Rose's face fell. "Will ye not be home to dine?"

"No, Rose. I have a very important account which will take up a lot of my time over the next few days, possibly longer." He kissed her again and rose to put on his jacket.

"Well I will keep myself busy Andrew. Mother has invited me out for lunch today and I have bridge this evening.

Andrew left Willowbank and climbed into his carriage with determination coursing through his veins.

*

That evening Sir Muir read the evening newspaper with interest. Sitting with his wife in their parlour he commented, "It appears that Mr Ross's grandson may be leaving politics after all. It talks of illness but I don't believe it. The timing is strange though as he was doing well despite the attempts at making him look foolish. I almost admired his tenacity."

"Perhaps Mr Ross found a way to dissuade him." Elizabeth answered.

Donald looked up. "That may well be true." He rose from his chair by the fire and rang the servant's bell. "I think I will pay a visit to my club."

"Is something wrong? Ye seem perturbed. Are ye not happy that the Independent Labour Party will lose a strong member?"

"I am, but it now seems inevitable that the party will prevail and changes will indeed occur within our realms. Politics and society are changing and I am not foolish enough to think that I can control that. It has been a welcome challenge to try and forestall its progress but, as I said, the timing of this occurrence confuses me and I suspect that Mr Ross has perhaps been complicit in some wrongdoing against his own grandson."

Elizabeth raised her eyebrows. "What do you intend to do?"

"Find out the truth."

Sir Muir entered the club where dark oak panelled walls and leather armchairs were imbued with the fug of smoke, a mixture of pipe and cigarette tobacco and that of the coal fire burning brightly in the large stone fireplace. Occasional tables holding glasses full of whisky, port and rum sat sedately between each group of chairs, the reflections flickering from the low lit lamps attached to the walls. There was a general buzz about the room, a low hum of conversation interspersed with an occasional laugh or voice raised in excitement.

About twenty men were present, fewer than normal for a Thursday evening, but it was early yet so likely to change. Sir Muir ordered himself a glass of port and sat down to wait.

*

Charlie flitted from room to room unable to settle. He knew that Alice was safe, but for how long? His father and uncles would do their utmost to sort out this sorry mess but knowing that he himself had no choice but to wait was tormenting. Time was a strange thing indeed as it could flow like the river in spate or be suspended like haar above the sea.

*

Robert read the evening's newspaper with a smirk on his face. The men he had hired had indeed done their job. It had been a long wait to hear news and of course he could not enquire. He had spent most of Monday indoors, lurking near the door in case a messenger arrived with a note from one of his kin but no such message had arrived which had both angered and confused him. Why had no one informed him of his grandson's beating? Ann had been in and out of the house as usual and had not returned with any news. Eventually Robert had had enough of waiting and decided to call in to the bank. James was not there. Robert was informed that Mr Ross had been in first thing but had left again on business. Robert then called in to see Andrew but it was the close of day and the office was locked. Becoming more and more frustrated he decided to go and see Gordon. If Gordon knew anything he would be the first to squeal but on arrival the foreman had told him that Mr Ross had been out for most of the day on business.

Robert's thoughts raged. *Business. All out on business. Well I did not think that my sons and son in law would ever collude but collude they are. Why all the secrecy? What is going on?*

His temper had simmered all Monday evening and Tuesday had brought with it no answers as his messages to his sons went unanswered. The arrival of the evening's newspaper had at last answered his question and his anger dissipated being replaced with victory. No one made a fool out of him and got away with it. Especially not family. Whatever his sons and Andrew were doing was no longer of concern. For all he knew it was completely unrelated.

It was time to celebrate.

Robert sauntered into the club. He breathed in polite society's air and felt his breast swell. This is where he belonged. It was where he had always belonged.

Sir Muir watched as Robert joined a group of peers, whisky in hand. Robert had not yet noticed him which gave Sir Muir time to observe his actions. He could hear snippets of the conversation. "Not at all, Mr Tate. Nothing serious. He will no doubt continue in banking and be very successful in it." Robert skillfully answered questions as if blowing the seeds of a dandelion into the air. He flitted from one group to the next sowing his seeds of lies amidst jovial tales and good humour.

Is it an act? thought Sir Muir.

Having watched and heard enough he decided to see for himself. "Mr Ross, come and join me, good sir."

Robert excused himself, his ego nurtured by the beckoning of Sir Muir.

"Good evening, sir. How does the evening find ye?"

"Very well, Mr Ross. And yourself? It appears you may have some cause to worry - an ill grandson?" The question was genuine with no hint of suspicion in it.

"All will be well, Sir Muir."

"So we have succeeded then?"

Robert smiled but the smile did not quite reach his eyes. It was a look that Sir Muir had seen before whenever someone tried to take credit away from Robert.

"I believe the matter to be dealt with although I cannot say that the Labour movement will not succeed."

"Quite. I do believe they have a stronghold but just how was the matter, as you put it, dealt with in the end?" Sir Muir's eyes were hard as they penetrated Robert's. "A beating perhaps?"

Robert batted his hand in the air. "Not at all. That was a foolish, passing thought that remained just that."

Sir Muir leaned forward. "And yet my own doctor attended to many cuts and bruises yesterday belonging to your grandson."

Robert faltered. "I know nothing of that. I know only what was written in the newspaper."

Sir Muir raised his eyebrows. "Really? You mean to say that no one in your family contacted you?"

Sparks of anger lit up Robert's eyes.

"Let me fill you in. A bloody face, with deep cuts to a lip and cheek and an eye swollen shut. Bruising on the torso and hands and knees badly scraped where he had been dragged along the ground."

Robert made as if to rise. "I must go. I know nothing of this."

Sir Muir grabbed Robert's arm. "Sit down Robert." His voice low and threatening, "Or do you wish me to tell one and all that you had your own grandson beaten to within an inch of his life?"

Robert remained seated. "You like it here, don't you Mr Ross? You enjoy the trappings of society; the theatre, the balls, the dinners, the mistresses. I don't imagine you would like to lose it. We are only as good as our reputation, are we not? Once tarnished it rarely recovers and the shame of it on our families - the humiliation, the lack of invitations. It can be cruel."

Robert swallowed and became aware of sweat in his armpits as his breath grew in pace. But still he kept silent.

"Your silence speaks volumes, Mr Ross." Sir Muir rose and left without another word.

Robert threw back the last of his whisky and he had the same thought that had entered his mind when he arrived. *I belong here.*

SEABANK

The Ladies' Society for the Rescue of Fallen Women in Aberdeen took it upon themselves to look after and reform women who had succumbed to the pressure of poor living and empty bellies by selling themselves in brothels. This was mostly achieved through charitable fundraising by the ladies as opposed to any contact with the fallen women themselves. The *Seabank Rescue Home* on King Street was once such place where women were compelled to redeem themselves at the hands of staunch religious women and visiting ministers.

The religious amongst them preached hell and damnation but others, more sympathetic to their plight, sought to help rather than judge.

Mabel, unbeknownst to most, chose to visit the home once a week, on a Wednesday. Having initially been shocked by the number of women there she took time to speak to them and was saddened to hear, first hand, how their lives had spiralled. She learned that there were those who chose their profession and thrived on it but for most it had not been a choice but an act of desperation with which to feed young mouths.

She arrived with a basket, as always. Sometimes it contained books, other times it held necessary undergarments. She also often arrived with flowers from her garden or some freshly baked cake. She would hand out her offerings discreetly to those she had spoken to the week before. Mabel had become a trusted lady to whom the women could approach to ask for small items they were in need of that would perhaps be ridiculed by the staff.

The door was opened and Mabel entered. Mrs Sim, who took charge of the home, barely concealed her dislike as she greeted her. "Good morning, Mrs Ross. It doesn't seem a week since yer last visit." Her voice dripped with sarcasm as she glowered at the basket in Mabel's hand. "I wonder what delights our quines are to receive today."

Mabel was used to Mrs Sim's disapproval but where she was often quiet in the company of her peers and indeed inlaws, here she came into her own. "Some items to improve their minds or dignity, Mrs Sim."

Mrs Sim folded her arms across her wiry frame. "The Bible is all they need."

Mabel gave her a small smile. "I will speak with those who wish to speak with me. Please bring a large pot of tea into the drawing room. The women will be due a break from their chores." She walked through the home to where the drawing room lay fully aware of two eyes boring into her back.

Presently the women could be heard coming down from the rooms in which they slept or from the kitchen, having spent the morning cleaning and scrubbing each room til their hands were raw. Cups were filled and the women blethered quietly amongst themselves, welcoming a break from their work. Mabel spoke quietly and now and then reached into her basket to retrieve an item to be given to one of the women. Most were secreted away in a pocket or bosom as Mrs Sim was known for her nosiness but the items would not be taken from them as Mabel had made it clear to Mrs Sim that there would be consequences if such action occurred.

Two women approached Mabel and asked to speak with her. Sometimes women required a personal item or wished to unburden themselves of a happening without the fear of judgement and Mabel was happy to listen. Jean was a slim, dark haired woman of around twenty years in age and her friend, Frances, was taller with red hair and a worried look in her eye. Mabel had spoken to them before on a couple of occasions but neither had ever requested anything from her.

Jean looked around the room making sure that no one was within earshot. "We wondered if ye could find a way to help us retrieve something."

Mabel nodded. "I will try my best to help. What is the item?"

Both women hesitated and moved closer to Mabel. Jean spoke again in a low whisper, "Someone took photographs of us and we want them back."

Mabel tilted her head to the right. "I'm not sure I understand. Do you need me to write to someone?"

Jean shook her head. "These photographs are dangerous for us. They need to be taken back."

"Dangerous in what way?" asked Mabel.

This time it was Frances who answered. "A man paid us… He took photographs of us…of a particular nature…"

"Oh." Mabel sat up a bit straighter. She may be of a particular class but she had been visiting the refuge for some time and heard certain stories pertaining to the lives these women once led.

Jean whispered, "He will show them tae other men and we need tae be able tae get honest work as domestics or in a factory and if one o' these men is an employer he might recognise us. The man told us that he would not take photographs o' oor faces but I saw them and he lied. We went tae his studio several times and the last time I saw the postcards o' us. They were on a wee table. He said that he might keep ours for himsel' in his personal collection as he thought we were bonny, so we were thinking that maybe they are still there in his studio. There is a desk with drawers but there is also a door to another room so perhaps they are in there." Jean stopped and looked straight into Mabel's eyes. "Please can ye get them back fir us?"

Mabel was at a loss for words. She dabbed her forehead with her handkerchief. "I don't see how I could possibly retrieve them. I cannot walk into such a place. Should ye not inform the police as surely that is not allowed?"

"Nay," Francis said. "That will make things worse. We can tell ye where the studio is but nae the man's name. He never telt us his name. We ken ye are a lady and could never go there yersel' but maybe ye could hire someone to go and we will pay ye back soon as we hae honest work." The two quines waited for Mabel to answer.

Mabel's mind was whirring and she could see no way of achieving such a thing. "Tell me everything ye know and I will go away and think about it. I cannot promise anything mind."

"The studio is on Belmont Street above the dressmakers. There is a door just tae the right o' the dressmakers which takes ye up tae it. There is nae sign on the door. We always went there in the evenings so I am nae sure if he is there during the day. He is a tall, handsome man possibly in his sixties or seventies, clean shaven. He is well spoken like a gentleman and dresses as such but we know nothing of him other than that he enjoys art and has often said that we would...what was the word, Francis?"

"Adorn. He said we would adorn the walls of the art gallery if he had his way."

Mabel squeezed each of the young women's hands and left somewhat dazed.

Answers

Gordon lifted his head from his paperwork, although no ink had left his pen as his mind had been elsewhere, when his foreman knocked and entered the mill office. "Ye wished for information, Mr Ross."

"Please sit, Mr Duguid, and tell me quickly what ye have found out."

"Well, word has it that a man was heard boasting about beating a gentleman on Sunday evening. He had been on the whisky and his two friends bundled him out the door afore he could say anything else but they are a shifty crew and well known in town as ruffians. It wouldn't be the first time they have beaten someone and even quines have been known to suffer at their hands."

"Any way of getting close to them to find out more?"

"All I ken is that they frequent The Black Bull public house most evenings. I get the impression that they would hurt their own mothers for a penny in their pockets."

Gordon shook Mr Duguid's hand. "Thank you. You have been very helpful."

Gordon called for his messenger boy. Andrew would know what to do.

The man hired to seek out the men in the public house bought himself a beer and sat down at a table in the corner. As expected the men were already there and the ladies of the house were being attentive. There were rooms upstairs where the men were entertained and Frank hoped that his wait would not be a long one. He had a wife at home and was not in need of any entertainment of his own. This was a job and nothing more.

Chrissie was sitting on Mr Stewart's knee. He could not hold his drink as well as the other two making him the easier target and she knew what she was required to do. The whisky flowed quickly and whispering in his ear Chrissie proceeded to take him by the hand and led him up the wooden staircase to the rooms above.

Frank waited, surrounded by revellers enjoying the jaunty music being played by a couple of fiddlers and watching folk dance and sing, their voices loud and their egos large as women teased. Whisky and beer was gulped and minds succumbed to desires as bodies were bought.

It had been a long time since Frank had entered such an establishment. The scent of whisky and bodies filled his nostrils and the music screeched in his lugs. He had never liked the sound of the fiddle and each note drove into him like a needle going through cloth on a sewing machine. Blending in he pretended to be enjoying himself, cheering on the fiddlers and raising his glass. He even danced with one of the quines whirling her around to a jig and falling back on his chair, feigning drunkenness.

A short time later Mr Stewart staggered down the stairs, Chrissie behind him. His friends were by now upstairs themselves and he made his way to the bar to order himself another drink. Chrissie sauntered through the room and plonked herself on Frank's knee whispering in his ear and laughing at an untold joke. She rose and moved on to another, and so the night continued for her. Frank slowly made his way through the crowd and out onto the street. He hailed a Hansom cab to Willowbank where Andrew was waiting for news.

A̲NDREW STARED AT Frank, his voice level. "Ye are sure?"
"Aye. Not the name ye were expecting, no doubt, and for that I am sorry."
Andrew nodded but did not utter a word.
Frank made his way to the door and stopped. "Ye hae my word that no one will hear it fae me."
"I knew that already but I thank ye for saying it."
As the door closed behind his trusted servant, Andrew breathed out a long sigh. He had wondered, but to have it proven was another thing altogether. And just what he would do with such information for the moment alluded him. He sat back in his chair clasping both hands behind his head and looked up at the ceiling wishing that the answer lay written above him.

*

T̲HE SUN SHONE brightly the following morning although the autumn air was cool. Crisp orange and red leaves scurried in the breeze, brushing shoes as they journeyed past. Mabel and her maid alighted from their carriage onto Belmont Street and Mabel took a second to take in her surroundings although she had been there many times before. The old Gaelic church towered above behind her and the elegant houses lined either side of the street. In front of Mabel stood the dressmaker's shop. Tucked neatly into one of the tall, proud buildings it boasted a large window in which sat two beautiful dresses of the latest fashion. Her eyes flitted across the window to the door that lay to the right. Green in colour it held a number but no plaque. Mabel allowed her head to tip up slightly as she skimmed the windows above the shop. Two symmetrical windows adorned the building, each covered with muslin and no light showed through.

A bell tinkled as they entered the dressmaker's shop and the earthy scent of cloth greeted them. Delicate embroidered cotton, and woven silks embellished long shelves and buttons of every colour rested in tall glass jars. A dark, maroon coloured curtain separated the shop from the back room where seamstresses toiled and the whirring of a sewing machine could be heard. The proprietor of the shop was serving a customer so Mabel perused the yards of cloth on large rolls as she waited.

Having completed her purchases the other lady left, pausing only to say good morning to Mabel. "Sorry to keep ye waiting, madam. How may I help?"

"I am in need of some alterations to a coat. The collar is no longer fashionable nor the length. My maid has the garment." Susan stepped forward with the coat wrapped in a cloth covering and placed it on the counter. "I also wish to look at some material. I have a wedding to attend in the spring so am in need of something elegant and of the latest fashion."

"Of course, madam. We have a selection just arrived yesterday in the most beautiful colours and I have acquainted myself with the latest fashions in Paris and London."

"Excellent."

She turned to Susan. "I may be some time so you can collect my ring from the jewellers and then wait for me in the carriage."

"Yes, madam."

Susan left the shop and Mabel began her quest of finding

both material for a dress and information. As she exclaimed over the beautiful silk she began to make conversation. Beginning with all things garments Mabel then turned the conversation. "Does your shop extend upstairs?"

"No, madam. I have a large room in the back for my seamstresses."

"Does someone live above you or is it an office of some kind?"

"I have been here for five years and have never known it to be an office. There is no plaque so I have always assumed it to be an apartment."

"It is such a lovely street. I have a friend who lives here and I must say I do envy her being able to access the department stores so easily. Now I really must choose or I will be here all day."

Mabel told the woman that she could not quite make up her mind and would return another day and left. The visit had not proved fruitful and she was unsure as to what she could do next. Frustrated, she did not enter her carriage but walked further along the street and turned down Little Belmont Street hoping that a little fresh air would result in some inspiration. A message boy was walking towards her and an idea formed in Mabel's mind. Stopping him she reached into her purse and withdrew a coin, and spoke to him. The loon nodded in answer and taking the coin made his way around the corner.

Mabel retraced her steps and stopped by the corner to adjust her hat. She watched as the messenger rang the bell on the green door by the dressmaker's and immediately left on his way. Mabel waited, her heart beating slightly faster. What was she expecting? A monster? A gentleman? The door remained steadfastly shut and Mabel tutted to herself and made her way to her carriage. Even if he had opened the door, what good would it have done? She still would have no name or more importantly no way of retrieving what he held.

*

Andrew rang the bell to the Buchan residence and was invited to wait in the drawing room. He had tossed and turned all night before finally deciding to speak to David Buchan in the morning. David entered and shook Andrew's hand before enquiring, "Do ye have news?"

Andrew nodded. "I do Mr Buchan but I am unsure as to how to proceed. I cannot find it in me to tell either James or Gordon Ross of my findings."

"So ye have come to tell me?"

"Aye. It would seem so."

David saw the dejected look in Andrew's eyes. "I can see that it is something of great concern so just take yer time. I will help in any way that I can. My first priority is Alice but I know her to be safe at the moment."

Andrew closed his eyes for a second and then looked straight at David. "The man responsible for the beating… was Robert Ross."

"Good God. His own grandson."

"Aye."

The two men were silent for a time, David shaking his head in bewilderment. "Nae wonder ye didn't want to tell his sons. How on earth would you deliver such news?" Then a thought struck him and his voice rose in anger, "And he threatened my Alice. When I think about how many times I have doctored his family and sat beside him at a dinner or in the club. My God I will throttle him with my own bare hands."

"I feel the same. For years I thought I had a handle on him. I saw how he treated his kin but I honestly believed that deep down he loved them. I should have done more years ago. When I think of how he spoke of Charlie. Never to my face, he knew better than that, but I know he ridiculed him, thought him an idiot and despised his poor start in life. How he must have laughed to have imagined Charlie in pain. My poor loon." Andrew put his head in his hands.

David quietly rose and poured some whisky into two glasses and handed one to Andrew giving him some time to compose himself.

"Robert Ross will not get his way. My future son in law is an asset to politics and must continue in his political career. What we need is something to prevent Mr Ross from carrying out his threat. We cannot involve the police as that will only lead to scandal for us all. This needs to be done quietly."

"I agree," replied Andrew. "I have spent the night trying to think of a way to do just that. I know of a certain mistress that he has but cannot see a way of using that against him."

"Would his wife have an influence? I do not wish to upset her but could she stop him?"

"No. He would not care if she knew of any mistresses or of the beating."

"We need to think of someone or something that he cares about. Something he would not wish to lose."

Andrew rose and went to the window. He looked out onto the garden and watched as a bee buzzed against the window and then turned and found its way to the flower bed. Delicate petals were nudged by the insect's body as it burrowed into the centre to collect the sweet nectar.

David joined him at the window just as a cat sprung from the undergrowth snaring its prey in sharp claws. "If only he were a mouse."

"Aye."

Andrew glanced down to where the morning's newspaper lay on the table. Left open on the news pages he read the heading, *'Her Majesty set to return to Balmoral.'* "That's it" he said. "Victoria. Victoria is who he would hate to lose."

David frowned. "I'm not with you."

"His granddaughter, Victoria, is the apple of Robert's eye. If we threaten to tell her of his antics he will back down. I am sure of it. He would not risk losing her." Andrew's excitement grew. "I will go to Redwood Manor immediately. If he is not there I will track him down." He turned to leave but David's hand clutched Andrew's elbow. "I am coming with you. I have a few words I would like to say to him."

Andrew saw the need for vengeance reflected in his eyes. "I understand Mr Buchan but perhaps we can have our own game of cat and mouse. I will make it known that I am not the only one who knows of his deed. Let him squirm a bit."

David hesitated but acquiesced. "What will ye tell the family?"

"That it was a disgruntled merchant who is now on a ship to Canada."

Cat and Mouse

Andrew decided to walk the short distance from the Buchan's home to Redwood Manor. He needed the air to gather his thoughts and work out exactly what he would say to Robert. His anger ebbed as he thought of Robert as a mouse to be toyed with, before claws ripped him apart.

Fortunately the servant announced that both Mr and Mrs Ross were at home and Andrew found them sitting in the garden. "Forgive me for coming unannounced," he said as he kissed Ann on the cheek. "Rose knew that I would be near Dee Street today and asked if I would call in and ask if you are free tomorrow Ann to visit her in the morning? The reason has escaped me but it is possibly wedding related."

"I can make time. Do you have time for some tea, Andrew?"

"Tea would be very welcome, thank you."

Ann rose to go into the house and request tea from her maid as Andrew addressed his father in law. "It is fine weather indeed and the flowers are in full bloom I see. I was reading about the flowers that grow in hedgerows in England called Bittersweet. Not so common here in Scotland - they symbolise truth. The berries are toxic though."

"I had no idea ye were interested in flowers, Andrew." His disinterest apparent.

"My interests lie in many places, Robert." The words held a threatening tone and Robert shifted slightly in his chair, unsure of its meaning.

Ann returned and sat herself down again on her wicker chair.

"Your garden is looking beautiful, Ann. Rose has a book detailing the meaning of flowers. It is quite enlightening. The yellow Jasmine you have growing there is very apt as it portrays grace and elegance."

Ann laughed. "You are charming me, Andrew. Have you misbehaved?"

Andrew also laughed. "Not as far as I am aware. Unlike a perpetrator I have had the misfortune of meeting through my work. Turns out he hired some scoundrels to badly beat a member of his own family." He caught Robert's eye as he spoke and saw a glint of surprise.

"Goodness." Ann tutted.

"Yes. It's a shocking business but he will be punished. I imagine his garden is full of geraniums. They represent stupidity."

Robert looked across his garden at a clump of geraniums now beginning to die away.

"I am sorry to hear that you have to deal with such people, Andrew," replied Ann.

"It is not a common occurrence. I mainly deal with business, not criminals. An acquaintance will take on the case. I have just held a meeting with him and all is in hand."

He looked at Robert and smiled. "Forgive me, I have dampened the sunny air with depressing talk. Tell me, will young Victoria be joining us on Sunday. I have some news that I am eager to share with her."

Robert paled but did not rise. His legs would not have held him up at that point. Glancing at his wife he answered,

"I believe she has sent word of her coming. Am I right, Ann?"

"Yes, she will be here. And Philip too. I am hoping that they will soon announce the coming of a child. I would like to have another great grandchild."

"Family is all important. And on that note I must take my leave as I promised Rose that I would be home early to dine and I still have much work to do in my office."

"Of course. We shall see you on Sunday. Robert, will you show Andrew out?"

"I will," Robert replied as he rose and for the first time felt the weight of his years in his bones.

The two men walked through the house and the front door was opened. Robert followed Andrew out onto the drive where he turned to face him. "Ye have forgotten who I am Robert. Telling Victoria is only the beginning."

Robert swallowed. "The threat will not be carried out and I will not have the loon harmed again. Please do not tell Victoria."

Andrew walked away, calling, "I will send ye a bouquet of Hyacinths. They signify games and play."

*

THE OPERA HOUSE was full as folk eagerly awaited the production of Gilbert and Sullivan's *Iolanthe* to start. There was a buzz in the air and the gentry, in all their finery, greeted friends and acquaintances as they took their seats. Ann and Robert had arrived in time for a pre performance drink and had mingled with their peers: the usual polite small talk and gossip shared. Only Robert had been aware of any change in welcome as Sir Muir had walked past without stopping and Lady Muir had turned her back on him. When the bell rang they had made their way up the staircase to the first floor and sat down in a box to the right of the stage just as the orchestra struck its first notes and a hush descended on the audience.

Ann was enthralled as the fairies flitted across the stage singing *'Tripping Hither, Tripping Thither…"* The costumes were stunning and the light allowed the wings to shimmer as if they were indeed flying. She lost herself in the buoyant, impish music and was unaware of the broad smile on her lips. To the left of her, Robert sat oblivious to the story unfolding on stage as his mind refused to settle. His thoughts scurried from Andrew's words to the lack of contact from his sons and Elizabeth's cold shoulder. Had he taken in the satire of the comic opera he may well have realised the comparison with his own life - where Iolanthe had been banished from fairy land he too was at risk of being banished from polite society.

*

James's drawing room was bathed in the light of the various lamps and by the flames from the fire flickering in its hearth as his kin, joined by David Buchan, assembled to discuss the latest news. Charlie listened with interest to what they had to say. "The merchant is gone for good so you can rest assured that no harm will come to either yourself or Alice."

"I am relieved indeed, and thank you to all of you. It has been frustrating having to be here and do nothing but wait."

David spoke up. "I have been thinking about yer political aspirations and as something like this is unlikely to happen again I think it would be prudent for ye to continue. Alice knows nothing of what has occurred but I feel that she would be somewhat disappointed in you if you gave up politics."

"He is right, lad," Gordon said, "ye have great promise and should continue."

Charlie stood by the fireplace.

"If ye are certain that Alice is not in danger then I will gladly carry on. She has ideas of her own as to our country's progress and together I think we can make a difference." An eager smile began to surface before being stopped with a wince as the cuts on his face pinched.

Backs were clapped and whisky drunk in celebration. Andrew shook his hand. "Well Robin Hood, as soon as yer injuries heal we will have it announced in the paper that your illness has passed and you will be returning to your duties with vigour. A message to your grandmother saying that you are out of town on business will take care of your absence on Sunday evening."

Glasses were again raised and Andrew took himself over to the fireplace.

'Any problems with your grandfather come and see me immediately,' he said outwith earshot of the others.

*

ROBERT LEFT HIS club and took his usual Monday evening ride in a Hansom cab to where Elizabeth awaited him. The rain fell heavily and drummed on the roof as the horse plodded through the streets. It was a dismal night and Robert was glad to be undercover unlike the driver who sat behind the cab with the driving rain battering his face. The horses reins were pulled half way along Albyn Place and the hatch above Robert's head opened allowing the rain to enter as he quickly paid, passing the money up through the hatch. The driver, checking that the correct fare had been received, pulled the lever by his side to release the cab door and free his passenger into the night.

Head down against the inclement weather, Robert strode along the path and turned left with a quick look behind him into the driveway. Four large pillars supported a grand semi circular porch atop eight stone steps. With a last look behind him he climbed the steps, shook himself off under the cover of the porch and placed his hand on the door knob. It did not turn. Robert tried again but still it would not turn and he realised that the door was indeed locked.

"Damn it," he cursed and turned on his heel. Elizabeth had always sent word to him if for any reason their plan had to change. Perhaps her husband was there or she had not gone to Albyn Place at all.

Or perhaps her turning her back on him at the opera signified something more.

Yesterday's family gathering had gone without incident. Victoria had greeted him warmly, as usual, and James and Gordon had not seemed angry in any way so he suspected that Andrew had not told them of his findings.

Andrew was a threat and Robert knew that there would be consequences for his actions.

He had no choice but to return home with his thoughts and hope that he could hail a Hansom cab as it was a very long walk otherwise.

*

MABEL WAS TROUBLED. It had been a week since her visit to the refuge and she was no further on in her enquiries. Could she involve Gordon or would he judge her for talking of such things and stop her from visiting the fallen women's refuge? She had thought of confiding in a friend but could not see how anyone in the same social position as herself could be of help. Hiring someone as the quines had suggested was an option as she possessed money, but as to whom she had no idea and no way of knowing how to go about it. The man may well be dangerous and Mabel felt very out of her depth.

She arrived at the refuge that morning disheartened with the realisation that she would have to inform the women that she was unable to help them.

Jean and Francis became agitated as they listened to Mabel's apologies. "Ye have tae help us. Please, Mrs Ross, there is no one else we can ask," pled Jean.

"I'm sorry, I just can't see a way to help."

Francis began to cry. "Ye need tae understand. Those photographs must be destroyed."

Mabel folded her hands under her chin and looked at the women just as Mrs Sim appeared. "What are ye snivelling about? Mrs Ross is not here to listen to you feeling sorry for yourself."

Francis left her chair and ran from the room.

"Break time is over!" bellowed Mrs Sim to the room, "Get back tae yer chores."

Jean rose, but not before Mabel touched her on the arm and nodded.

*

THREE WEEKS AFTER the beating Charlie read the letter from Alice stating her return to Aberdeen.

… and being whisked away by Mother and taken to London was such a wonderful surprise. Folk here are so fashionable and Mother has kindly purchased several gowns for me and the most beautiful silk for my wedding dress. Staying with uncle Harry has been exciting and enjoyable. He has escorted us to the museums in South Kensington, the Theatre Royal in Covent Garden to see the Royal Italian Opera and the National Gallery of British Art. I have seen so many

wonderful sights that it will take me a month to tell you all about them! A carriage ride took us past Buckingham Palace which is a magnificent building but what a treat to be taken to dine in London's newest hotel, The Savoy. Its grandeur was breathtaking and I ate food which I confess to having no idea what it was and the tables all had pink table cloths. Pink!

It has been a whirlwind holiday but I am very aware that beyond the affluent streets in which I have visited lies poverty and hardship, as it does in every city. I have felt guilty at times indulging in such treats. It is down to luck, to whom we are born, and what life we will lead. A bairn is born and more often than not its life is already chosen for him or her. I honestly believe that we can change that by helping to change our country's laws. I am rested and full of vigour to continue alongside you, my darling, to fulfil our goals of a fairer world.

I have missed you.

We intend to take the train back on Tuesday stopping over in Edinburgh for the night and continuing our journey home on Wednesday....

He had missed her too and could see that his family had been right to encourage him to continue in politics. There was so much to be done to improve the lives of many and by having a wife such as Alice by his side he knew that together they would make it their life's work to succeed.

The bags were packed and the carriage waited to take him back to his own apartment in Golden Square. The newspapers had printed a statement in which it claimed that there had been an exaggerated account of his ill health and that '*the young gentleman banker will indeed be continuing with his political work.*' The bruises were now gone and the cuts had healed so Alice, like most others, would be unaware of the beating.

Charlie left with a smile on his lips and Alice in his heart.

*

Mr Murray sat at his desk and pondered. Over the years he had kept an ear to the ground regarding the Ross family. His loathing of Robert Ross, due to his injured hand, had remained but had not festered into hate. Mr Murray was very aware of the good fortune he had encountered in life as a direct result of becoming a messenger but this in itself had resulted in him straddling two worlds. If he was honest with himself he was comfortable in neither class setting.

He had the mind of a gentleman with the heart of a working class boy.

He had allowed his journalists free rein in their writings of the Rosses, especially politically, and being paid by Sir Muir had been advantageous, but as a man with a curious mind he was intrigued as to what Andrew Milne had said regarding a beating. It pricked his conscience that anything he had printed in his newspaper could have in some way caused the loon physical harm.

Perhaps the two were not related in any way at all but Andrew had seemed sure that they were connected. He would keep his ear to the ground and be more careful in what he allowed to be printed in his newspaper.

*

Andrew mingled in the parlour of the Music Hall following a late supper. No other members of his family were present which made it the perfect evening for his plan to unfold. The atmosphere was congenial and tongues danced to the rhythm of the conversation: a steady pulse within polite society's chant.

Slowly, a carefully constructed whisper altered the tempo

and flutters of excitement hopped from one tongue to the next. Society loved nothing more than gossip - as long as it was not pertaining to them personally. Snippets were past and fans quivered and flitted across ladies' faces as gentlemen cocked their heads.

The ladies, he knew, would gather around Ann, protecting and nurturing as a bird would its chick. No words of acknowledgment would pass their lips as society knew better than to admit to listening to gossip, so Ann would benefit from many invitations without ever knowing the cause.

His work done, Andrew slipped away. The mouse would be toyed with for a while yet.

PATRIARCH

THE MONTHS PASSED and life settled into a rhythm again. Charlie spent his time ensuring that Alice was safe and content and keeping a close eye on all things political. Work had begun on knocking down houses unfit for human occupation in the poor areas of Aberdeen but with a lack of better or new houses in which to move them, folk ended up sharing accommodation resulting in yet again, overcrowding and substandard living conditions. It frustrated Charlie to see folk lacking in food and a clean bed. His own humble beginnings never having been forgotten.

More often than not Charlie attended the Sunday evening gatherings at Redwood Manor which continued to both entertain and aggrieve him. Knowing he had never been accepted by his grandfather he had asked himself why he continued to visit but his answer remained the same - because he loved his grandmother. He saw all too easily the two sides of the city; the wealth and opulence of one and the deprivation and squalor of the other.

He saw all too easily the two sides of his grandfather.

The unwritten rules within polite society were often overlooked at the Sunday family gatherings, with Robert enjoying nothing more than stirring the political pot with jibes against the Independent Labour Party but since

Andrew's warning Robert had been on his best behaviour, though it pained him to do so.

The family gathered as usual one Sunday evening in November but it was James who started a political argument over the newly started Boer War.

Britain had sent ten thousand troops to South Africa in September following the unsuccessful Bloemfontein Conference in May/June which had been set up to try and diffuse the growing conflict between Britain and the two African republics over the discovery of diamonds and gold. An ultimatum was issued by the Boers and subsequently war was declared on Britain on 11th October 1899.

The day's newspaper lay on the small table by the window in the drawing room and James noticed it as his wife, Edith, moved from beside him to sit with Rose. "It will be a quick war," he said to Andrew, indicating the newspaper heading.

"I wouldn't be so sure, but let's hope so. I fear Britain has become greedy. I think there is some unease nowadays towards Britain having an empire and ruling over other countries."

Robert started in surprise and snapped at Andrew. "Surely ye are not saying that Britain should relinquish its power?"

"We have little trade with the countries that we rule so one could argue the benefits, Robert. This is a colonial war and lives will be lost needlessly."

Robert felt his hackles rising, "Needlessly? I would not say that protecting our interests is needless. Should we just let the Boers take all the gold?"

Charlie waited to see what would be said next but Ann intervened. "Please, Robert, Andrew, this is not the time or place for a political argument."

"Of course, Ann. I apologise." Andrew answered.

Robert spoke through gritted teeth. "Ann, I will speak as I like in my own home."

He glowered at Andrew and Charlie wondered where this would end. James tried to diffuse the situation, feeling somewhat guilty at having started it. "Did you hear that the SS St Paul has become the first ocean liner in the world to use wireless telegraphy when she arrived at England's coast? It's in all the newspapers and hailed as a great invention."

"I did read that, James," Rose replied. I would like to travel on an ocean liner one day."

"Perhaps you and Andrew will emigrate, Rose," added Robert.

Rose looked hurt and Andrew sat forward speaking in a low, steady voice, "As much as you'd like that, Robert, it will not happen."

Charlie moved to sit by his father and Robert turned on an easier target. "What say you, Gordon, would you like to travel on a ship or do ye have too weak a constitution?"

Gordon looked his father square in the face. "I would gladly travel, Father, but there is too much work to be done here."

Charlie felt his anger rise as he listened to his grandfather. Someone had to put him in his place.

"I have joined the Stop the War Committee. William Thomas Stead is doing a good job persuading people to stand up against the Boer War and Keir Hardie is a prominent member. Will you be joining us, Grandfather?"

The barb struck. "And be a pacifist who is too cowardly to fight? I do not think so. Mark my words, lad, you will not survive politics as a pacifist and feminist lover. Ye may have survived thus far but ye will fail and where will Alice be then with a husband who is a laughing stock?"

"And where will you be, Grandfather, if economics, like nature, to quote Herbert Spencer, is 'the survival of the fittest'?"

Andrew laughed. He looked at Robert. "Ye are right lad. The world is changing and only some of us will survive."

An awkward silence descended to be filled with the chattering of the women concerning general society functions and the men poured themselves another whisky as Charlie smiled in the knowledge that his grandfather was beginning to lose his title as the formidable patriarch.

*

Ann was delighted when yet another invitation was received inviting her to afternoon tea. There had been a flurry of both callers and invitations from female friends and acquaintances and Ann found herself ensconced in the bosom of friendship akin to her young married years when she had felt herself at the heart of polite society.

As she read her latest correspondence over breakfast Robert appeared. "Good morning, Robert. Did you sleep well?"

"No I did not." he barked. "There was a banging noise that kept me awake. Goodness knows what was going on outside."

"I didn't hear anything."

Robert harrumphed and poured himself some tea. "This tea is cold. Harriet! Harriet!" he bellowed.

"For goodness sake, Robert, must you shout. The tea is cold because you are late down for breakfast."

Harriet appeared. "Yes, sir, sorry sir."

"Fetch more tea. This is cold."

"Of course, sir."

Ann rose from the table. "I will leave you to your breakfast. I have been invited to call in on Mrs Smith this morning."

"Ye have been out every morning this week and most afternoons." His tone was petulant with a hint of anger.

"Yes, I have been very busy and to be honest it has given me a new lease of life. I am old now, Robert, as you yourself have pointed out on numerous occasions, but recently I have been going out and about more and I am enjoying life..."

Something slid across Robert's eyes that made Ann stop. His voice was low but he spat his words, "Enjoying life? And just how exactly is *my wife* enjoying life?"

Ann stiffened. "Whatever do you mean?"

Robert's eyes flitted down her body and up again, from the dainty feet and slim waist to her face, deeply lined with wrinkles and hair, long since grey. He shook his head and laughed. "Nothing, my dear. You may leave now. Give my regards to Mrs smith."

Ann left feeling perturbed as her husband's laughter echoed in her ears as she walked along the hall.

On hearing the front door close Robert ate his breakfast alone with his thoughts. *My own invitations have been slim of late and have I sensed an atmosphere in the club recently? I can't quite put my finger on it but I feel shunned, although the gentlemen converse with me, the usual geniality is missing. Men who would normally stop to speak now walk by or conversation is cut short and they hurry off.*

The eggs and bacon on his plate began to congeal as his thoughts dragged his attention away.

I have done as Andrew required and the family are as congenial as ever. Surely that is done with now. Am I seeing things that do not exist or am I being naive? He shook his head. *I have never been naive.* He took a bite of cold bacon.

But Andrew has power. I have always known that.

Only half finishing his breakfast Robert decided to take himself out. Perhaps a walk would refresh him. On passing the hall mirror he paused for a second taking in the jaw line that now sagged a little and the wrinkles etched on his face. There had been no further liaisons with Elizabeth. No notes or messages or explanations. Thinking of Ann, laughter no longer rose up in him.

The man looking into the mirror felt young, fearless and virile: his reflection said otherwise.

Nymphs

Gordon and Mabel strolled around the art gallery pausing at each painting in turn. "It's funny how folk become more popular after they die. I always think it's such a shame that they are not appreciated whilst still alive and die believing that they are not very good at what they do."

"I think I may have something in common with artists, Mabel. Father was in the mill yesterday in a foul mood. Perhaps if I die before him he will appreciate the work I have done."

"Oh, Gordon, don't talk like that. Ye will live a long life and yer father is just a tyrant of a man."

"He is. But I have known no other." The couple continued on, nodding to acquaintances and making a point of praising the paintings of those still alive. They crossed to the second picture gallery and found no other than Robert Ross himself standing still as a statue in front of a painting of naked nymphs. Mabel sighed and turned to leave but Robert saw movement out the corner of his eye and looked over spotting them. "Gordon. Come and be educated," he beckoned.

Gordon took an in breath and walked towards his father with Mabel at his side. "Afternoon, Father."

Robert did not return the greeting. "Look at the light here." He pointed to the left of the painting where two women were emerging from the shadow. "See how it contrasts with the light here on the right which accentuates the milkiness of the skin. And see this nymph's expression as she leans over towards another nymph. Where are your eyes drawn, Gordon? Do you see the light or their nakedness or their expressions?" His words were serious and Gordon was unsure how to respond. He hesitated which of course always infuriated his father. "Gordon. Have you no appreciation of art? Ye have a wife so I am assuming ye have seen the female form naked?"

Mabel gasped and Gordon snapped. "For goodness sake, Father, ye cannot say such things. Apologise to Mabel."

"Apologise for what?" He looked at his daughter in law. "This is art. I am appreciating the work and the female form."

"I am going to look at the landscapes in the other room," Mabel replied and walked away.

"I don't imagine yer mistress is quite so timid."

"My God, Father." Gordon turned and followed his wife out of the room.

Robert shook his head and continued on to the next painting, taking in the light and the colours of the landscape and losing himself in the blueness of the sea. Mabel glanced back and noted how intently her father in law studied the work of art in front of him. "I had no idea that yer father enjoyed art."

"His study is full of paintings. No one is allowed in there without him being present, probably not even Mother. I saw them once as a lad but of course I was thrown out and told never to go in again. They were all paintings of nymphs bar a couple of landscapes behind his desk."

Mabel did not reply but something niggled at the back of her mind.

*

MABEL HAD MADE an appointment with their family solicitor having come to the conclusion that he would keep their conversation confidential. Several times she had opened her mouth to tell Gordon of the plight of the women in Seabank and immediately closed it again. She could not find the words, and berated herself for it, but something in her told her that it was the wrong thing to do.

She alighted her carriage on Union Street and entered the door to Hall and Woodburn solicitors where she was shown upstairs and into Mr Hall's office.

"Good morning, Mrs Ross. Please take a seat."

Mabel sat down. She had given herself a stern talking to before arriving in order to be calm and confident in her dealings with Mr Hall. She did not want to fail in her mission.

"Good morning. I will come straight to the point. I need to find out who owns a certain property in Aberdeen."

"I see. Are you hoping to buy the property?"

Mabel hesitated as she was unsure if answering 'no' would hinder things. "Possibly, Mr Hall. Our son is looking for an apartment and I said I would make enquiries as he is so busy. If you could give me some information regarding it I would be very grateful. It is an apartment on Belmont Street above the dressmakers."

"I do remember helping with the sale of that shop a few years ago now. Let me have my secretary bring me the papers." Mr Hall rose and left the room.

Mabel looked around the large office with its mahogany desk and panelled walls. The window looked out onto the bustle of Union Street below and she could hear the hooves of horses and the trundle of wheels as carriages and carts were pulled and steered over cobbles to their destinations. The occasional raised voice could be heard over the rumbling din and Mabel wondered at who was there and where they were going. As a child she had enjoyed sitting at her window and watching the street and that same curiosity had never left her. Not being a social butterfly she was one of life's observers and folk fascinated her. She liked to think that that made her a good judge of character as she sometimes saw what others missed.

Mr Hall returned and sat down somewhat excitedly, "Well, Mrs Ross, on looking at the papers I also found the ones pertaining to the apartment above the shop. I was involved with the selling of the shop to its current owner but also with the buying of the apartment for a client of mine some fifteen years ago." He hesitated and took off his glasses.

Mabel leaned forward, "Yes, Mr Hall. So can ye tell me the name of the person who owns it?"

Mr Hall hesitated again. "Have you asked anyone in your family about the apartment in case they can inform you of the owner?"

Mabel shook her head. "No, I have not."

"I am sorry but I am unable to tell you who owns it as I suspect he would not wish me to." He rose from his seat and Mabel realised that the meeting was now over.

She found herself outside and a growing sense of vexation and unease mingled within her mind. Climbing back into her carriage she directed the driver to the dressmakers on Belmont Street.

The shop was busy which suited Mabel. She needed time to think so she sat down and waited as her mind whispered particles of information that she could not yet grasp. Seeing some paper and a pen on the side of the counter, Mabel took them and began to write a short note as an idea formed in her mind.

Dear Sir,

I am interested in being photographed by you. Please meet me tomorrow at ten past two in the Art Gallery by Henry Fantin-Latour's painting of roses in a vase.

Sincerely Miss Constance Smith.

Satisfied at what she had written she excused herself saying that she would return and walked out through the door and back onto the street.

She found a messenger boy on the corner and handed him the note and a coin. Mabel watched discreetly as he posted the note and then returned to her carriage.

*

At two o'clock the following afternoon Mabel arrived at the Art Gallery. She had arranged to meet a friend there but not until half past two. The gallery was busy and she wandered around pretending to look at the art in the room whilst observing each gentleman she saw. Jean and Francis had described him as a tall, handsome man around the age of sixty or seventy and clean shaven, which could well be the majority of the gentlemen present. They had said he had a love of art so she hoped that by suggesting a meeting here he would be happy to oblige. Mabel ascended the stairs to the second floor where the Fantin-Latour painting hung in the gallery to the left of the staircase. She made her way to the other gallery on the right and hovered by the door where she could see folk coming and going in the gallery opposite. Most people were in pairs so she made a point of watching for gentlemen walking in alone.

Her timepiece which was pinned to her bodice showed the time as seven minutes past two. Her plan was to ask the gentleman for some assistance, feigning faintness, and in the aftermath of his help she would enquire upon his name and then leave. Surely he would be expecting someone much younger and not of her class so would not suspect her in any way.

A small group of young gentlemen appeared together with their tutor and Mabel had to move from her position to let them pass. Glancing back across the hallway she saw the back of a gentleman go into the other gallery. Mabel slowly walked across the floor and she could see two men and a woman standing by the rose painting, their backs to her. She positioned herself near the corner along from the door and waited. The woman turned alongside one of the gentlemen and both looked to be around thirty in years. The other gentleman remained standing in front of the painting and did not move. He was tall in stature but she had no clue as to his age. He carried no walking stick but an overcoat hung over his left arm.

She observed him as he took out his pocket watch and checked the time. He made no sign of moving and stood as motionless as the statues in the lower ground floor. *'Surely this must be him,'* she thought. *'It is not the most interesting of paintings to stand there for so long.'* Mabel walked slightly further down the left hand wall to see if she could catch a glimpse of his face but as she neared he turned to his right and looked at the painting of the nymphs about which her father in law had been rude to her. Mabel again moved slowly down the room. The group of young scholars entered with their tutor who was educating his pupils on various painting techniques. He sent them on a task to look around and make notes as they went. The tutor approached the gentleman still standing by the painting of the nymphs and said something which Mabel could not hear but caused both men to laugh.

Mabel recognised one of the laughs.

She knew before he turned that it was her father in law

who was standing with the tutor. *'Damn. Where is the other gentleman?'* She glanced at her timepiece and it showed twenty past the hour. Ten minutes late. *'Is he not coming?'* Mabel walked back up to the other end of the room. Robert had not seen her and she would wait a while yet. Her friend was not arriving till half past so she had time.

Over the course of the next ten minutes four people stopped to admire the painting of the roses but none were older gentlemen and no one appeared to be waiting for anyone. Robert hovered between paintings but remained in the far corner close to the nymphs and the roses. Mabel knew she would have to go down and meet her friend but good manners forced her to acknowledge her father in law's presence so she walked over to him. "Good afternoon."

Robert turned. "No it is not a good afternoon, Mabel. Some folk have no idea how to keep an appointment and like to waste my time." He brushed past his daughter in law who clutched her hand to her stomach, and stood motionless as his words thrust into her mind and the realisation of their meaning drew her breath from her.

GAMES

THE END OF 1899 drew near. Some folk lamented the passage of time and others embraced its fast pace. The Trades Hall on Belmont Street was predominantly used for meetings by the Labour movement and Charlie spent a lot of time there listening to plans, debates and speeches by older members of the party. With the end of the year nigh surely the new century would bring better lives for the poor. There was to be a Labour conference held in London at the end of February 1900 and all were busy forming plans in preparation for it. Conversations were full of excitement and expectation as Charlie sat amongst them.

"This is an opportunity to bring the Labour movement together and see a cohesive union with which to succeed in parliament."

"Done right, we will succeed in doing just that, Mr Forbes. We have been on the sidelines for too long."

"Aye," replied Mr MacDonald. "The anticipation I feel is akin to waiting for my favourite dish to be served. I can almost taste the victory."

"I'm sure our Robin Hood here would rather compare it to the anticipation of his wedding night."

Laughter erupted from the group before the men settled and continued in earnest with their plans.

*

The final lavish dinner on polite society's calendar before Hogmanay was hosted just before Christmas. The guests had gathered in the drawing room and the host called out the names of which gentleman was to escort each lady into dinner. Robert's name was called followed by the title Lady Muir. He glanced towards her and felt a mixture of both anger and excitement. It had been seven weeks since their last assignation in her aunt's home and Robert was none the wiser as to why.

He left Ann, who was to be escorted by a Mr Adamson, and walked towards Elizabeth who turned and greeted him. "Good evening, Mr Ross."

Robert bowed his head. "Lady Muir. So lovely to see you. Shall we go in?" and he offered her his arm.

"It will be my pleasure," and they walked together towards the dining room. Robert immediately relaxed believing that Elizabeth was on good terms with him and that she would find a discreet way to explain the lack of contact. Within a few minutes all were seated and Robert found himself near the end of the table opposite Sir Muir. Ann was at the other end. Conversation flowed up and down like the fiddler's bow and, like a reel, the atmosphere was buoyant. The gentlemen served their female partners, spooning delectable morsels onto plates as the ladies talked of social activities. Being December the hunting season was in full swing and although most women did not take part it was popular in the upper classes for women to enjoy such sports. Queen Victoria was often involved in hunting when she stayed at Balmoral.

After half an hour Robert grew impatient as his need for answers rose, " Have you and Sir Muir been away recently?"

Elizabeth smiled, "No, Mr Ross. We have been at home since September."

Robert continued, "And is your aunt quite well?"

Elizabeth smiled again, "She is fine, thank you. I visit her every week."

Robert was unsure what to say next as he digested this information.

Elizabeth asked a question of her own, "Have you been enjoying the hunting and shooting season, Mr Ross?

"I have been on a few grouse shoots which were enjoyable and I have another on Saturday."

"Does your wife shoot?"

"Goodness me no. Guns were not intended for women!"

"Is that right? I am rather a good shot. Isn't that right Sir Muir?

"What's that, dear?" her husband leaned towards her.

"I was just saying to Mr Ross that I enjoy hunting and am good at it."

"You are indeed. Careful, Mr Ross, she likes to shoot beasts." Sir Muir laughed at his own joke and Robert was unsure how to respond.

Elizabeth leaned in to Robert and lowered her voice, "I especially like to shoot beasts who are cruel to their young."

The penny dropped for Robert. *I am being punished. But for how long, I wonder?*

He looked at Elizabeth who had been his mistress for several years. He had missed her over the last few weeks. Life was off kilter and he wanted it on an even keel again. He was surprised that Sir Muir had told her of the beating. Perhaps they were closer than he had believed. Conscious of those around him he continued the conversation, "The hunting season for the stag is past now though."

Elizabeth leaned in again, "So is the rutting season."

Robert took a long drink from his glass, finishing his whisky. He motioned to the servant for another as light hearted conversation continued all around him and the sound of laughter mocked him.

*

It just so happened that the last day of the century landed on a Sunday so Ann had decided that she would host a lavish dinner party for her family and closest friends so they could toast the new year, and indeed century, together. She had the printers design invitations with gold lettering and embossed with the Ross crest - a hand holding a garland of laurel representing success and victory.

For days the food had been carefully prepared with deliveries of meat, game, fish and vegetables arriving alongside ingredients for puddings. Various cheeses were also purchased and the finest wine, port, brandy and whisky awaited the palettes of the guests. Ann had instructed her staff to clean the silverware and her best china and a new linen tablecloth had been bought for the occasion. The table was set and Ann entered the dining room to check that all was perfect before going upstairs to change into her evening gown.

The long, dark, oak table was covered with a crisp, white, linen cloth and decorated with a lavish centrepiece of green foliage and winter flowers. Candles held in silver candelabra were placed precisely on the table and lay in wait of being lit and the heavy, long stemmed, small bowl wine glasses stood elegantly to the right of each place setting. Ann clasped her hands together and smiled. It was perfect.

Mabel had taken time to digest the fact that Robert was the photographer on Belmont Street. Her mind had gone back and forth between acceptance and denial of the facts. He fitted the description, the solicitor had been unforthcoming with a name and hinted at asking her family and Robert had been the only gentleman to appear at the art gallery and state his anger at a missed appointment. *But my husband! How can I possibly tell him of his father's behaviour? I have always disliked Robert's treatment of Gordon but now I loathe the man and he is certainly no gentleman! The scandal it would cause if it were to be known. And poor Ann. How would she bear to know of her husband's photographs?* Mabel's thoughts jolted from one side of her brain to the other. *And I still do not know how to retrieve the photographs of Jean and Francis.*

Mabel closed her eyes and tried to calm her mind. A week had passed and she had to find a way to deal with what she had discovered. She pushed her thoughts away as she readied herself for the Hogmanay gathering at Redwood Manor. How she would tolerate being in Robert's company she had no idea. She just prayed that she would not have to speak to him very much at all.

Mabel had the advantage of always being quiet at family gatherings so as no one expected much of her so she could observe proceedings at her leisure. The only one to notice her scrutiny that evening was Charlie as he himself was doing the exact same thing. He had met Agnes, his grandmother's friend, once or twice and he disliked her. Although it was an informal, intimate gathering of family and close friends, Agnes, to Charlie's mind, acted as if she were the hostess. There was just something about her manner that he did not quite understand. Had he been able to read Mabel's mind he would have noticed the same thought.

Robert had been the perfect host on arrival and as charming as he could be. He had complimented his daughter and daughters in law on their dresses and had warmly welcomed his guests. John Fraser had been a business acquaintance of Robert's and he and his wife Eliza had been friends with him and Ann since their children were little. Mabel had not been present when Agnes and the Frasers arrived but as they all gathered in the drawing room for pre-dinner drinks the atmosphere was buoyant and light, holding within it the potential of an enjoyable evening.

Charlie moved from person to person, being entertained by the conversation. Alice was dining with her own family but arrangements were in place for the younger family members of households to meet at the concert hall later where the Hogmany party would continue into the wee hours. There would be chaperones of course but they would either be young and wish to enjoy themselves or old and would fall asleep. Either way, young lovers would have some freedom and time to enjoy themselves.

The family and friends of Ann and Robert were escorted to the dining room and on approaching the table looked for their names on the place cards. The cards had been printed in the same design as the invitations with gold lettering and the Ross crest embossed at the top above each name. Ann and Robert sat at each end of the table and their guests between them with their partners for the evening. Charlie positioned himself beside his grandmother and Agnes sat down by Robert who had Mabel on his other side. Robert was irked that Victoria was not present, her being the one person in his family that he liked the most, but she was married now so he had no say in where she should be. Ann was irked as James and Edith's daughter, Eleanor, had not felt well enough to attend, a slight cold her mother had said, so the table was off kilter with no female now seated between James and John.

Mabel was not pleased to be sitting beside her father in law so intended to keep conversation with him to a minimum and give her attention to her youngest son, Joseph, the only one of her bairns in attendance as he was not married.

The first course was served and the meal began in earnest. The candlelight flickered and reflected off the silverware and glasses and the low, ambient light accentuated and softened the faces of those in their autumn and winter years. Champagne was sipped delicately by the ladies and Rose, who no longer overindulged, savoured each bubble that fizzed on her tongue and every morsel of delicious food. She looked across at Andrew who raised his glass to her and smiled.

Mabel and Charlie, unbeknownst to the other, subconsciously sniffed the air, as a connoisseur would wine.

Both noted overtones of gentle tenderness imbued with warm affection.

Both noted an undertone of precariousness with a frisson of danger.

A{NN SOAKED IN} the atmosphere and congratulated herself on the appearance of the room and the delectable food and wine. As her eyes flitted around the table she observed the attractiveness of her guests, dressed in all their finery, and although her children had at times been of disappointment to her they were at least very handsome and beautiful.

Ann looked across to Agnes whom she had deliberately placed next to Robert. *You are ageing well,* Ann thought. *Your auburn hair contains little grey, unlike my own, and your skin has defied the ravages of age but your dress is like that of a younger woman: too low in cut for a mature woman.* She had pondered on Agnes's revelations regarding having had lovers over the years and although a part of her had been shocked another part had envied her. *I always thought of Robert as being a good husband but I have nothing to compare him to. I do not know whether I have regrets in my life or not. Surely I should know whether I have been happy or otherwise.*

Ann's eyes moved to Eliza, *You on the other hand, have the skin of a prune which ages you beyond your years. Your kind eyes soften your appearance but I am glad that I have aged better although I feel unkind in admitting it. I wonder if you have been happily married.*

Agnes's voice rose above the general chattering of the table. "Ye are quiet, Ann. What is that mind of yours pondering?"

Ann was wrong footed. It was not the place of a guest to hold court the conversation and certainly not to ask so personal a question. She faltered as Agnes laughed. "Goodness, Ann, I mean no offence. Ye just looked so deep in thought."

Ann recovered herself. "I am pondering, as you put it, on how wonderful everyone looks this evening in all their finery." *And here you are playing the part of the lady of the house. I can see now how you have always envied me.*

Agnes smiled. "We are indeed a handsome gathering. We should have a toast to our splendour and its trappings."

Mabel was outraged, *Agnes is acting as if she were the hostess. And what on earth does she mean by trappings? To be so forward is unseemly!*

Robert laughed and raised his glass. "I quite agree. Here's to splendour and its trappings."

Edith laughed, as did her husband, whereas the others were a little reticent in their rejoicing. All glasses were raised and the toast made but there had been a shift in the atmosphere and the frisson of danger that had earlier alerted Mabel to its presence vibrated softly in the air. Charlie could not decipher the look in his grandmother's eyes.

John took the room back to normality by turning to Ann. "Can I offer you some more vegetables, Ann?"

"No thank you. I have quite enough." She was perturbed and decided to put the conversation on a surer footing. "What are your thoughts on the coming century, John?"

"I admit to feeling a tad auld," he bellowed, being deaf

in one ear and afflicted with an arthritic knee.

"Never cow tow to age, John. That is what will age ye," replied Robert.

John chortled, "It's easy for you to say when you sit there no rounder than ye were in yer twenties and able to play a day's golf."

"Joseph, you are the youngest here, what are your thoughts on the coming century?" Ann asked her grandson.

Joseph thought before answering, his timid nature like that of Mabel's. "I am excited to be working under Father in helping to expand the mill and I feel that our efforts to improve working conditions and wages are placing us at the forefront of progress."

Charlie was delighted to hear such words from his cousin.

"I will drink to that, Joseph."

"And I to you, cousin. Ye have shown us how best to better the lives of those less fortunate."

Several glasses were raised and Andrew made a toast, "To progress."

Robert drank heavily from his glass but did not utter a word. Andrew, in a playful mood, continued the conversation. "I too am excited for the next century. I have decided to offer a scholarship to a young working class lad for him to study law. I have been in touch with the master of a school in a poorer area of town and he has introduced me to a loon who shows great aptitude for learning."

Gordon smiled. "That is very generous, Andrew, and I am sure the lad will do ye proud."

"Alice has mentioned something similar to me. I am doing well and obviously any future children of ours will be highly educated but we hope to contribute to the education of someone from the lower class - perhaps a female." He lifted his place name with the Ross crest embossed upon it. " Look around ye, Grandfather. It is indeed a clan of success and victory."

Ann sensed that Robert may well explode so moved the conversation on. Mabel observing Robert's disapproval found some gumption of her own and leaned in to her father in law. "I myself will be employing a young girl from Seabank as a maid in my home."

Robert felt his anger and bitterness rise so much so he could almost taste the bile in his mouth. This was *his* table in *his* house that he had worked hard for and he was being made a fool of. His thoughts pummelled his brain, *Why can't folk see that the poor make a choice. If they have no work - they are lazy. I gave them jobs and look how I was repaid - with insubordination! They want money for doing nothing.* He looked at Andrew, his eyes burrowing into his face. *My family had respect for me until you brought that idiot into our lives. Charlie made you blind and you defied your own class. Charlie was born into his father's class and had no right to be a gentleman. His father was a coward and his mother an idiot.* Robert took a long, slow breath and allowed his heart to right itself. *I will not allow this to continue. There will be no political career and no marriage to Alice. I will see to it, if it's the last thing I do, and Andrew be damned!*

He raised his glass. "A toast, dear family and friends. To a better future."

FOLLOWING DINNER, THE party again gathered in the drawing room to raise a glass to the year 1900 as the clock struck midnight. Agnes stood by Robert and lowered her voice. "Time has flown away from us." Her tone was wistful which was not lost on Robert.

"Aye." His reply was short but not curt and the word was soft to Agnes's ear.

"Will ye visit tomorrow?" she asked.

"I will."

DISCOVERY

THE YEAR 1900 arrived with much jubilation and Charlie celebrated the establishment of *The Scottish Workers' Parliamentary Election Committee* that January, through which the election of working class representatives to the House of Commons who could act independently of the existing political parties, was made possible. This was a milestone in Labour's advancement.

Wedding preparations were in full swing and Charlie was delighted with how happy Alice appeared. The majority of the Ross clan were looking forward to a family wedding although no one would have dared say so in front of Robert who was forever coorse mannered, at least in private.

The new century had the effect of raising expectations but some wondered if it could indeed deliver on its promise of change and betterment. The women in Seabank looked for forgiveness and charity, although some required the taking back of their dignity, either stolen or paid for.

Mabel, all too aware of her own promise, sat with Gordon at breakfast and the couple talked of what they hoped the new century would bring. "I am hoping to be a grandmother again. Victoria has hinted at such a happening so perhaps we can expect an announcement soon."

"That would be good news. Ruth's young loons are growing fast so to have another young child amongst us would be something to celebrate indeed."

"Are you happy with Joseph at the mill, Gordon?"

"Aye. The mill is prosperous and Joseph has a good understanding of how business works. Andrew has been drawing up some papers for me concerning some new contracts abroad."

"He has been a great asset to ye has he not over the years, both as a friend and a business associate?"

"He has, Mabel. In business he has a way of dealing with Father when he is pig headed and ignorant which I would like to emulate. I have always wondered at their relationship. It intrigues me but I have never quite managed to work it out. As for friendship - I would trust him with my life."

Mabel's thoughts began to knit together much like the cloth on the loom and when Gordon left for the mill she sent a message to Andrew requesting a meeting which was answered immediately and at eleven o'clock Mabel found herself entering the solicitor's office.

Andrew greeted Mabel with genuine warmth and invited her to sit as he requested some tea to be brought in.

"I am intrigued as to why ye wish to see me, Mabel. I hope that ye have not had a bad service from your usual solicitor?"

"Not at all, Andrew. I…I wish to speak with you regarding a delicate matter and I have come to the conclusion that you may well be the person to help me."

"I will try my best, Mabel. Ye can be sure o' that."

Mabel took a long breath. "Gordon trusts you completely." She looked straight at Andrew, "He doesn't know that I have come here today and I must stress that he must never find out what I am about to tell you."

Andrew nodded.

"First, I need to ask ye some questions. Would ye do

anything to prevent a scandal within our family even if that meant…upsetting Robert?"

Andrew raised his eyebrows. "I would, Mabel. In fact, upsetting Robert would be rather enjoyable."

Mabel felt a shimmer of relief. "Would ye help to take something from him that is causing distress for others?"

Andrew cocked his head. "That is an intriguing question, Mabel. I would gladly help those in distress but does this involve breaking the law?"

Mabel could not discern his expression and she closed her eyes. "It likely does, Andrew. It would be stealing." She rose from her chair and turned towards the door, "I am sorry I should not have come. I realise now that I can't possibly ask ye to help me."

Andrew rose and walked around his desk. "Mabel. Please don't leave. Come and sit down and tell me exactly what ye need me to do. I know what kind of man Robert is and if I can stop him from hurting others I will do it."

Mabel bit her bottom lip. "But ye are a solicitor. A man of the law."

Andrew placed his hands on Mabel's arms. "Let *me* decide what I am willing to do."

Mabel nodded and returned to her chair. She took a sip of her tea, giving herself a minute to sort her thoughts before proceeding. Her words were slow but concise. "I have found out that Robert has an apartment on Belmont Street, above the dressmakers, that he uses for…illicit purposes. There are…items in there which I must retrieve on someone's behalf. Please do not ask me what those items are…I could not possibly say it aloud. I need someone to enter the premises and retrieve them."

Andrew took a moment. "I can see that this is distasteful but how can I retrieve something if I don't know what it is?"

She looked at Andrew and could see that more was needed to be said. Mabel rose again and took herself to the window so her back was to him. "I visit Seabank every Thursday to offer what help I can to the women there." Andrew remained silent. "Two of the women told me of a man who has something pertaining to them that they wish back. I only found out recently that the man in question is Robert and it came as quite a shock." Mabel stopped. "Ye need to… find photographs of them… of a certain ilk. They were taken last year in the apartment." Mabel leaned her hands on the sil to steady herself as she waited for Andrew to speak.

Andrew did not move. "I understand, Mabel. It will be done. I will let you know when I have them."

Mabel straightened her back but did not turn. "Gordon must not know of his father's behaviour. It would destroy him."

"Of course. Ye have my word."

Mabel turned and made her way to the door. "Thank you," she uttered as she left.

*

The invitation had been sent, as requested, and accepted. Edith's father, George Grant, was of the same ilk as Robert in terms of character, but of higher status, so it massaged Robert's sense of self importance to be invited to a dinner hosted by the Grants where those in higher circles moved.

It had pleased Robert that his son had married well but although he enjoyed the association, Robert was aware that he was not quite one of *them*. He knew how to socialise and how to charm, as did Ann, but for Robert it was an act. He played the part as if in a play: knowing what to say and how and when to say it but never being included in the after party. He had spent his life striving to reach the top in business and class but of course, good breeding and respectability being the entry requirements, Robert only possessed the latter.

Ann possessed both which was one of the reasons he had married her.

Had her parents been alive at the time he wouldn't have stood a chance, being of a lower class and with his business only in its infancy, but he had wooed Ann and gained a nubile, naive, young, upper class woman with a large inheritance.

His children had all married well and as a result his grandchildren were afforded the label of good breeding stock.

A fact that stuck in his throat like dry bread.

George Grant, to Robert's mind, had the mind of a woman. He enjoyed gossip and spread it as if buttering his toast with the creamiest butter. Many a soul had suffered as a result of his loose tongue. He took particular pleasure in the demise of a woman's reputation but tonight, following the gentlemen separating from the ladies after dinner, the butter melted on the knife in relation to a Mr Yule. There had been talk of an upset in the Yule household: some marital disharmony but no one was quite sure who was to blame. Mr Yule, a prominent young merchant, was currently residing in his mother's home.

"Some gentlemen do not deserve the title of a husband," Mr Grant declared. "What respectable man would allow his wife to be the one who remains in the marital home? I do not care of the circumstances, a man should be able to rule his wife and have the ability to satisfy her. I have had enough mistresses to know that women enjoy the pleasures of the flesh almost as much as men, so clearly he is weak in his masterings of husbandry."

Much laughter ensued that comment but several men looked from the corners of their eyes at each other, sympathising with the ridiculing of Mr Yule and breathing a sigh of relief that it did not concern themselves. Some even held the thought, *I must do better.*

Robert sat in his study on returning home from what had, in the majority, been a tedious evening. It had felt a rushly planned affair so soon after Hogmanay. He looked at the paintings of the nymphs on the opposite wall. Often his best ideas came to him whilst observing art. His mind went into another realm where light, shadow, colour and contour both calmed and intoxicated and allowed a feeling of anticipation to course through him. Observing the curves of the nymphs he took a sip of his single malt whisky and it too had the effect of calming and intoxicating. It too caused a fire in his belly.

He lingered on Mr Grant's comments pertaining to Mr Yule. His thoughts swirled, like his whisky, and slowly a plan began to form itself in the coils of his conniving mind.

*

The dark nights and inhospitable weather of January aided Andrew's quest. The dressmakers had shut up shop and a quick look around the back ensured that no seamstresses still laboured in the back room. The street lamps offered what light they could onto the narrow, cobbled street but with the blinds and drapes drawn in the surrounding houses and apartments no prying eyes were visible.

Andrew checked his pocket watch and cursed. It was quarter past the hour and the blacksmith was supposed to have been there at nine. His carriage had been pulled into Gaelic Lane by the church, between Belmont Street and

Back Wynd, discreetly out of the way but Andrew was becoming impatient. Presently a horse and cart arrived and slowed to a stop behind Andrew's carriage.

"You're late."

"Sorry, sir. My horse was lame and I had tae see tae her shoe afore I could leave."

"Right, follow me," he snapped and proceeded back along the lane and onto Belmont Street carrying a small lamp. He paused to look down Patagonia Court where sometimes reprobates lingered but it was empty so he continued on. It was fortunate that the apartment was opposite the church which afforded the perfect cover. Andrew stopped at the green door next to the dressmakers.

"This door first."

The blacksmith nodded and proceeded to try various skeleton keys into the lock, achieving success on the fourth one. He turned the handle and pushed open the door which emitted a low groan. The blacksmith stood back and let Andrew enter before him and the two men walked through the door closing it behind them. Andrew lit the lamp in his hand and as it flickered into life they found themselves in a narrow hall with a stone staircase in front of them. No other doors led off the hall and the two men mounted the stairs.

"May I have the lamp, sir?" asked the blacksmith.

Andrew handed it to him and the man peered at the door lock. "Aye, aye." He pulled a screwdriver from his bag and set about unscrewing four screws. "Nae much work in that one," he declared as he held the lock in his hand and pushed open the door with his other.

"Wait here, Please, Mr Clark."

Andrew took the lamp and walked into the room. It was not what he had been expecting.

The room was of medium size and elegantly decorated with floral cream and green wallpaper with hints of gold and pink. A green chaise lounge was positioned at an angle to a small lady's chair and a leather chesterfield in a deep mahogany brown stood proudly opposite. A large rug languished beneath the legs of all the seats and on the wall behind the lady's chairs a beautiful cast iron fireplace nestled on its hearth.

It had the pretence of a parlour belonging to the elite. The camera on the stand in the middle of the room was the only hint at something other than what it looked like. There was a small desk in the far corner by the window where a hand held 'detective' camera lay. A lamp and inkwell were the only other items on the desk but as Andrew approached he saw three small drawers sitting snuggly underneath. Expecting them to be locked he was surprised when the top one slid open in his hand revealing some paper and a pen and some more ink. The second drawer revealed a pile of envelopes but the third was empty.

Leaving the desk he ventured to the other side of the room where a door stood and turned the handle. Locked.

"Mr Clark. Your assistance please."

The blacksmith entered the room and walked towards the other door. He had no idea whose apartment they were in but it was not his place to ask and Mr Milne was paying him handsomely. Taking out his bundle of skeleton keys he set to work once more, finding success with the second one that he tried. The door opened with no noise and Andrew walked through taking the lamp with him. He was faced with a long bench on which lay various camera and developing equipment and on the opposite wall hung five long shelves. The upper three shelves held small narrow boxes with lids. Each one had a number and date on the end and two metal handles either end of the long box. Andrew took one of the boxes from its home and opened the hinged lid where inside lay a long row of fifty glass plate negatives. Carefully removing one of them he held it up to his lamp and saw the image imprinted on to it. He replaced the glass plate and proceeded to open the other boxes one by one and view sporadic negatives. All were of women in various poses and all were naked. A quick calculation and Andrew surmised that Robert owned over two thousand glass plate negatives. He turned his attention to the lower shelves. The second one from the bottom contained boxes of hundreds of photographs catalogued according to pose and four ledgers. Two of the ledgers contained the names and addresses of what Andrew supposed were customers with columns corresponding to number of photographs sold, type and cost. The other two contained a list of women's first names, dates and fee paid.

The bottom shelf held a continuous row of small, green, leather bound albums with metal clasps. Each one was highly decorated and embossed with the Ross crest with thick gold edged pages. Unclipping the small clasp on one of the albums revealed twenty pages each containing the photograph of either a single woman or two or more in a group. No names were written anywhere in the albums but there were dates. The earliest was dated 1885. Andrew cast his mind back and remembered the day that Ann had arranged her surprise and a photographer had arrived at Redwood Manor to take their photographs. Charlie had been five years old and they were the first photographs ever taken of him. Andrew also remembered Robert's fascination and endless questions directed at the photographer and was in all likelihood when the hobby first piqued his interest.

Conscious of Mabel's request, Andrew was unable to discern if any of the albums pertained to the women in Seabank or not. Having no knowledge of their appearance did not help matters. He had assumed that there would be some sort of studio but had not reckoned on the amount of photographs and negatives stored there. The ledgers appeared to hold names and dates so perhaps he could ascertain which photographs were the ones pertaining to the Seabank quines.

Andrew stood for a minute in deep thought. Various scenarios played out in his mind before he left the room and locked the door, having ensured that all was in its proper place and appeared undisturbed. "Mr Clark, I wish ye to make a copy of the keys needed here. I will pay ye well and I trust ye to be discreet."

"I will have them done in two days."

The men left and made their way back in silence to the lane by the church where they parted ways.

Threats

Charlie was delighted on hearing the words spoken by the chairman in the Trades Hall on Belmont Street.

"We have elected you to be one of the delegates at the conference in London."

"It will be an honour and I thank each and every one of you for putting yer faith in me. The 1900's will indeed be a time of change."

"When you marry Alice you will be seen as a man of responsibilities which will heighten yer regard and her suffrage work makes ye a powerful couple. Ye will go far in politics and we are glad of it."

The men continued in discussing Labour's goals and aspirations for the future and how that would be achieved in the new century. Anticipation pulled folk forward as the Moon did the Earth.

Charlie was somewhat concerned as to an invitation his grandfather had sent requesting a meeting and following the end of the discussion in the Trades Hall a Hansom cab was hailed and directed towards Redwood Manor.

Robert invited his grandson to sit. He closed the study door and proceeded to sit himself down behind his desk. A hand proceeded to open a small drawer under the desk and an envelope was removed. "I have here a statement drawn up by my solicitor which declares that you are having an affair with Mrs Gregory Yule. It will be used in court as evidence in the divorce case. Your name will be blackened, your political career will be over, due to the scandal, and Alice will no longer marry you." Robert leaned back in his chair, placed his hands behind his head.

The papers were removed from the envelope and Charlie saw that what was written there was indeed as Robert had indicated.

"Alice will not believe it."

Robert laughed. "It makes no difference. Her family will not allow the marriage to go ahead. If you read the second page it talks of your frequency in attending brothels and of a witness who is willing to testify to that. The oh so high and mighty Labour Movement would not approve of that. Oh, and for extra insurance, shall we say, there may be a rumour spread regarding Alice's virtue." Robert stood up and looked down at his grandson. His voice was low and full of venom. "There will be no marriage to Alice and no political career. Now get out."

The loon staggered from Redwood Manor and out into the dreich, cold Aberdeen street with one thought in his mind, *Alice*.

A second Hansom carriage of the evening was hailed by a dazed mind and Charlie sat inside with all thoughts on Alice. His grandfather had proved just how despicable he was but to ruin Alice's chance of happiness in the process was a cruel and unnecessary act. The driver had been instructed to go to Golden Square but as it trundled down Union Street a memory surfaced and the instruction changed. Winter darkness had descended on the streets of Aberdeen and a lack of light had the power to change its demeanour.

Charlie sat in his father's study as Andrew pondered the

information he had just received. "Nothing that man does surprises me but he will not have his way."

"But how is it possible to stop the papers being produced in court?"

"They are obviously fabricated and I know Robert's solicitor, so he will be dealt with." What he didn't say was, *That is the easy part. Robert is the loose cannon.* "I have heard rumours of the Yule situation but I will find out when the court session is to be held. Hopefully Robert is planning to just wait for it to happen which will buy us some time."

"It makes no sense to me. He was up in arms about how I was embarrassing him and the family by pursuing my line of politics and yet here he is about to expose me in an outrageous scandal which is surely a lot worse. And what of Alice, how can I stop him from ruining her?"

"He may well not be planning to carry out his threat regarding Alice. I think that may be a bluff but I will ensure that those papers are destroyed." Andrew's thoughts ran on, *Robert may well feel that he has nothing to lose and that makes him very dangerous.*

Charlie moved to the window as he took in his father's words.

"He hates me." The words were but a mere whisper.

"He hates what you represent. He hates that he came from a lower class and he does all he can to forget it. Your political leanings force him to remember."

"I saw him with a woman once. I was about twelve in age and I walked into his study and there they were half undressed with her lying over his desk. She tried to turn away but I saw her face. I called her a harlot. I didn't really know what it meant but there were stories of them at school and I knew that what I saw was wrong. Grandfather roared at me to get out and to wait outside by the front door. I wasn't going to wait, but I did, and when he appeared he flung me against the wall and said that he would kill me if

I ever breathed her name to anyone."

Andrew shook his head. "If that had been a recent event perhaps we could have used it against him but it was a long time ago and who knows who it might have been."

The loon turned. "Oh I know exactly who it was but ye are right, it holds no weight now."

"Are you going to tell me her name?"

"No. It serves no purpose. Now what am I to do?"

"Send word to your grandmother tomorrow that ye will be unable to visit on Sunday evening. That will keep Robert happy. Say nothing about this to anyone and I will let ye know when the papers have been dealt with."

He shook Andrew's hand. "Thank you. I look forward to hearing that this is all over."

"Aye, loon. I share that thought. Tell me, do you think your mail is still being tampered with?"

"No. Not since I was beaten."

"Good." Andrew took a long breath as his study door closed. His father in law could not be allowed to threaten anyone again.

Consequences

THE HORSE DRAWN delivery wagon pulled up outside the dressmakers shop just as it was closing for the day. Passers by were used to seeing all sorts of wagons delivering and picking up goods so no one on seeing one by the shop would have thought anything of it. The four closed sides of the wagon afforded both protection from the elements and privacy as to what lay inside. The driver had been directed to stop the wagon right by the door leading to Robert's apartment and to wait.

An hour before, another wagon had stopped in the same location and several trunks had been delivered to the apartment. Andrew and two trusted men were in the process of filling each one with the contents of the second room within the apartment. The men had been instructed not to open the boxes but to pack them carefully ensuring that no one but Andrew knew of the contents. When all five shelves were empty the trunks were carried down the stairs and deposited into the waiting wagon. The final things to be packed included the cameras, developing equipment and the ledgers leaving nothing but a bare room.

Andrew surveyed his work and wished he could be there to see Robert's face when he next visited the apartment. He relocked all the doors and left with the wagon which was instructed to deliver its cargo to an address on Rubislaw Terrace where it was unloaded swiftly and efficiently.

All was packed away in a locked room except for the ledgers which Andrew took up to the drawing room and studied carefully.

*

Robert arrived in Belmont Street and sauntered through the door to his apartment. As he climbed the stairs leaving the front door unlocked he congratulated himself on his latest acquisition. She would arrive shortly and he was eager to see her. He would stay late and develop the photographs straight away if she pleased him.

His key slid into the lock and turned and on entering the apartment Robert lit the lamps in the room. It was cold and his first task was always to light the fire to warm the room as shivering bodies did not bode well for preventing a blurry photograph but he stopped short as he surveyed his room. Everything was in its place except his camera. He turned towards his desk and his detective camera was also gone.

Robert's chest tightened and his head flinched back at the scene in front of him that made no sense. He removed his bunch of keys from his pocket and with some apprehension walked towards the locked door within the room. The key opened as it always had and Robert could see no signs of the door having been forced.

As he entered the room he raised the lamp in his hand and his eyes beheld a scene of desolation. He fell back leaning heavily on the door frame.

The doors to his world were being locked one by one.

*

Andrew had his driver take him to his club where he knew Robert's solicitor would be. A creature of habit, as most men were, he was to be found there every Thursday evening between the hours of ten and midnight. The club was busy and Mr Hall was lounging in a chesterfield chair with a large whisky in his hand talking rather loudly of his new acquisition that he had recently purchased thanks to a prosperous business deal. Andrew knew only too well where the money had come from.

Approaching the solicitor Andrew spoke jovially, "Ah, Mr Hall, just the man I am in need of. May I speak with you for a minute?"

"Why, of course, Mr Milne," he replied. He rose from his position and followed Andrew to the corner of the room.

Andrew let his smile fall as he leaned into Mr Hall. "I have in my possession proof of your association with pornographic photographs and your part in helping a certain person to buy the property in which they are produced. It wouldn't be hard to have a jury believe that you yourself are producing such material which as we both know is a criminal offence. You will destroy all fraudulent papers relating to a certain divorce case or I will personally report you to the police."

Mr Hall's face lost its colour and he swallowed hard before nodding.

"Good. So we understand one another. One more thing - you will tell Mr Ross that all is in hand so that he believes the court case will go as he wishes. Good night, Mr Hall." Andrew left the club and returned home. His work for now was done. Robert would be dealt with in the coming days.

*

ANN WAS AWOKEN by shouts of profanity and the breaking of glass. Clambering from her bed she hurriedly donned her dressing gown and took herself out of her bedchamber and onto the landing. Below her rose the bellowing voice of which she recognised as belonging to her husband accompanied by the quieter, calm voice of their butler. She descended the stairs with haste and entered the open door of the parlour to find a drunk Robert trying to pour himself a whisky whilst the butler was sweeping up the remnants of a bottle of brandy.

"What on Earth is going on, Robert?"

He swayed on his feet as he turned to his wife, the whisky in his hand spilling over the side of his glass which hung from his hand. Dark eyes stared at Ann as he spat, "They're gone. They're all gone."

Ann dismissed the butler and approached her husband. "What is gone?"

Robert lurched towards her and shrieked in her face, "They were mine."

Ann flinched and stepped back as Robert staggered to the fireside chair where he collapsed into it. He swigged the last of the whisky letting the glass fall. "I will find out who did this."

Ann stood motionless and on seeing Robert's eyes close she left the room and closed the door behind her.

*

THE FOLLOWING MORNING Andrew called upon Mabel knowing that Gordon would be at the mill. He was invited into the drawing room and tea was sent for as Andrew and Mabel sat either side of the hearth.

"I am sorry to have taken so long to contact you, Mabel.

The apartment was not as I expected it to be and I am unable to give you the items you require for the women in Seabank."

Mabel's face fell. "Oh, I am sorry to hear that, Andrew, but thank you for trying. I will explain to the women that it has not been possible to retrieve what they wished to have."

Andrew shook his head. "No, Mabel. You can tell them that although they cannot have them back, they have been destroyed."

"But I don't understand. Why not give them to me instead of destroying them. I think they would have wished to destroy them themselves."

Andrew hesitated. "As I said, the apartment was not as I expected it to be. I do not wish to shock you or make you feel uncomfortable so I will not divulge what was there but you have my word that the photographs in question have been destroyed."

"Very well, Andrew. I know ye to be man of your word. I will inform the women and I know that they will be extremely grateful."

"Ye were right to come to me, Mabel. I know it was not easy and that finding out what Robert has been doing came as a shock."

Mabel's brows pinched together. "I have nothing but contempt for the man. If it were not for Gordon and my bairns I would have reported him to the police."

"He will get his comeuppance, never you fear. I will not allow him to tarnish our names but I will make sure that he is punished."

"What will ye do?"

"I am undecided but for now, Mabel, know that he is a worried man."

"Am I awful to say that that gives me some pleasure? If ye could see how it has affected the women in Seabank."

"It gives me pleasure also. His behaviour has been despicable."

Mabel poured some more tea into both cups and for a moment neither spoke.

"Can I help in any way, Andrew? It seems unfair for you to do this alone."

"Bless you, Mabel. That is kind but I will gladly handle… actually, Mabel, there is something you could do but only if you are comfortable doing so."

"Go on."

"Perhaps you could drop something into the conversation at Sunday evening's gathering. Something pertaining to Belmont Street. He will never suspect you of anything but it would rattle him."

Mabel smiled. "Gladly. Now tell me exactly what ye wish me to say."

*

The message from Andrew was very clear and Charlie was once again thankful that his father was a good man who stood for justice. The bank was busy, as usual, and the continuing taking and leaving of ledgers from the records room was common practice. With an hour to go before the bank closed for the day all were busy finishing the day's business. The correct ledgers were found and as a pen was dipped into ink various monetary contractions were entered into one ledger, withdrawal after withdrawal, and in the other ledgers there appeared deposit after deposit.

When the last transaction had been recorded Charlie grinned and left the bank as the clock struck six.

*

Robert was late in rising the morning after his drunken

outburst and Ann was readying herself for leaving the house when he appeared. She took in his sunken eyes and pale skin and for once could see how much her husband had indeed aged. Leaving her coat in the hall she addressed Robert, "Come into the drawing room. I will have some tea brought in for you or would you prefer coffee?"

"Coffee," he mumbled.

The maid was called for and instructions given whilst Robert slumped into the fireside chair. "Tell me what has occurred, Robert. I have never seen you so angry as you were last night and I must admit to being rather scared."

Robert shook his head but his voice was low with no anger in it, "It is none of your concern, Ann. Some business gone wrong that I will deal with."

Ann's eyes narrowed as she listened to his words. "Should I be worried?"

Robert again shook his head. "No, Ann. Now leave me and go about your business."

Ann left without saying another word and could not decide whether to be worried or angry. But one thing she knew was that she was suspicious.

*

Andrew was pleased with how his plans were enabling the cat to ensnare the mouse. Alice's father sat himself down in Andrew's office and took a sip of his coffee. "I take it that something of importance has happened in order for you to have summoned me here?"

"Aye. I am sorry to say that Robert has yet again used threats against our families and it is time to ensure that he never has the opportunity again."

David sat forward, his anger rising in him at the thought of Alice being hurt in any way, "What kind of threats?"

"Blackmail involving false allegations of involvement with a married woman to be heard in court and vile rumours pertaining to Alice's virtue. That would of course ruin the chances of a political career and marriage for them both."

David rose from his seat and began to pace the floor. "My God, that man makes my blood boil." His voice grew louder with every step his feet took. "How dare he. How dare he."

Andrew gave David some time to rant and subsequently calm himself again before proceeding.

"I have a plan, Mr Buchan, but ye may not like it."

David looked Andrew square in the eyes. "I will like it, Mr Milne. I will break every law in the land if I have to, to protect Alice. Now tell me your plan."

*

SUNDAY EVENING BROUGHT the Ross and Milne families to Redwood Manor, as had been the way for nearly thirty years, but this was the first time that no grandchildren were in attendance. Ann sighed with the realisation that time was ploughing on and as each grandchild grew and forged themselves new lives and families she knew that her Sunday gatherings were coming to an end. Perhaps her children would continue to attend but she could not be sure if they would wish it.

She surveyed her brood. *Have I been harsh in my criticism of you? I have always deemed you weak in nature, Gordon. You were a sensitive child but you have proven yourself worthy in both business and as a father. I feel now that being kind, honest and fair and making good judgements are traits of a strong man.*

Her attention turned to James. *So like your father in looks and character. You always seemed stronger than Gordon: forthright and outspoken like Robert and looking down on your older brother.*

Now I can see that perhaps you have been envious of Gordon, taking on the mill and making a success of it. Envious too of his marriage as any one can see how happy Gordon and Mabel are. You and Gordon have appeared on easier terms the past few months and I am glad of it.

Ann glanced at Edith whom she had never liked. *I have never trusted that you have tried to make James happy.*

Moving her eyes to her daughter, she smiled. *How strong and brave you have proved yourself to be. I like to think that you gained some of that from me.* Her mind suddenly conjured up a picture of Grace which caused Ann to flinch. *It has been so long since I thought of you.* She pushed both the image and thoughts away. *I will not allow myself to return there. The past is the past and I must live with the consequences.*

Robert turned from the cabinet, having poured himself a large whisky. The last days had passed in a blur as his mind had tried to make sense of what had happened on Belmont Street. He had not one clue as to who had taken his belongings or how they had managed to enter his property. He had the only set of keys which he kept locked in his desk in his study.

He hadn't planned to attend tonight's gathering but decided to see how his family behaved towards him. Surely if one of them was behind this he would have been confronted. He, like Ann, surveyed his offspring. Gordon, he dismissed, *You are too scared to have carried out such a theft and wouldn't have the means to do so. James, you would have confronted me and made demands of your own.* He turned towards Andrew and paused. *This is exactly something I would expect from you but to what end? No threat of blackmail has come forth and you, usually one to quickly confront me, have not been in touch and are sitting quite naturally in my parlour with no hint of condemnation or malice.* The solicitor had confirmed that all was in hand for the forthcoming court case so his grandson could not have informed anyone of the blackmail. Robert smirked. *I am somewhat disappointed. I thought ye may have had some backbone.*

Robert sat down none the wiser as to whom had taken his photographs. Years of work gone, but he could start again.

It was the ledger that worried him.

Andrew noticed how Robert eyed each of the men in the room and he could hear the thoughts running through his father in law's mind. He must not react to it though. It was imperative that Robert did not suspect him.

The evening was an amiable one. The conversation flowed from one safe topic to another and Andrew observed how much better James and Gordon appeared to get on. Coming together the year before, united as a family, had strengthened a bond that had previously been made of thread.

Rose interrupted Andrew's thoughts. "I am looking forward to the wedding. Alice will make a very bonny bride and her mother was telling me that they purchased the material in London which had actually come from Paris."

"Yes. They had quite the spending spree there." replied Edith.

"My dress is being made by a dressmaker in Belmont Street. Just opposite the Gaelic Church. She has all the latest fashion patterns from Paris."

Robert's ears pricked.

"I have not been there, Mabel. Mine has always been satisfactory but I notice that she is perhaps falling behind with fashion. She is older and I get the impression that she does not approve of the current shape of dresses."

"The one on Belmont Street is young and also quite entertaining. Always seems to have the latest gossip." Mabel looked at Robert as she spoke and just as quickly turned away again.

Robert felt a prickling sensation on the back of his neck and froze for a second before it passed. He shook his head quickly ridding himself of the absurd thought. *Mabel indeed.*

Don't be such a fool, Robert.

"I might pay her a visit then but I fear it may be too late to have a new dress made with the wedding being only a few weeks away."

"It's worth popping in, Rose. She might be able to do the work in time," added Mabel.

The conversation shifted again to the theatre and the coming of spring and eventually it was time for all to leave. Coats were donned and farewells made and when the house was again quiet Robert was no further on in working out who had stolen from him. He wondered if perhaps someone in the dressmakers had seen him go in or out of the apartment but even if they had they would have no way of knowing what it contained and the women only ever visited in the late evening long after the shop had shut. Mabel's look towards him must have been sheer coincidence. *Perhaps it would be prudent to sell the apartment and buy another elsewhere.*

*

David Buchan had sent word to James to ask him to visit him at his home the following evening. "Thank you for coming, Mr Ross. I'm afraid that I have some news to impart concerning your father's health."

James sat up straighter in his chair. "Is he ill?"

"Not physically, no. He is of strong heart and I believe he may well live a good number of years yet. The problem lies with his mind, Mr Ross. He has been having bouts of anger followed by, according to himself, periods where he has no recollection of his behaviour. He claims that he has spent money that he has no memory of spending so I wondered if perhaps that is something that you should look into at the bank. The last thing anyone wants is for your mother to suffer if she suddenly finds herself penniless."

"Good God. I heard that he had been drunk in his club last week and had become angry there but to think that..."

"I am sure that with plenty of rest things may settle but the mind is a complex thing and I feel he needs to be protected from himself. I have suggested some time away, perhaps to his property near Inverness. The country air would be most beneficial. Meantime are you happy to see to the financial side of things in order to protect your mother? I am happy to provide a letter to your solicitor."

"Of course. I will see to it first thing in the morning."

*

JAMES OPENED THE ledger pertaining to his father's account and was horrified to see a large sum of money had been paid on several occasions to various charities. Had this been anyone else such charitable donations would not have concerned him but knowing his father loathed giving to charity, believing that the poor stay poor by choice, he knew that his father's mind was indeed affected. He immediately sent word to his own solicitor whom he would instruct to draw up papers allowing James to transfer all of his father's funds into his mother's account. She had to be protected.

*

THE DAY OF the divorce proceedings regarding Mr and Mrs Yule arrived and Robert was waiting eagerly for a telegram from his solicitor informing him of the outcome. Although not present himself Mr Hall had informed Robert that the solicitor dealing with the case would let him know the outcome. Divorce cases could only be heard in Edinburgh and although Robert would have liked to have sat in on proceedings he wished to distance himself from the coming embarrassment. It was unfortunate that the family would suffer some humiliation but he would deal with it and Ann would be instructed to hold her head high. It was not the first time they had had to ward off unpleasantness. Grace had brought shame to their door but it had been dealt with.

The Yule's were a prominent couple within society so he knew that the newspaper reporters would be there in their droves. His solicitor had informed him that all relevant papers would be read out to the court.

As the hours passed Robert became increasingly agitated. Why was there no word? Perhaps there had been some delay and the case was to be heard another day. He sent Ann out for the afternoon as he could not stand her continual questions asking what was wrong with him. Another two hours passed before he sent a message to his solicitor who immediately returned one of his own.

Mr Ross,

>*Papers not sent. I am no longer your solicitor.*
>
>*Regards, Mr Hall.*

Robert's anger soared as his blood pumped through his veins causing his eyes to bulge and a vein in his forehead to throb erratically. He had been crossed again. The papers on his desk flew across his study followed by a paperweight and inkwell. As the bottle smashed, the black ink ran down his favourite nymph portrait pooling along the bottom of its gilt frame. He roared in anguish and anger as he watched the ink destroy his beloved possession.

*

JAMES HAD INFORMED Gordon of the doctor's news and

Gordon had insisted that they call in that very day. They were greeted with an anxious butler who told them that their father had been in his study but had now left. "He was very angry. I have not been into his study as I am forbidden but I fear it may be in some mess."

The brothers exchanged a look and made their way to the study. Gordon placed his hand on the door knob and opened the door. Taking in the floor strewn with papers, books and glass and seeing the destroyed painting they took a second to let it all register. "The doctor is right about the anger then."

"Aye, Gordon. I am glad that I acted quickly to save Mother."

"Save Mother from what?" Ann demanded.

Her sons turned to see their mother by the door. Her eyes scanned the room. "What on Earth has happened? Where is your father?"

Gordon took his mother by the arm. "I'm sorry that we did not see how things were. Has Father been awful to live with? Please tell me he has not hurt you?"

"Hurt me? Of course he hasn't hurt me. What are you talking about?"

"Let's sit down, Mother. Father has gone out and I'm sure he will return when he has calmed down."

James asked the butler to organise some tea for them all and gave him permission to tidy the study. Ann paced the drawing room floor and demanded to know what was going on. James explained his conversation with the doctor but Ann was having none of it.

"Your father may well be angry at the moment. I have seen it. But he is not losing his mind. Something has gone wrong in business. I don't know what, as he would not tell me, but he has lost something, perhaps money. He has ranted about things being taken from him."

"Mother, I have looked into his bank dealings and he

has given a substantial amount away to various charities," James said.

"Perhaps he is mellowing in old age. That is hardly a crime and certainly not proof of losing his mind," Ann snapped.

"Perhaps, but to be on the safe side I have transferred his money into your account for safe keeping."

That caught Ann's attention and she stopped pacing. "Do you really believe that he is ill?"

"Aye. We do," answered Gordon.

Ann sat down on the floral couch and clasped her hands together. She was fearful of saying something inappropriate so allowed her son to pour some tea whilst she sat in silence. Her mind was like that of a kaleidoscope where fragments were moved and displaced and mirrors reflected back a new way of seeing.

*

THE CLOSED CARRIAGE stood outside Redwood Manor in wait of Robert's return. The trunks had been packed and had already been taken to the train station. Gordon and James sat with their mother in the drawing room and the butler had been instructed to inform them of Robert's return following which a message was to be sent immediately to Dr David Buchan.

Robert walked through his front door at six in the evening. Having spent the last two hours in the art gallery his mind had calmed itself again and he was determined to get his life back on track. *I will ingratiate myself once again into society. That will be my first priority. Whatever the problem has been I will ensure that others view me with respect through being benevolent and charming. Elizabeth will not hold her grudge forever so will soon want me in her bed again. The rest I will deal with in time. There is nothing that either my charm or my money cannot buy.*

He was greeted by his butler who took his coat. "Yer wife and sons are in the drawing room, sir."

"Are they now?" Curiosity pricked his mind and he made his way to the drawing room. On opening the door he found all three sitting having tea.

Ann rose to greet her husband. "Robert, would you like some tea? Gordon and James have come to visit regarding good news about the mill."

Robert took a seat on the couch beside his wife. "What news do you have?"

Gordon recounted his well rehearsed words. "Profits are up again, Father, and James has arranged for a loan with which I can expand the business."

"It is a good investment for the bank therefore a profitable situation for all concerned," added James.

"I am very pleased to hear it. I trust you will keep me informed?"

"Of course."

The conversation flowed as Gordon and James kept to the topic of profits and society functions knowing that it would keep their father's interest until such time as the doctor arrived.

Ann observed her husband but could see no sign of an ill mind and worries began to surface. *Perhaps I have been too hasty in allowing my sons to persuade me of this plan. Robert has certainly been angry but I don't believe him to be of danger to anyone or himself. The charitable donations are certainly unusual but often age brings with it a softening of the heart.*

She took a sip of her tea which was now cold and placed it back onto the table with a grimace. *Robert will be incensed to find out that I have control of his money. Women have no place in running their husband's affairs.* Ann's memory took her back to when her mother had died and she had inherited the family home and a substantial amount of money. *But I had my own money once and handled it well. Really I am just taking back some of what was already mine.*

"Ann! I have just asked ye a question. Are ye going deaf?" Robert's raised voice caused her to flinch.

"I'm sorry, Robert, I was miles away." She kept her tone light as her sons had advised. No one wished the situation to be harder than necessary.

Robert laughed. "Head in the clouds, as always. That is why women have no place in business. I was asking if you had heard from Lady Muir regarding an invitation to the spring ball?"

Ann bristled. *Another of your mistresses if I am not mistaken. My head may be in the clouds but my eyes see and I have a nose for perfume.* "Not yet, dear, but I am sure it will arrive soon."

Satisfied, Robert continued his conversation and Ann's thoughts turned to mistresses. *How could I have been so naive? I know it to be a common occurrence, accepted even, by wives that their husbands take pleasure elsewhere but I honestly thought that you had never strayed. You visited my bedchamber for almost fifty years and I took that to mean that you were satisfied. I have been a fool! And when I think of Agnes….No! I will not think of her.*

Ann looked at her husband and saw a man who had deceived her. *Enough*, she thought and she rose from her chair as she heard the faint sound of the front doorbell. "I am going up to change for dinner," she announced, and she nodded to her sons who understood its meaning. She did not look at Robert and she left the drawing room, closing the door behind her. Mr Buchan was in the hall, his doctor's bag in his hand, and she merely nodded to him and ascended the stairs to her room.

Ann shut her door. She had no wish to hear any noise from below - would take no pleasure in it. She trusted that the doctor would administer something to prevent any outbursts and Robert would be accompanied on his journey by carriage to the station and then on the evening train to Inverness. They all seemed so sure that Robert was of unsound mind but she had lived with him for nearly fifty years and she knew that that was not the case but she was complicit in going along with it. *I have made my choice and must live with it.*

Ann stood by the window and watched as the carriage trundled along the sweeping drive and out through the gate.

Revelations

Ann sat with Agnes in the drawing room belonging to her friend of fifty years. "Yes, thank you dear, I will have some cake."

"You are looking very well, Ann. Have ye discovered some new lotion?"

Ann smiled and her words had a teasing quality to them. "No. I am using my usual cold cream but perhaps it's the effect of some new found independence."

"Really? And what might that be, Ann?"

"I have gained my husband's wealth," she stated.

"But….but surely he is not dead? Oh, Ann, tell me he is not dead?" Her words were desperate which did not go unnoticed.

Ann patted Agnes's hand. "Oh no, dear, he is very much alive."

Agnes stared at her friend with a furrowed brow. "I don't understand, Ann. What are you telling me?"

"He has not been himself and the doctor recommended some country air. My sons organised it all. They have been magnificent in looking after me. Robert was being a bit careless with his finances - between you and me of course - and so James very sensibly took charge and now

I have control of everything."

Agnes's mouth was agape. "But surely Robert would not allow such a thing...all his...his property...and such like."

"As I said, he has not been himself so matters had to be taken out of his hands. My solicitor is going through his papers and I will soon be informed as to property and other business interests. The money of course is at my immediate disposal." Ann took a sip of her tea from her saucer. "I apologise, Agnes, it is vulgar of me to talk of money. I just wished to confide in my oldest, dearest friend."

Agnes faltered. "So where is Robert?"

"In Talla Cluaran, my family home. I believe it to be a healing place, as you know, so I am positive that Robert will rid himself of all that ails him there. There is a doctor in attendance and no visitors are advised at the moment. He will be unable to attend the wedding which is unfortunate but his health must come first."

"Of course," stammered Agnes. "How long do ye think it will be before he returns home?"

"I have no idea."

The two ladies conversed for half an hour before Ann decided that she had had enough of playing. "I really must go, Agnes. Thank you for afternoon tea." She rose from her chair and took herself over to where Agnes's family photographs lay. "Such a handsome family, Agnes." She picked up the photograph of Agnes's daughter. "Isabella looks very like you, dear. Her son, John, is the double of his grandfather is he not?"

Agnes's eyes widened and she swallowed.

Ann leaned in and kissed her on the cheek, "Good afternoon, Agnes," and she left the parlour with a spring in her step.

Agnes slowly lowered herself back into her chair.

*

By the end of the second day of the Labour conference in London, on twenty eighth of February, a Labour Representative Committee had been formed which enabled a distinct Labour group into Parliament with its own Whips. Charlie danced in the streets alongside fellow supporters in celebration of real progress. At long last something substantial had been formed and the future of politics would go on to be quite different for the working classes.

Alice was overjoyed at the news and as her betrothed twirled her round and round in her parlour, after returning from London, both looked forward to their wedding and an exciting future. David looked on and not for one second did he regret his actions which went against his nature. Robert had been a real threat and had had to be dealt with. He would be forever grateful to Andrew Milne for his trust, discretion and wisdom.

Charlie was full of gladness as he saw the look of genuine happiness in Alice's face. David cleared his throat and his daughter was released, "There is something that we have decided to tell ye Alice. Many would keep this news from a lady's ears but we both agree that ye are a woman of great strength and you value honesty."

Charlie agreed with that sentiment and knew that Alice would not like to be lied to.

"My grandfather plotted and schemed to derail my political career and it saddens me to say that he stooped so low as to try and blackmail me with the threat of using false information against me, to be produced in a court of law, stating that I was having a relationship with a married woman."

A look of horror passed over Alice's face. "But that is despicable."

"It is, but I am afraid that there is more. He threatened to ruin your reputation, again through false information.

Both would have resulted in our being unable to marry. He is deemed unstable and is currently convalescing in our country house by Inverness."

Alice looked to her father. "Does unstable mean that his mind does not belong to him?"

"I believe that, yes. I have written to his doctor there stating my diagnosis."

Alice's face softened. "Your grandfather is obviously ill and would surely never have behaved in such a manner had he been of sound mind. Scandal has been avoided and so he must have our sympathy."

Both men showed initial surprise but of course this was Alice speaking.

"Ye are the most forgiving woman I have ever had the pleasure of knowing and I will be so proud to call ye my wife."

David seconded Alice's praise and asked her to fetch her mother so that they could toast to the coming marriage yet again.

"Do not be fooled, lad. I am sorry to tell ye that it was yer grandfather who had ye beaten and threatened to harm Alice. It is best ye know so as ye will always be on yer guard."

Charlie could see that David had not wished to impart such awful news but it was best for all that it had been said.

He walked to the window, his back to David. "How do ye come to know it was him?"

David hesitated. "I was told in confidence. There is no need for it to go any further."

He nodded. "I am not shocked. My grandfather has loathed me for a very long time. Thank you for telling me."

Alice returned with her mother and glasses were raised to the future. Charlie was glad that David had imparted what he knew. Alice had to be protected at all costs and it had been the right thing to do. Forewarned was forearmed.

Later whilst lying in her bed, Alice revelled in the excitement of her coming wedding. She pushed aside the thought of what could have been, had Robert Ross managed to carry out his threats, and whispered, "Goodnight Charlie."

Charlie

As I look upon Alice and hear her words of betrothal my mind travels back to our first meeting. She had burst into the room at the tender age of five and pummelled straight into my heart. Her enthusiastic, boisterous nature cocooned a loving heart and an understanding mind far beyond her years. She was my closest friend and she healed my troubled soul - so bereft of my family - with her joyful spirit.

I was seven in years when I fell from that tree. My arm was broken but so too was a rib that pierced my liver which slowly bled. My mother and father sat by my bed, their tender words comforting to my ear as my wee wooden rabbit was placed in the palm of my hand. My final breath released me from the pain and as I floated upwards Mama and Papa were waiting for me. And here I am still: cocooned in their warmth and love.

I have watched over those, whom I loved in life, ever since.

I wander through the lives of the living. I watch and I listen. I think and I feel.

But I do not speak.

I have seen my cousin, Archie, grow into a fine man and hearing his words of betrothal to my beloved Alice I smile. Alice is happy and safe and each night as she bids me goodnight I whisper it back, though she cannot hear me.

I may have died but I live in that moment between sleep and waking.

Look for me, for I am there.

My name is Charlie and I am dead.

The End.

Epilogue

Alice held the letter and wiped away tears as she read the words written there so long ago. Rose had found the letter in a drawer in Charlie's room where it had lain undiscovered for many years.

Dear Charlie,

I hope that you are reading this as a man and not just a man but a gentleman. I could not save my other bairns from a life without a mother but you have a chance, Charlie, and I have to give it to ye. The chance to be a gentleman and to make something of yourself. I have failed your Mama and for that I pay the price with my life - for I do not deserve to live. The scattering of my bairns has broken what is left of me.

I ask one thing of you, my loon, and that is that you go out and seek your brothers and sisters. Find them, Charlie. Be family to one another, and remember your Mama and Papa fondly. I cannot ask your forgiveness for the taking of my life but I ask you to find your true family. Ye are a stag now.

Your loving Papa.

*

Glossary of Scots Words

Bosie	Cuddle
Loon	Boy
Quine	Girl
Dicht	Clean
Coorie	Snuggle
Coorse	Bad
Ken	Know
Dreich	Grey, wet weather
Dinna	Don't
Winna	Won't
Bide	Live
Lum	Chimney
Greeting	Crying
Girning	Whinging
Reek	Smoke
Breeks	Trousers
Boosey lip	Sulking, pouting lower lip
Bickering	Arguing
Auld	Old
Lugs	Ears
Haar	Sea fog

Seel	Happy
Sleekit	Sneaky
Thrawn	Stubborn

Printed in Great Britain
by Amazon